The
Epiphany
Crystals

Short stories
by L. Wayne Goodin

"Devil's Choice"

"Monkey Shines"
Published in the Storyteller Magazine

"Dream Maker"

"Letting Go"

"Change of Heart"
Winner of the second prize for short story in
the prestigious Ozark Creative Writers
44th annual competition November 2011

The Epiphany Crystals is also available for many digital book
readers including Nook, iPad, and Android.
It is also available from Smashwords.com

You may see Wayne's latest work at
www.lwaynegoodinpublications.com/

The Epiphany Crystals

by
L. Wayne Goodin

Wire Road Press
Republic, Missouri

Published by
Wire Road Press
PO Box 663
Republic, MO 65738-0663

Cover photography Copyright by Ioannis Pantziaras
Licensed by Shutterstock Images

To Lori, Kristen, and Philip

"As long as there are sovereign nations possessing great power, war is inevitable."

~Albert Einstein, November 1945

CHAPTER 1

The moisture laden clouds crackled, pierced by the blistering sizzle of a basketball-sized sphere moving from the northwest. The sphere dipped from cloud level and zipped along just above the treetops in the woods near Harrison, Arkansas, vaporizing a trail in the atmosphere. The sphere slowed deliberately as it approached Max Gibson's cabin on top of Radford Mountain south of Harrison. As the sphere passed the security light in the front yard, the light abruptly went out, leaving the house and grounds totally dark. The chrome-colored device slowly rotated as it came to a stop at the front porch then gently floated up to the door, which opened with a click. The sphere entered the house. Effortlessly the shiny object, which an observer might have described as an oversized Christmas ornament, traversed the stairs to Max's bedroom and hovered just above him. A fluorescent green wave of light emanated from the sphere and scanned Max, momentarily illuminating the room with near daylight intensity. Without waking, Max sat up in bed as if someone had just called his name, and then he quietly laid back down and continued to sleep soundly. The sphere then reversed its path, the door closing behind it as it left the house on Radford Mountain. The power came back on at Max's place as the object sped down the valley toward Harrison.

The only two police officers on patrol duty in Harrison that night sat in their cars, one facing east and the other west, in the Edwards Grocery parking lot, their vehicles about a foot apart so the men could converse through their open windows. As usual, there was not much going on in town after midnight. The idling cars emitted a plume of vapor in the calm dense air of the valley that rose up creating an artificial fog around them. Billy and Ray sat quietly in a relaxed conversation reminiscent of campfire stories of the past.

"Billy, you gonna deer hunt durin' the black powder season in January this year?"

"Oh, I don' know, Ray. I just about froze my keester off last year, and all I got was that little ol' doe 'bout the size of my red-bone hound, Benson. In fact, I think Benson's got more meat on him than that there deer had." A swiftly moving flash of light, soon followed by a sizzling sound and a severe crack, dramatically interrupted him.

"Jesus, Lord in heaven! What was that? Did you see that Billy? Something jist flashed by goin' down Highway 7. And what the hell was that crack? Did you hear that?" He noted his dash lights were out and reached for his keys in the ignition. "Billy, see if your car will start. Mine jist went as dead as a hammer."

"Naw, my car is dead too! Look yonder, Ray. The lights in the grocery store are out. Hell, the lights in the whole damn block are out. I'm callin' this in." He reached for his mike and held the button. "Car three to base, over. Damn it, Rafe! Come in! This is Billy! Shit! The radio is dead too. What the hell is goin' on here?" he asked as he craned his neck to look out the car window in the direction the flash had seemed to travel.

As the officers sat in their cars in utter bewilderment discussing whether to walk to headquarters, the sphere continued to progressively blackout Harrison. It was headed toward Susan McKinney's apartment in the northeast part of town. The sphere gained access to her second floor apartment through the deck's sliding glass door, which moved silently aside to allow entry. Like Max, Susan's scan was accomplished quickly, she too sat up as if called and then laid back down, breathing rhythmically as one deep asleep.

After the glass door quietly slid closed behind it, the metallic sphere accelerated straight upward through the cloud cover, and then it moved out of the atmosphere as quickly as a rocket. The sphere did not make the slightest sound until it exceeded the sound barrier, which caused a rumble of muffled thunder high in the atmosphere. In a few seconds, the power and all electromagnetic functions were restored to Harrison. The time was 3:10 a.m., and the entire elapsed time of the sphere's visit to the town was just under ten minutes.

Nute, the Topek governor and explorer of this sector, was conducting a meeting in the captain's ward room aboard ship. His briefing to the Galactic Council was a formal affair, and there was an obvious air of importance about him to match the stakes, which were quite high. The entire Council was aboard, having traveled from across the galaxy to the edge of the frontier just to visit Earth, and he was quite mindful they were here solely at his request. He was in fact a bit nervous, and he wanted to give them a clear presentation and be attentive to their questions and careful in his answers. His presentation would be augmented by holographic images to clarify each point as he spoke and to emphasize what he judged to be most important. He reviewed the material mentally as he waited for the Council to take their seats, hoping the results of the scans of his test subjects he ordered would arrive in time for his briefing.

The Council members filed in dressed in their traditional yellow robes and took their seats facing Nute in a semicircle. When everyone was seated, Clacton, the head of the Council, gave Nute a nod to begin.

"Councillors, I would first like to give you a brief history of the events leading up to our trip. As you all know, we have observed many species and inventoried several cultures in this sector. Of these studied species, we found the Earth people to be the most interesting and paradoxical. On the one hand, they are brutal in warfare, barbaric in the wholesale slaughter of their enemies. Conversely, they can be compassionate and even produce beautiful art and music. In a few words, they are full of surprises and thus always interesting."

As Nute spoke, vivid images of Earth and its inhabitants filled the room, the brutality of war contrasted with the beauty of art. Symphonic music accompanied the holographic images. Images of the Sistine Chapel were accompanied by Tchaikovsky's "Waltz of the Flowers," and these images were interspersed with beheadings and brutal dismemberment of prisoners, even children, with machetes. There was an audible gasp when the hologram of a child having his arm cut off during a recent tribal ethnic cleansing in Africa appeared.

"We began to monitor this species more closely about two hundred thousand Earth years ago, when in our routine observations we saw them using fire and stone tools."

Obviously disturbed by the visions of the violence, Clacton interrupted. "Nute, let's go back to their violent nature for a moment. Did you find their tendency toward violence to be learned or innate?"

"That is an interesting question, Councillor. It seems their original propensity for violence was nurtured by competition for food and territory, but over time, dominance over their environment and over more primitive species evolved into conflict with other humans for the same scarce resources and territory. Unfortunately, even local conflicts among humans have grown in significance over the last hundred years because their technology has allowed them to become more and more accomplished at killing each other."

"When you say they are growing more and more destructive, do you feel they are reaching critical mass with regard to their war-making technology?"

"Absolutely. About seventy-five Earth years ago, they detonated the first nuclear explosion at a place called Trinity in the American desert. Since then, they have improved on this technology, increasing the yield from the equivalent of twenty kilotons of TNT to a thermonuclear device with a yield of five-hundred megatons."

"Nute, are they continuing to increase the yield of these devices?"

"The yield has stayed about the same for the last fifty years or so. But, during this build up and experimentation phase, several countries have detonated weapons in the atmosphere, underwater, and underground—a total of some four-thousand devices. The technology has spread to many governments, religious groups, and to ethnic extremists. Given the increasingly wide spread capability to use nuclear weapons, we believe the Earth's inhabitants will effectively destroy themselves within the next twenty-five years, which would follow the well documented pattern of other K-10 cultures we have studied."

"Do you believe the Earth people are a true K-10 culture, Nute?"

"Yes, but I believe they have more potential to change than other species we have studied. They are still aggressive and desire to dominate others, the hallmark of the K-10 classification, but I have lived among the Earth people twenty-seven times over the last two hundred thousand Earth years and am always impressed by their creativity and adaptability. I truly believe the species is worth saving, perhaps even more than saving."

"What do you mean, Nute?"

"It is too early to say if the Earth people are worthy of our further investment, but because we believe their self destruction is eminent, my team has devised a test to see if they are capable of handling Level-Eight technology. Twenty-two Earth years ago, we started a planet-wide search for outstanding representatives of the species, and we have been following a fairly large group of candidates since they were children.

"Our final two candidates are intelligent and have passed all of our health requirements. We quietly arranged for them to be employed by the same company, what they call a 'diversified high tech' company, known as Astrolabe Systems, Inc."

As Nute spoke, his two superstar selections appeared before the Council members as three dimensional holographic images, like lifelike mannequins, the images produced based on the results of the scans made in Arkansas. The two figures rotated nude in front of the council members, all aspects of their bodies revealed along with their specifications: age, blood type, and disease history.

"Do they know each other yet?" asked one of the Council members.

"Not really. They met professionally a few times and once at a company picnic. As you can see, these magnificent physical specimens are in peak physical condition. Their mental abilities are also outstanding, especially the male. These two clearly stand out from all other human candidates we have studied."

"How did you come to select this particular pair?"

"We had access to all educational databases in the developed countries, and we searched them for students who had been identified as gifted by early childhood measurements. Originally, we had approximately four-hundred youngsters to evaluate, and as the children got older, we gradually reduced the number of subjects until we were left with just these two. Some of our team members were able to pose as teachers and later as the subjects' coworkers to evaluate them firsthand. One of our team members, presently posing as Dr. Pete Bradley and working at Astrolabe, has been sending us regular reports. Based on his input and the other data, we all agreed that these two were the best we have studied. These two humans have very different personalities, but both have excellent mental and physical abilities for their species."

"Nute, let me remind you of our rules when dealing with other cultures. As you know, this is long-standing Council policy. First, you must let them solve their own problems with their runaway nuclear technology. Second, you may not give them more information than they need. In this case, I think we all agree that Level Eight will be quite sufficient. Third, and most important, the subjects must agree to be a part of any of your projects of their own free will, if and when we deem their participation worthwhile."

"Yes, of course, Councillor. We are prepared to help them with Level-Eight technology only and to insist that they make their own decisions on all aspects of any project. We have found the Epiphany Crystals to be the most reliable tool available to us. As you know, we have used many ways to nudge the humans along in the past, but the Crystals seem to be the most comfortable way for the humans to interface with us. Moreover, the Crystals can provide a communication link to the ship as well, and this tool has the added benefit of not requiring one of us to be physically present for long periods, which presents its own problems, of course."

"Good luck, Nute. The Council will be observing the outcome of your plan from here on the ship with great interest. The Earth people may be worth further study, but we will have to see. Your test is a logical way to evaluate them and give us that answer. Nute, we are proud of your commitment to this project. It has taken you a long time and many trips to this remote area of the galaxy, and we are all depending on your success. You seem to have developed an affinity for these Earth people, so I hope your time and effort have not been wasted on them."

"Thank you, Councillor. I am pleased that the Council entrusted this important mission to me."

After the meeting, the huge spacecraft decelerated as it approached the solar system, then took a static position near Jupiter to await the unfolding of Nute's plan. The Council was keenly interested in the performance of Nute's protégés.

CHAPTER 2

Max was up early that Friday morning, energized without apparent reason as he breezed through his morning routine to get ready for work. He was totally unaware of the encounter he had the night before or that he was the subject of such intense scrutiny. He was only mildly annoyed when he had to reset his clock due to the power failure during the night. He casually slurped a bowl of cereal as the early news began.

"Good morning, this is Howard Scott with the overnight news roundup for December 9, 2022. The international community was shocked late yesterday by the revelation that Iran exploded a third nuclear device in underground tests in the desert southeast of Tehran. Initial reports indicate the blast was in the fifty megaton range, raising fears of seismic activity in the earthquake-prone area. The government of the recently installed religious right would not confirm or deny the reports, replying to queries that it is no one's business what they do on their own soil. The United Nations has filed a formal complaint with the Iranian ambassador, but diplomatic sources say there is little chance it will have any effect on the Iranian government. The list of nuclear powers now includes the USA, United Kingdom, France, Russia, China, the Ukraine, Israel, North Korea, India, Pakistan, Iran, Australia, and Libya. Experts say there may be yet more members of the nuclear fraternity, countries or even non-aligned factions that may have obtained nuclear weapons secretly.

"United Nations weapons inspectors have been banned from all of the neophyte nuclear players' territories since the 2017 international meeting on nuclear proliferation. The newcomers insisted at that time that the international body did not have the right to enter a sovereign country for any purpose whatsoever, including to inspect nuclear capabilities. This raises speculation in some quarters that a preemptive strike against the upstart powers is more likely.

"General Bernard Potter, the Air Force's top weapons procurement officer, testified before the Senate Armed Services Committee yesterday, reassuring the senators that our military has the capability of defending the United States and its allies against any adversary. General Potter said, 'The new space-based weapons and detection systems are very capable of identifying and destroying any threat to our territory.' The general added, 'We can handle anything they have.'

"In other news, outspoken Senator Sam Stone, Republican of Alabama, fueled speculation about his bid for the presidency when he was quoted last night at a black tie political fundraiser as saying: 'I don't see why we keep pussy-footin' around with these Middle Eastern religious fanatics. I wonder how they would react if we turned their oil fields into a radioactive cinder. Who do you think would buy their righteous indignation or even care about them then? The only reason anyone listens to them at all now is because of the oil, period. Hell, some of our fly boys could stop this thing right now. All we need is a little political will and the guts. I say nuke 'em before we get blasted ourselves or bled completely dry of cash buying four-hundred-dollar-per-barrel oil. We need to take charge of our own destiny. Their political buddies in the oil business here in the States have kept us dependent on those guys far too long just for their own profit. How much do you think the CEO of Exxon-Mobil cares about the ol' US of A when he is making a fifty-million-dollar salary off Mideast oil? Big oil has put their profits ahead of the national interest of the United States, to the point we have practically given our country away to those sheikhs and religious wing nuts for the bottom line of the big oil companies.

"'Those Middle Eastern lunatics nearly own us now, boys. Having a religious leader run the country is a big mistake. How would you like to have the Pope running this country? He can't even keep his priests from molesting the altar boys, for Pete's sake. This country was founded on religious freedom; both freedom *of* religion and freedom *from* religion.'

"When asked if he was interested in a presidential bid in 2024, Senator Stone simply laughed and said, 'Aw come on, fellas. You know the election is too far away to say. Ask me next year.'

"In other news, officials at NORAD are trying to quell speculation about a UFO scare in northern Arkansas over night. NORAD spokesman Colonel James Baxter said the electromagnetic-pulse phenomena, commonly known as an EMP, that was recorded around 3:00 a.m. was probably due to solar activity. He added that the activity has been elevated the last few days. Police reports out of Harrison concerning power outages, which occurred at about the same time as the more serious electromagnetic pulses were observed, are being dismissed as a hoax.

"Wall Street reacted unfavorably to the news from Iran . . . "

Max had seen enough and turned off the TV, deciding to go on to work. As he got up from his chair, he mumbled to himself, "These lunatics will blow us all to hell. It's just a matter of time."

Bundled in his down jacket, he slid behind the wheel of his BMW sedan and headed for the office. A mixture of light rain and sleet pelted the roadway as he leaned into the curves on the winding asphalt snaking its way through the Ozark Mountains. The valley leading to the entrance of the Astrolabe Systems complex was shrouded in a cold fog that obscured the treetops in the depths of the valley, making this high security area appear even more mysterious. Pale gray white oaks and dark green ponderosa pines scrolled by as he powered his way up the last long hill leading to the security gate.

Dressed in full military garb with polished boots and yellow raincoat, the gate officer approached the car as Max rolled to a stop. The imposing twelve-foot electrified fence spoke volumes about how seriously Astrolabe took security. The guard tower officer, an ex-Marine, glared from above as he dutifully turned his M-60 toward the car in the clearance area.

As Max rolled down the window of his car, the guard greeted him with crisp military efficiency, "Good morning, Dr. Gibson. Could I trouble you for your clearance imprint?"

"Hi, Joe. Did your wife enjoy the herb garnish I sent home with you yesterday? You did take it home, didn't ya?"

"Uh . . . well, sir. I was planning to take it, really I was, Doc. I just . . ."

"Never mind, Joe. I'll bring you a new one next week. Where's Harv today?"

"He's working inside the shack, keeping out of the weather as usual. You know how it is: rank has its privilege."

Max removed his glove and placed his left thumb on the wireless tablet as Joe patiently looked on. In a few seconds, the print analyzer made an identification and the electronic voice droned: "Access granted to Dr. Max Gibson, December 9, 2022, 7:50 a.m. Good morning, Doctor. I have no messages holding for you. You may enter. Have a productive day."

With the security routine completed, the waist-high four-inch thick steel barrier blocking the entrance retracted into the ground. Max drove into the executive parking lot, giving a wave to Joe as he passed the gate. He pulled his BMW into his marked and canopied space, which was situated closest to the building and indicated his considerable status. He got out of his car and bounded up the short staircase to the back entrance of his lab.

Later that morning, Max sat in front of his computer terminal scribbling on a yellow legal pad with a pencil. Crumpled paper flanked both sides of the terminal, representing the morning's efforts. He mumbled to himself as he worked, occasionally stopping to key in the salient results of his extensive calculations.

Standing just over six feet two, Max's slender frame was clad in his usual uniform of jeans, sports shirt, and well-worn Reeboks. His purposeful antithesis of a fashion statement was topped off by a moderately well-kept beard and over-the-ear length hair that he constantly fussed with as he worked. To be sure, Max's persona didn't belie his status as the head physicist at one of the most clandestine high-tech companies in the nation. In fact, more than one observer had noted that he looked more like an undergraduate cramming for a final exam.

Astrolabe had courted Max in a highly competitive recruiting war, lavishing perks as well as money on him, after he finished his PhD in astrophysics at Caltech six years before. The company desperately needed him to head up their optics department because of his brilliant work with the Hubble space-based telescope, and so did Nute. Max was an expert on the area of space where Alpha Centauri is located, and he had discovered several previously unknown properties of dark matter and the black hole in the vicinity.

Max had only been with Astrolabe a year when disaster struck during the quake of 2017, destroying the optics lab in California. The company already had a modest facility in Arkansas, which had been built during the Clinton years, so Max's lab was moved there for safety reasons in late 2017. This formerly small outpost near Harrison had become a sprawling complex housing biomedical research, genetic engineering, supercomputer design, and Max's baby — the most advanced optics lab in the world.

Although Max had nearly free rein in determining what to work on, Steven Clark, the site administrator, tried to keep him interested in projects with commercial value. Often, his ideas would end up in military hardware or a spy satellite, but as far as Max was concerned, the sky was the limit for him in terms of discovery and it was up to the MBA types to make the company money. He only worked on things that interested his inquisitive and resourceful mind.

Like most brilliant people, Max was able to work for hours on a project, oblivious to everything around him, which meant people who did not know him well thought him aloof. As a child, he had learned to entertain himself by playing mind games, often becoming lost in his own thoughts, and consequently, he had become something of a loner. During conversations, his mind would drift to something else entirely, mundane small talk insufficient to hold his attention.

When he was seven-years-old, Max's mother bought him a math book — *1000 Problems to Solve* — to keep him occupied while on a trip. As a result of falling in love with those problems, he taught himself algebra and geometry. When he was still in grammar school, he was known to his teachers as a real pain, routinely embarrassing them with questions they couldn't answer. To keep his mind occupied when in his early teens, Max spent his summers taking college math and physics classes, and he became somewhat of a celebrity as a child prodigy on the campus of Caltech.

For his thirteenth birthday, Max's father took him to hear a lecture by Stephen Hawking, who Max was astounded to see in a wheelchair and able to speak only with the aid of a computer. Hawking's insights immediately struck a chord with Max, and Hawking became his hero. Max devoured everything Hawking wrote and was inspired by his idol's intuitive thought processes and his concept of the universe. At fifteen, Max began to publish his own articles and essays, which prompted insiders in the physics community to take note, many considering him the heir apparent to Richard Feynman, the Nobel Laureate and savant at Caltech. Frequent publications since that tender age had made Max, if not a household name the world over, renowned within the international physics community.

Dr. Frank Kelso, Max's colleague and assistant, was ten years older than Max but clearly subordinate to him when it came to physics. Frank, conversely, was more pragmatic and made a good interpreter of Max's theoretical visions, translating them into the everyday world of commercial physics and engineering. Max and Frank were good friends in the purest sense, enjoying a mutual respect for each other and their complementary assets.

Max had spent the morning working on a scheme to couple two land-based telescopes at the Keck Observatory in Hawaii via computer link-up to dramatically improve their image quality. He was improving on work done in the 1990s on interferometers to take advantage of newer and more powerful supercomputers. If he could make it work, Astrolabe would be able to retrofit existing hardware to extend the life and quality of optical telescopes all over the world.

As Max worked away immersed in his thoughts, Frank interrupted from across the room.

"Max, do you suppose a person could make money at blackjack using mathematics, ya know, probabilities and stuff like that?"

"I don't see why not, provided the game is honest and the dealer moves straight through the deck, but it has been tried. It takes a near photographic memory. They call those guys "card counters," and they are banned from most casinos. Why? What's up?"

"Well, I was just wondering. If someone were to write a computer program that would give the relative probability of certain cards being drawn, over time, he should be able to beat the house."

"You must be kiddin', Frank. There's gotta be twenty-five books written on that subject. The theory has been around since Pascal and Fermat published it in 1650. What ya got up your sleeve anyway? Get it? Up your sleeve!"

"That's not funny, Max. I'm talkin' some real money here! I'm takin' Jenny over to the new paddle wheel casino at Branson tonight, and I'm coming home with a bundle of cash. You just watch me. I'm gonna beat their system."

"Don't you think those casino guys are wise to people like you? All they want you to do is keep playing. The longer you play, the closer you get to the law of probability, and I'm sure they know what the odds are. Remember, Frank. There is no system when it comes to gambling. There is only probability. If you play, the house will win ultimately. Those hammerheads keep track of people like you for a living, and from what I hear, it's a pretty good living too! Did ya ever check out how many Porsches and Ferraris are parked over there?"

"I know. I know. But just once, I'd like to come into some easy money, spend some time in Barbados or somewhere like that. Ya know, with good-looking native chicks bringin' me a rum swizzle every time I ask for it. I'd like the ones with the grass skirts and just enough long black hair to cover their . . . Well, ya know what I mean."

"What about your wife, Frank? You gonna take her to the beach too?"

"No way. If I'm dreamin' I certainly don't want my wife around taking notes to nail me later. She'd definitely not go for the babes in the grass skirts with their boobs sticking out through their hair. Besides, she always cuts me off after one swizzle anyway. Here's the dream buddy: money, babes, rum, beach — and NO WIFE! Now that my mouth is watering, how about some lunch? I hear the cafeteria is serving salmon croquettes today, my favorite!"

"My God. I don't see how ya can stand to eat those overcooked lumps of cat food! You go on. I'll be down in a minute. I want to finish these last few lines of the program."

Max briefly looked up from his calculations to acknowledge Frank's departure and then continued entering data into the terminal. As Frank got close to the door, Max let out a loud "meow" just to torment his friend.

About fifteen minutes later, Max arrived at the cafeteria, which was buzzing with the din of normal Friday afternoon discussions about weekend plans. Crowded as usual, the place was a far cry from when Max came to Arkansas five years ago. An original workforce of fifty had exploded to nearly seven hundred employees, three hundred added just last year when the genetic engineering lab was converted from pure research to full production. The Harrison area was an ideal location for top secret work. It was remote, centrally located, and the local population had no idea what went on there, reminiscent of the Los Alamos nuclear lab for the Manhattan project during World War II.

Threading his way through the tables, Max made his way to where Frank was seated. As he passed their table, two young women checked him out and casually discussed him in a muted conversation.

"Susan, do ya know that guy, Gibson?"

"Of course, I know him, Marilyn. What about him?"

"They say he is so smart he got his PhD before he was twenty! But he is not too hard on the eyes either. Sexy, even."

"He's okay, I guess. I met him last summer at the picnic. He seemed a little nerdy."

"Nerdy? You must be kidding! He could be my nerd any time. Besides, you're just jealous because his brain has a bigger rep around here than yours."

"Don't be ridiculous. All I'm saying is he seems way out there on the very edge of being human sometimes, but you're right about one thing — he is one smart cookie. Some of the stuff he presents at our staff meetings is brilliant. About a month ago, he presented a talk to the staff about black holes and event singularities, whatever that is. He spoke for about twenty-five minutes and filled both chalkboards with formulas. Then he asked for questions and the room was totally silent. Not a single person had understood a thing he said. We're talkin' forty-five PhDs here and ya coulda heard a pin drop!"

"Do you think he is married?" Marilyn was acting as if she had not understood a word Susan just said.

"Married? No way! Just look at him. He couldn't possibly be married and dress like that. His socks don't even match. His back side does look pretty good in those jeans though. I guess you're right about that too."

"Oh, God! Don't look, Susan. Here comes that creep, Todd Gilroy, from Genetics."

Todd was making a beeline for the empty seat next to Marilyn, and they were trapped. Rather than make the situation worse by ignoring him, Susan blurted out, "Hi, Todd. Won't you join us?"

As Todd eagerly pulled out the chair, his lust for Susan was not well disguised. His eyes pored over her sleek athletic body, and he nearly dropped his tray when she leaned over to move the salt and pepper and her lavender silk blouse flared open slightly, exposing part of her more than ample endowment. Marilyn, obviously unhappy about Todd's untimely arrival, slid her chair back abruptly and said in a businesslike tone, "I will see you back at the office, Susan."

When Marilyn got behind Todd, she stuck her finger down her throat as if to make herself vomit. Susan could hardly keep a straight face and began talking to keep from laughing.

"So, Todd . . . Uh . . . how's it goin' over in Genetics?"

"Great! Say Susan, how's about you and me going over to Hot Springs this weekend for some indoor tennis and to hit the hot mineral baths?" Todd leaned closer as if he had some private thought to communicate, whispering, "I hear those hot baths really loosen up the old bod, if you know what I mean."

Susan simply ignored his sophomoric suggestion and said, "I didn't know you played tennis, Todd."

Todd was clearly irritated at the change of subject, his expression going from leering to angry for a brief moment, but then leering returned and he went on. "Well, a little. I've been taking some lessons, and my instructor says I'm getting pretty good. He thinks I might be ready for a real match. Do you play?"

"I played some at Stanford. How many lessons have you had?"

"Three. You don't mean you played for the school team, do you?"

"Actually, I was all PAC Ten. I had a chance to play on the professional circuit, but medical school was taking so much time that I had to give up competitive tennis. I still enjoy playing for fun and to keep in shape though. We should play sometime."

Todd, looking completely disarmed and suddenly feeling totally inadequate, quickly tried to extricate himself from the uncomfortable realization she would easily kick his butt in a tennis match. "Gosh, Susan. Is there anything you don't do well?"

"As a matter of fact, I'm not much of a cook. Actually, I hate to cook. I like to eat but hate to cook. A paradox of a sort, I guess."

"I don't like to cook either, so I eat out a lot. Burger King is my favorite." Todd could barely sit still; energized by being so close to Susan and getting this one-on-one time with her. He continued nervously, "So, what do you think about the hot baths? We could make a weekend of it."

Susan wanted to firmly dump his butt, but her social training kicked in and she made a valiant attempt to be polite. "Todd, I don't think so. My sister might come to visit this weekend, and I have a lot of laundry to do. Maybe some other time. I'll take a rain check. Okay?"

Susan then got up, dropped off her lunch tray, and headed down the hall to the elevator. Todd looked dispirited when she told him no, but his expression was all lust when he turned to view her back side and legs as she walked away in her smooth confident stride. As Susan got on the elevator, she couldn't help thinking of Todd sitting alone in a Burger King dining room with one of those silly paper crowns on his head eating a hamburger.

The others on the elevator gave her a puzzled look as she chuckled without apparent provocation. The elevator door opened on the third floor in front of her office. The sign on the door read:

SUSAN J. MCKINNEY M.D., PhD
BIOMEDICAL SYSTEMS

As Susan walked in, Marilyn began to laugh. Susan found no humor in what had just happened and complained, "Why did you leave me with that jerk? You know he's been pestering me for months!"

"Ah, come on. Todd's awkward advances are good for your defenses. It keeps you quick on your feet and off your back."

"And just what do you mean by that? You are not my romantic counselor, ya know."

"What I meant was . . . uh . . . You just have to watch your step with Todd, that's all."

"Yeah right. Anyway, I've gotta get this program finished before I go home this afternoon. I'm going to work on it in the inner office, so don't let anyone bother me. And for God's sake, keep those guys down in telemetry busy. We've got to get this interface for the Mars landing done before the end of the year, and they're already two weeks behind. Call that little weasel Wilson down there and tell him to get his butt in gear. I want that data on my desk Monday morning."

"Do you want me to quote you directly on that, boss?"

"Yes, and if he gives you any back talk, remind him that he's the one who is late — not us!"

"Yes, Ma'am."

Susan began her career with an eighteen month stint at NASA, working in telemetric physiology for deep space voyages. She soon became bored and decided to take Astrolabe up on their persistent lucrative offers to head up their biomedical department. After working only two years for Astrolabe, Susan had quickly established herself as a talented and capable head of her department. Physically imposing and stunningly attractive, her athletic background made her a brutal competitor and hard-nosed about her work. She really didn't have any problems dealing with suitors like Todd. Actually, she intimidated most men with her good looks and virtually all men with her brains. Consequently, she didn't date much and stayed home most evenings with her cat, Cosmo.

Men like Todd, attracted to her physically and too stupid to recognize her intellectual superiority, were merely an inconvenience. She remained polite and aloof, letting them know she was not interested as subtly as possible. Privately, however, she often wondered if she would ever find someone to be her soul mate. It seemed only men like Todd ever approached her, but she knew the rest were simply afraid. Where would she ever find someone who was not intimidated by her beauty but also smart enough to be her equal, if not here among so many of the best and brightest? Her question was always rhetorical, and it remained so now, as she headed for the inner office.

Max spent most of the afternoon plowing away on his Keck telescope problem. About 4:30, Frank finished calibrating the spectrum analyzer and said, "If it's all right with you, I'm going to knock off a little early. These casino chips are burning a hole in my pocket. I can't wait to get to the blackjack table and work on my system. Do ya wanna come along?"

"No, you and Jenny enjoy yourselves. Shall I book your trip to Barbados?"

"You better hold off 'til Monday. You may need to bail me out of the Stone County jail for losing my shirt at the casino and sellin' my wife into bondage."

Just then, Harvey, the chief security guard, tapped on the door and stepped inside.

"Sorry to bother you, Dr. Gibson. A special messenger left this package at the security shack at the front gate a few minutes ago. It looks important, and so I brought it right up. We gave it a routine sweep, and it doesn't have any metal devices or explosives in it. We could see a latch and a couple of precision hinges on the X-ray. It looks like some kinda box with a long metal bar in it. You want me to open it downstairs in the explosives cage?"

"Who's it from, Harv?"

"I don't know. It doesn't have a return address. If it means anything, Dr. McKinney up in the Biomed lab got one just like it only a little smaller"

"That's okay. Just leave it on the desk, Harv. I'll take care of it."

"Whatever ya say, Doc."

Frank took his coat out of the closet and prepared to leave. As he was putting on his scarf, Max asked, "Frank, do you remember Susan McKinney?"

"You mean the one with the big brain and the world class body? Sure. How could you forget a babe like her? Gilroy says she's an iceberg, but you know Mr. Macho. He thinks anyone he hasn't slept with is an iceberg. She's one of those dual degree whiz kids, trained as a physician but too smart to be wasted on a medical practice. She got her PhD in aerospace physiology a year later. She's a real hotshot on computers too. I hear the guys from NASA are always calling her to fix their screw-ups with the telemetry on the space station. Well, if there ain't anything else, I'm taking off to get rich at the casino. See ya Monday."

Max gave Frank a wave as he left. "Have fun and don't spend your whole check!"

Max pulled the package across the desk, surprised at how heavy it was. He took out his Swiss army knife and cut the cotton string securing the brown wrapping paper and folded it back. He uncovered a rich dark colored wooden box. "My God," he quietly exclaimed. "This box is beautiful!"

It looked like the box had been carved out of a single piece of ebony. It had no joints or seams and gave off a faint aroma of cedar. On what appeared to be the top, Max recognized the gold inlay of an ancient Egyptian amulet in the shape of an ostrich feather. He had seen these when his dad had been stationed in the Middle East. The insignia fit so precisely it looked like it was part of the wood. The box was so well crafted that the top and bottom halves appeared seamless, it was not obvious how to open it. On what Max judged to be the front, a gold oval about the size of a quarter was inlaid into the wood. He picked up the box and inspected it carefully. The surface had a sheen, smooth but not glossy, and it had obviously been hand rubbed with some type of cedar oil. Max thought the box absolutely exquisite.

Unable to readily open the box, Max set it on the bench and just admired it. Then, somewhat frustrated, he pushed firmly on the gold oval and the box popped open. Inside, the wood on the upper and lower halves had been precisely carved out to fit the shape of the most beautiful object Max had ever seen. Nestled in the lower half was an eighteen-inch long hexagonal crystal rod that looked like a diamond. It fit so precisely in the cavity that Max had a hard time getting the crystal out. When he finally dislodged it, he inspected the crystal rod carefully and held it up to the light. It sparkled brilliantly!

After a few minutes of playing with and admiring it, he realized that Susan probably received something just as exciting. He fumbled through the company directory and located her three-digit extension. Hurriedly, he punched it in and waited impatiently for someone to answer. "Surely, she hasn't gone home yet," he thought to himself.

Finally, an answer: "Yes?"

"Is Dr. McKinney in, please? Oh sorry, Susan. I didn't recognize your voice. Did you get a package in the past few minutes? No, I didn't send it. No, I don't know who sent it. Did it have a dark wooden box in it? I think I may have received one like it. Listen. Why don't you bring your box down to my lab on the first floor and let's compare notes? Right. See you in a minute."

Max carefully took the crystal rod to the scale. "Unbelievable," he muttered. "The scale says 5.5076 kilograms, but there is no way this thing could weigh over twelve pounds!"

He took the crystal to the workbench, where he tried to pass a laser through it without success. The laser merely reflected off the surface as if the crystal were a mirror. "Impossible," he muttered. "I can see through this thing, so how can it reflect the laser?"

Susan came to the door clutching the box under her coat, instinctively concealing what she had and a bit surprised at herself for doing so. She bounded across the room and asked excitedly, "Do you have any idea what this is?"

"Not a clue. Let's see what you've got."

As if it were a Christmas present, Susan placed the box on the countertop and proudly opened it for Max. To his surprise, it was not a crystal rod like his at all, but round, about the size of a baseball, and with hundreds of facets. The object sparkled and glistened in the light, flashing blue and red pulses of reflected light as Max turned it. Standing speechless and dumbfounded, the two admired what appeared to be at least a twenty thousand karat diamond. All either could manage to say was simply, "Wow!"

Holding a crystal in each hand, Max asked, "Can you believe how heavy these things are?" He then carefully placed Susan's on the analytic scale, and they watched the readout come to rest at 5.5076 kilograms. "Yours is exactly the same weight as mine!"

As Susan looked more carefully, she noticed that her round crystal had a small indentation on one of the facets. She and Max looked at each other as if to say, "*Why not?*"

They took their respective crystals and placed them together. At the moment the objects touched, there was a "click" like two strong magnets popping together and the crystals were joined. To Max and Susan's amazement, the two objects began to glow with a pale pink sparkle. Suddenly, across the room, a printer zipped out a quick burst of information on the paper. Susan jumped. "Did you do that?"

Max, who was also startled, exclaimed, "Are you kidding! I nearly dropped these things. Let's see what it printed."

They went over to the printer on the south wall and read: "Does anyone know you have received your special gift?"

Max and Susan answered in unison, "No." They were spellbound and felt ridiculous talking to a computer printer, but as if in answer, there was more printing!

"Excellent! You are requested to take your gifts to Dr. Gibson's home. The person who sent them will meet you there at 1930 hours."

They read this message, and then there was more printing: "Destroy this transmission."

As soon as the printer stopped, the crystals separated in Max's hands and the pink glow faded. He and Susan stood looking at the printer as if it were the Oracle of Delphi. After exchanging glances of disbelief, Max cleared his throat and said, "If this is one of Bradley's practical jokes from down at the lens grinding lab, I will kill him."

"Bradley?" Susan questioned. "No way. This is way beyond him. He has trouble making a fist let alone pulling off something so elaborate. I had a date with him once and, trust me, he couldn't have done this!"

Max glanced at his watch. "I guess we should get moving if we are going to comply with . . . Well, with the printer's request, for lack of a better way to say this. It is well after five o'clock. Maybe we will get some answers at my house at 7:30." Max carefully placed the crystals in their slots inside the boxes and secured the lids with a "snap." Max then turned, collected the printout and stuffed it in the shredder to destroy the evidence.

Max quietly asked, "Did you really go out with Bradley?" Susan turned slowly and gave him a look that could have stopped a truck. He didn't pursue the topic further.

Gathering up their treasures, Max and Susan put on their coats and headed out into the storm, not knowing they were about to embark on the most important journey in the history of Man.

CHAPTER 3

Winter's precipitation barrage had left a two-inch layer of slush on the streets, making the usual twenty-minute drive to Max's house almost half an hour. Max led the way in the BMW and Susan followed closely in her Jeep. Their brief journey led to the wooded area that sheltered Max's cabin, which looked rustic but was obviously designed to appear that way. The cabin was about three miles off the main road, which was only poorly laid asphalt known locally as chip and seal, and so the access road to his property was, to say the least, primitive. Max owned two hundred acres of land on top of Radford Mountain overlooking the Buffalo River Valley just west of Hasty, Arkansas. Situated to face west, the cabin had a wide covered deck that flanked the entire south and west side with a view of the valley and river below.

As they started up the sidewalk, Susan commented, "This is really neat. Did you build it yourself?"

Showing no small amount of pride, Max replied, "Yes. The architect and I had quite a time getting the plans the way I wanted, but I was happy with how it turned out. Come on in and see for yourself."

He led her up the wooden plank steps onto the spacious front porch. Built in the old southern style, the front porch was almost like an outside room, suitable for porch swings and relaxed enjoyment of the spectacular scenery on cool summer evenings. Each corner and roof support was made of a sturdy eight-inch pine post that had been stripped of its bark and roughly hewn, giving the modern house a rugged and backwoods appearance. Precisely cut horizontal timbers formed the walls and gave ample room for the two large triple glazed windows that, together with the front door, completed the front façade of the house. As they entered, they were greeted by the homey aroma of a wood burning stove and the unmistakable smell of Ozark cedar.

The front door opened into a large vaulted room with exposed roof trusses made of single pine timbers spaced about every six feet. Susan noted that tongue and groove cedar covered the inside of the roof structure and was the source of the delightful aroma inside the great room. To the left, an expertly designed and well-equipped kitchen dominated the north side of the room. The six-burner stove was recessed into a wall nook and a ceramic tile countertop surrounded the burners. Concealed beneath the surface, a large burner for a wok was situated in the traditional Chinese style so the wok could be placed over the heat and be level with the stove top. A brick arch completed the professional cooking area, which would rival any restaurant's. A high-volume exhaust system and fire suppression equipment let everyone know this kitchen meant business.

Toward the back of the main room, facing the front door, a stairway led to the upstairs sleeping quarters. A downstairs guest bedroom, bath and utility area formed the back wall and hallway to the back door. Susan remained wide eyed, stunned at the beauty and primitive elegance of Max's home. Max helped her with her coat and then took the crystal boxes and carefully placed them on the coffee table. As he casually tossed his own coat on the sofa, he remarked, "It's only six o'clock, how about I fix us some dinner before our guest arrives?"

"Great. I'm starved."

Then, as if he were a head waiter offering the daily special, Max inquired, "Would you care for some Chinese style orange beef?"

"That sounds great. I love Chinese food. Do you cook for yourself often?"

Max lit up as he said with confidence, "I guess you could say I enjoy cooking. In fact, I relish it far beyond its true importance. I consider good food part of the meaning-of-life category. Why don't you put on some music, and I'll get started on dinner?"

Eager to be of help, Susan went to the stereo and looked over his collection. "What are you in the mood for?"

"Anything is okay with me. There are some classical pieces on the top shelf over the stereo."

Susan leafed through the flash memory cards on the shelf and finally came to something that interested her. "How about some Rachmaninoff?"

"That's super. I had to play the Paganini once for a recital, so believe me, I know every note. It is still one of my favorites." As they talked, Max removed ingredients from the refrigerator in preparation for his cooking exhibition.

Susan found *Rhapsody on a Theme of Paganini* played by Philip Entremont and the Philadelphia Philharmonic. The music would be a splendid accompaniment to the spectacle that was about to unfold in front of her as Max began to prepare their dinner. It was as if he had been transformed from a mild-mannered physicist into Super Chef. He waltzed around the kitchen, never making a false move. It seemed to Susan that he had the focus and game face of an Olympic diver just before leaving the ten meter platform to do a triple summersault for the gold — pike position of course. He chopped. He diced. He shredded. All this without missing a stroke with his razor-sharp Chinese cleaver as it did its work on a dazzling array of vegetables, fresh ginger root, and a half pound of beef brisket. He retrieved the usual Chinese staples of soy sauce, star anise, dried orange peel, garlic as well as a jar of orange marmalade and a can of Mandarin oranges from the pantry. The ingredients assembled, he took the wok from the overhead rack, put it on the stove, and started the rice maker.

"The rice will take a few minutes. What's your pleasure for some wine? I have a selection in the basement."

Susan, not being a connoisseur, replied, "Whatever you recommend to accompany the meal is fine with me."

"Come downstairs and we'll pick something together."

Susan followed him down the stairs to what seemed to be a whole new house. The basement contained not only a wine cellar but what looked to Susan like a complete dry goods department: canned goods, freeze dried food of every description, and to top it off, a walk-in freezer!

Susan pondered a moment and then said, "Max, why do you have all this food? You live alone, don't ya?"

Her question caught Max a little off guard. Hesitating a moment, he finally said, "Actually, I hate to shop. No, that's not right. I really loathe shopping. So, I go into Little Rock about every six months and try to get all of my stuff at once. Most of the specialty items are only available there anyway. I might as well get it all done in one fell swoop and just stock up so I don't have to shop again for a long time."

"I guess that makes sense, but since I love to shop, I never have more than two days' supply of anything. I find shopping relaxes me somehow, and so I go every couple of days. I'm on a first name basis with every clerk in Harrison."

While Max reviewed his selection of vintage wines, looking for the perfect choice, Susan strolled around the basement as if shopping, taking stock of the myriad of goods Max had laid in so he, as he said, "does not need to shop again for a long time."

"What's all this mechanical stuff at the end of the room, Max?"

"Oh, that. It's the solar storage and heat transfer unit to control the temperature of the cabin when I'm away. There are twenty thousand gallons of water in a storage tank beyond that wall, which is heated by the solar panels outside in the winter. During the summer, I circulate spring water through the system to keep the cabin cool. I designed the system myself. It's controlled by a small computer that has sensors that do most of the work. Actually, the cabin is completely self sufficient. I could last a year and never leave this room. Ah, here we are: a good California wine, a '12 Pinot. This will be perfect."

His selection made, they returned to the kitchen for the real show. After the rice had finished cooking and the oil in the wok was nearly smoking, he plunged a pile of slivered red onion and diced ginger root into the wok, creating a heavenly aroma that prompted Susan to say, "Wow! What a delightful smell. I hope it tastes even half as good as it smells."

Max confidently continued to work his magic, constantly stirring as he added the paper-thin slices of brisket to the mixture. Susan leaned on the counter that separated the kitchen proper from the dining area and watched with wonder. The beef cooked quickly in the hot oil, and then he added the vegetables. For the final touch, he added the orange peel, marmalade, and Mandarin oranges. The food cooking over a blistering hot fire created copious steam that billowed up from the wok. The sauce was completed with a little soy, sherry, sugar, corn starch, and Cointreau Liqueur. "Absolute perfection!" Max muttered to himself before he proudly presented the dish at the dining table. He dished up the rice on his plain white china and finished the setting with two sets of chopsticks.

As they sat down, Susan said, "My God, Max. Where on Earth did you learn to do that? You didn't measure a thing!"

"You mean where did I learn to cook? Oh, it seems like I've always done it. My mother let me play around in the kitchen when I was a kid, and I just sort of fell into it. My dad was in the Air Force, and we traveled a lot. So I learned as much as possible from the local people wherever we were stationed. The Asian stuff I picked up from a roommate I had at Caltech, who was Chinese and enjoyed cooking as well."

After taking her first bite, Susan had the look of someone having her shoulders rubbed after a bad day, a look of total ecstasy. "Max, this is wonderful! I've never tasted anything like it. That stuff they sell at Master Wong's carryout certainly doesn't taste like this."

Max thanked her for the compliment and said, "Let's eat!"

Susan was relishing every bite as they sat quietly with Entremont playing the mood variation to Rachmaninoff's powerful rhapsody. Max began their dinner conversation by asking, "Where did you grow up, Susan?"

"In Canton, Ohio, about an hour from Cleveland. My dad is a physical chemist and head of the metallurgy department at Diebold Safe and Lock Company. My mom is a secretary to the CEO of Hoover Sweeper Company."

"Isn't the Pro Football Hall of Fame in Canton?"

"Very good, Max. I'm glad to see you didn't spend all your time looking through a telescope. Canton is also the birthplace of President McKinley. It's still just a small town though, with a population of only about two hundred thousand people, but it was a nice place to grow up. I guess, with your father being in the military, you had lots of hometowns."

"Yeah, we lived all over the place: Europe, the Middle East, and Colorado as well as other places. It seemed like a lot of moving when I was a kid. I think we lived on fourteen bases before I went away to school at Caltech. I had gone there during summer sessions, so it was as much home to me as any place. I think that is why I love this place so much. I built it for myself, and it's a permanent home, at least as permanent as anyone gets these days. How about your family, any brothers or sisters?"

"I just have an older sister who lives in New York City. How big is your family?"

"I have a sixteen-year-old sister who still lives at home with my parents. My older brother, Steve, was a test pilot for the Air Force. He was killed in a flying accident. My dad was teaching at the Air Force Academy when Steve was killed. We all took it pretty hard. My dad retired from the Air Force shortly afterward and has never been quite the same. The whole family lives in Colorado Springs now, and my dad still does some consulting work for the Air Force and has a civilian teaching position at the academy. I still miss Steve. He was my idol and my best friend. It sure left a big hole in the family when he was killed."

Max seemed caught up in his memories for a moment, but then he smiled to lighten the mood. "How about some more wine? When did you get interested in medicine?"

"I guess I got started like most kids who take that path, with a Barbie doll stethoscope and a burning desire on the part of my parents to have a doctor in the family. You know, the usual stuff. When I was about nine or ten, I began to think seriously about being a doctor. I thought it would be fun and exciting. Now look at me. I spend nearly all of my time working at the same thing I thought was so much fun as a kid, and sometimes, it really is fun. Unfortunately, most of the time, it's just plain hard work."

Max remembered, "I got started with telescopes when I was about eight. My dad bought me this little twenty-power telescope. I thought the universe belonged to me. With my first trip to Palomar, I was hooked. After that trip, all of the math and physics were just an excuse to get into the observatory and see what was out there. Do you ever regret spending so much time at your work?"

"The amount of time I spend working bothers me all the time. When I gave up tennis to finish medical school, I truly missed the competitive action and social interaction of the game. You have to be pretty tough in medical school, because it is so competitive, and you can't afford to be very lady like, which means one's social life suffers. But mostly there just isn't much time for a decent social life. When I was in school, I became just one of the guys, and most of my female classmates were so jealous they hated my guts. Being first in the class didn't help much either. Women tend to be that way, jealous of someone who excels. The bottom line is I didn't develop much of a social life in college when most young people are reveling in theirs."

"I know what you mean. It's really hard for people like us to meet anyone. I mean, with work and all here in the middle of the Ozarks, I envy Frank and Jenny, the fact that they have each other. They have already started their family and seem to be really happy. Frank talks all the time about missing his social life, but I think he is happy just where he is, with Jenny. He talks a good game, but he loves being a daddy and having a stable home life."

"I sometimes wonder if I will ever find someone," Susan said. "It isn't easy, you know, for a woman who is five feet ten inches and works all day with computers and lab rats to find someone compatible. My sister is married and has two great kids, and I really enjoy being around her family."

After Susan's remark, neither said anything for a while. They just enjoyed the food, each quietly within their own thoughts.

After they finished every morsel and Max had poured the final bit of wine into their glasses, Susan said, "Why don't you let me do the dishes. It's the least I can do after this magnificent meal."

"Sure. That would be great. I'll clear the table and get ready for our guest, whoever that will turn out to be, maybe a walking printer." They both chuckled uncomfortably, both curious and a bit wary of the strange gifts and what happened with the printer.

Living alone, Max was all but fully domesticated and so he cleared the table and helped put away the dishes and utensils. It was obvious they were a natural team, and they seemed to enjoy working together. When they had finished, they moved to the front part of the great room and sat down to finish their wine.

"Max, what do you really think the crystals are all about?"

"I've been thinking about that, and to be honest, I simply don't have the slightest idea. They certainly are high-tech. Before you came down to the lab today, I tried to scratch the surface of the crystal rod with a diamond drill — nothing. And the material is so heavy it must be a high molecular weight matrix of some kind. But I don't understand how something could have the mass of a metal and be in crystal form. To weigh that much, the crystals would have to have a molecular weight of at least two-hundred or be made of a crystal alloy of some type. The material is certainly not like anything I've seen before. It's not radioactive either. I checked. It really is a puzzle."

"My dad's company makes bank vault doors and armor plate for military vehicles, and so they work with hard metals and ceramics all the time. He's never mentioned anything that would stand up to a diamond drill. A tungsten alloy is the hardest metal they make, and it's still a lot softer than a diamond drill."

Just then the doorbell rang. Max looked at his watch — exactly 7:30. He and Susan glanced at each other with a look of anticipation as Max went to the door to greet their mystery guest. When he opened the door, he was surprised to see a short, slightly-built man with about a three-day growth of beard, the type worn by many Arab men in the Middle East. He was wearing a Russian style fur hat — it appeared to be dark mink — and a heavy coat.

"Hi. I'm Max Gibson. Won't you please come in?"

"Thank you," the man said with a slight British accent.

As he shook the visitor's hand, Max said, "I'd like to introduce my colleague, Dr. Susan McKinney. We've been waiting to meet you." The man shook her hand and then removed his dark tweed wool coat, which was covered with snow from the continuing storm. He was dressed in a simple white linen shirt buttoned all the way to the neck and a pair of black pants. The only peculiar aspect of his dress was a heavy metallic belt, which looked like finely braided stainless steel or polished aluminum and didn't seem to match his rather ordinary attire.

"I'm afraid the weather is still quite dreadful. Sorry to get your floor wet." The man took a seat across the dining table from Max and Susan. "I trust that no one knows about my gift to you?"

Max and Susan answered in unison, "No."

"Very well then. We may begin. My name is Nute. I'm also known by many other names, but you may call me Nute. This will be hard for you to believe, but I'm what you would refer to as an

44

alien. I'm from a faraway place, and I represent our United Galaxy Council. Your planet has been under observation for nearly three-million of your years."

Totally captivated, Max and Susan both sat motionless. Nute continued to speak, sounding very much like a father telling his children a bedtime story.

"Long ago, during one of our regular observation trips, your present life form was noted in northeast Africa. You were the most successful descendants of a now extinct species of chimpanzee. We became more interested because we noted the first signs of intelligence: the use of tools, primitive speech, and especially, your species' clever dominance over other life forms.

"So, we began to keep notes on your development, visiting periodically over the next several hundred thousand years. We began to see campfires along the eastern rim of the Mediterranean Sea, a significant development, and eventually, two hundred thousand years ago, your species was assigned to me as governor of this sector. I have since kept a more detailed catalog of your activities."

Max blurted out, " How can you personally have observed us this long? It seems impossible for anyone, no matter how advanced your species might be, to live for hundreds of thousands of our years."

"I know this is difficult for you to understand right now, but you must simply accept that our life form has a much longer lifespan than yours. We must leave it at that for now. Okay?"

Max was not satisfied with the answer, but he and Susan gave each other a look that seemed to say, *"Let's hear him out, no matter how strange this tale is thus far."*

Nute continued, "One hundred thousand years ago, I spent ten years living among your ancestors and several similar species. After much observation and documentation, it was determined that your species was indeed developing as a K-10 culture, a level of cultural development we have seen many times before in this sector and throughout the galaxy. What this basically means is that your species would dominate all others but eventually become extinct.

"Let me explain. Your evolution from lower primates was successful because you were able to overcome your environment and successfully compete with other predators and species similar to your own. This very fact, however, planted the seeds of your destruction. Your success was based not only on intelligence and the use of tools but on territorial dominance and aggression toward your enemies. This worked well when you were fighting for survival against lower animals. It did not serve you so well, however, when your enemies became members of your own species.

"Eventually, as technology developed, your ability to inflict death and destruction on your enemies became more effective. First, it was a club, then the bow and arrow, and eventually your species achieved thermonuclear capabilities."

Max tried to interrupt with a question, but Nute held up his hand and said, "Please be patient. I will answer your questions later."

The strange guest continued. "It was decided that your civilization and thirteen others in this sector would be selected for special intervention: we would try to help you *not* destroy yourselves. In time, it was hoped that you might join with us and become productive members of the Council. The rules for our help as laid down by the Council, were simple and very specific: We cannot intervene or participate in any warfare; we cannot provide information you are not capable of understanding; there will be certain levels of assistance we can offer, specifically Levels One through Ten; if you are to be successful, you must achieve success yourselves. Simply put, we cannot tell you what to do to stave off extinction, but within certain limits, we can answer your questions about how to do it."

Nute then asked, "Are the crystals available?"

"Of course," Max replied, and then he brought them to the table from where he and Susan had left them in the other room.

Nute opened the boxes as if they were old friends. He put the crystals together and pointed the round end toward the open part of the room. With the crystals glowing, he began to tell his story:

"In 40,000 BC, by your way of reckoning the past, I came to live with the nomadic people in northern Africa, where we had observed them for tens of thousands of years. They were proficient with fire and very good hunters. Having the mental capacity for more advanced technology, and with an improving climate, we decided they were the place to start in your species' attempt to avoid its end. I had a wonderful time living among these people. I taught them pottery making and basic metal working with copper, and I taught them to improve their stone tool making capabilities. I also came to appreciate their social interaction and the workings of tribal life."

As Nute spoke, the crystal projected a hologram so lifelike that it was like being on the northern plains of Africa themselves. Max and Susan saw Nute living among the tribal people and teaching them what amounted to high technology for their time.

He went on, "Since the ice was now receding, marking the end of that particular ice age, I continued my travels to Europe, China, India, and Central America over the next thirty-five years, teaching Level-One technology. Also during this stay, we did a genome inventory and identified the five basic racial types of your species. An observation satellite was left in place to monitor the planet and communicate the findings to our space-based control center.

"I made my next trip in 6500 BC. My mission was to help your species start agriculture."

As Nute went on to describe his many trips to Earth, Max and Susan were spellbound. He revealed how he was present at nearly all intellectual achievements over the millennia. These earliest cultural advances, which he hoped would stabilize human civilization at any given point in time, were spread to the indigenous people from Stonehenge to Australia and Central America.

During subsequent trips, he introduced writing to all of the Middle Eastern cultures, first with pictographs and later with phonetic alphabets. As time went on, the scope and intensity of the cultural advances he had introduced grew exponentially.

Nute continued, "I had been working with a farming community near what was later called Memphis in the Nile River Valley and had to leave for an emergency. So I left the crystals with a member of your species for the first time, with Narmer, a local chieftain. I didn't know what I would find on my return. I didn't get back for seventy-five years, and to my surprise, when I returned to the Nile River Valley to help the descendants of my old friends, the culture had developed rapidly. The tribe was quite advanced in terms of farming techniques and the establishment of a fledgling government and many new religions.

"Narmer had been succeeded by Hor-Aha, and the new Egyptian nation, with its capitol at Memphis, had been formed. I was impressed by the people who used the Level-Three knowledge the crystal imparted. I was particularly impressed with a builder named Imhotep, who took a simple concept of construction using mud bricks and began what was later to become the most grandiose use of the triangle in architecture ever known on Earth — the building of the Great Pyramids. Although I was skeptical about the use of this information for further development, it was obvious progress had begun. So I took the crystals and headed for my next stop on my regular rounds.

"I returned periodically until 1741 BC, when a new assessment was made, and we noted some civilizations had progressed and others had not done so well. The Egyptians, Babylonians, and Chinese had fared the best, and so we continued to teach them. Some of the cultures we found in Central America were removed from our help list because of their continued practice of human sacrifice, especially of children. In fact, this practice was so abhorrent to us that it was decided to never help those peoples again. We then became more discreet with our assistance. Since the societies had now developed central governments, the leaders jealously guarded our knowledge, not only from their enemies but from their own people as well, so that they could remain in power by virtue of their subjects' relative ignorance. Unfortunately, during my travels, I mistakenly became known as a court mystic with god-like attributes. But since we continued to make good progress, we accepted your species' misplaced platitudes.

"During this time, we wanted to teach the concepts of law and mathematics and introduce more advanced astronomy. All of the improving cultures were receptive to our teachings, and I was particularly impressed with the Babylonian king, Hammurabi. Since he did not know how to explain my wisdom, he mistakenly referred to me as the lawgiver god, Shamash. My elevation to a deity notwithstanding, this was a very good trip.

"During the previous fourteen hundred years, the cultures of the Middle East had flourished but they had also fought many wars and remained fragmented. Religion had consumed enormous amounts of energy to the aggrandizement of their leaders. Religion and the kinship of the kings and pharaohs to their gods had subverted the advancement of these civilizations, which were then merely preoccupied with the warrior-king-god succession scenario.

"This led to the self-indulgence that produced the pyramids, obelisks, and any number of enormous self-serving artifacts on a grand scale. Most of these grandiose edifices and accompanying ceremonies were designed to provide immortality to the leaders. For them, life was good and they wanted it to continue forever. Wars came and went. Religions came and went. Kings and pharaohs came and went. Since the kings basically kept nearly all of the technology from the ordinary people, often that technology was lost after a war because the survivors were mostly illiterate. We felt what was needed was political unification and integration of the cultures of these relatively advanced civilizations."

Susan, obviously growing impatient with their odd guest, interrupted. "I don't understand. What does any of this have to do with us?"

"Be patient, Dr. McKinney. In due course all this will make sense." Nute seemed a little amused by Susan's question, but he quickly continued his tutorial in the same fatherly tone as before.

"During the intervening centuries, the world's population advanced and was again diminished by a succession of wars only to be built back up again. The Chinese were a notable exception to this build-and-destroy cycle. I was pleased to see relatively steady progress, the civilization reaching a high degree of development with only occasional help from me. I believe this advancement was due to a rather strong government and the level of order the society achieved because of the religious philosopher Confutza. He was later to be known in the west as Confucius. I felt the other regions could benefit from this type of order and stability, so I looked for the opportunity to concentrate on this aspect of development in the Mediterranean area.

"In 336 BC, I became a confidant to a young man from Macedonia named Alexander. I advised him on military tactics and the political goal of the unification of his empire, which was later to encompass the entire region from Italy to the Indus Valley. Rather than keep technology secret, I advised that books be written and made available in libraries and that the social intermingling of Middle East cultures be encouraged to strengthen them and develop political order. Alexander was very successful and made a great contribution to the advancement of civilization. After his untimely death from malaria, I left to attend other business on my regular rounds.

"Over the next several centuries, I gave help at Level Five where I thought appropriate. After two years of evaluation, the Council decided to move to Level Six, and I spent the summer of 1775 with Isaac Newton in his country home, mostly answering questions about the work of others such as Kepler, Descartes, and Galileo. I also answered Newton's questions about calculus and the laws of gravity. He was a rather unpleasant and arrogant fellow, but he was intelligent. So our time together was well spent. Once again, I had to tend to other business and left the Earth's civilization to develop on its own for a while.

"In 1903, the Council approved Level Seven, and I spent about three months with Albert Einstein, answering his questions about Plank's work with quantum mechanics, relativity, and Brownian movement. Unfortunately, I was unable to stay with him, and he misunderstood parts of my explanation."

Nute sighed at this point, almost wistfully it seemed to his listeners.

"But, all of this is just history, and I mention it only to give you some background to our current situation. I am really here to talk to you about my current trip. We are coming to the crux of our management of your planet. I say this for the following four reasons:

"1. Your technological advancement is accelerating, and as we predicted long ago, it will far outstrip your ability to manage it politically.

"2. Weapons development and the expertise to use them are fast becoming dispersed worldwide, which was also expected, just as all technology eventually became dispersed in the past.

"3. The warrior-king-god complex is still prevalent in many parts of your world, and it is only a matter of time before religious, ethnic, economic, or national interests trigger a conflagration that will extinguish your species. We estimate this will happen in the next twenty-five years.

"4. We have been impressed with your progress in some areas, the United Nations, for example. However, there is no real commitment by the member states and it remains a weak and ineffectual organization overall. Our hope is not that we will eliminate the arrogance, pomposity, and burning desire of the world's leaders to dominate others of your species — these attributes are all part of your nature. It is, however, impossible for you to survive without the ability to control those among you who wish to pursue their prehistoric inclinations to subjugate their enemies. Even if those among you thus inclined have no one to subjugate, we realize they will invent an enemy if necessary.

"For these reasons, we are at a time in your history when something must be done or *all humanity* will perish. The two of you have been selected to accomplish this task. We have studied you over the past several years, and you have been given clearance to receive information to Level Eight. This is a great responsibility. You will be assisted by the crystals you received today, and you will have one year to show the Council that you can prevent your species' self-destruction. If you fail, I will return in one year and take you away from this planet to a safer place where you will be the seeds for a new civilization. At the very least, the Council wants to save the genome of your species, as your kind has many outstanding and unique qualities. On a personal note, my time here has been very enjoyable, and I have a genuine affection for the people I have met along the way in your civilization's journey. Additionally, the vast diversity of plants and animals found on your planet has great value in their uniqueness and should be protected from extinction.

"By way of explanation, the crystals are here to help you. They can provide information and guidance, but the rules of the Council are firm: You may not receive information beyond Level Eight. However, I think you will find the information at Level Eight to be of great use to you. But, remember, you must do the job yourself."

This odd little man then folded his hands in his lap and peered at the two of them, smiling broadly.

"Before I answer any of your questions, and there are always many, you must decide if you want to participate in this endeavor. You must also agree to the stipulations of the Council. You will have twenty-four hours to reach your decision. I will leave you now and return tomorrow evening at the same time to get your answer."

Nute then got up, put on his coat and hat, and left the cabin without another word.

CHAPTER 4

Having endured an hour of one shock and revelation after another, Max and Susan were exhausted. They sat at the table without saying a word, mystified by the "story" they had just heard. Neither knew if it was just a story or the truth of human history. After a few moments, Max deliberately and thoughtfully turned to Susan, "Did you hear a car?"

"What did you say? I didn't hear you."

Max repeated his question as he got up and went to the window to look out at the driveway. "Did you hear a car leave?" He quickly got his coat and went outside to see if Nute had left in a car. Stumbling headlong down the steps, he caught himself on the railing and narrowly avoided burying his face in the slush.

Looking out of the open doorway, Susan yelled out maternally, "Are you all right?"

Brushing the mixture of snow and sleet off his knees, Max said, "Yeah, I'm okay." When he had gathered himself, he located Nute's footprints in the snow and followed them intently for about twenty feet, where they took an abrupt and unexpected turn to the south and headed toward the bluff. Max called back to Susan, "Toss me that flashlight that's in the closet next to the front door."

Susan quickly complied and dropped the light over the porch railing as he waited below. With the aid of the flashlight, Max followed the prints all the way to the edge of the sheer cliff face, which dropped straight down seven hundred feet to the valley below. The fence that Max had built to protect strangers from accidentally wandering off the precipice was intact, and the prints simply stopped two steps beyond the fence. Max got a chill on the back of his neck as he realized what had happened. Nute had gone off the cliff! He began to panic. He felt like someone had just punched him in the stomach, a tight nauseous feeling rising in his guts. He nervously climbed over the fence, and while holding on to the top wire, he directed his light down into the brush that covered the cliff face. There was no sign of Nute, and in fact, the snow was completely undisturbed. There was no sign he had fallen. The prints in the snow just stopped, and then nothing — no body and no prints and no fallen debris. Max's heart was pounding.

"What is it, Max?"

"Nothing, I'll be right there." He slowly climbed over the fence and made his way back to the cabin. Ashen and somber, he walked up the steps, past Susan, and into the cabin without saying a word.

Susan was growing more agitated by the minute. "What's the matter? You look as though you have seen a ghost!" When Max was unresponsive, she exclaimed even louder, "Max, what's wrong with you!"

Susan shut the door and followed Max, who went to the liquor cabinet, took out a bottle of 101 proof Wild Turkey Kentucky Straight Bourbon, and poured about two ounces into a tumbler. He gulped it down. He was transfixed, like he had been hypnotized. Then he seemed to shake himself into the moment. He finally turned to her and said, "Do you want a drink?"

Fear was beginning to creep into her voice as she asked, "What did you see out there?" Staring straight ahead again, Max didn't respond. Instead he poured himself another drink. She stood in front of him, took hold of his shoulders, and said, "Max, talk to me. WHAT DID YOU SEE?"

He picked up the bottle and slowly walked to the couch, sat down, and finally began to speak. "I don't know what you think we saw and heard here tonight, but I think we may have just witnessed a legitimate miracle. Nute has flown away."

"WHAT? You don't mean that he actually flew away."

"Yes, I mean he just flew away."

"How do you know that?" she inquired in her best scientific, no-nonsense tone, which was nevertheless tinged with nervousness.

"I just followed his footprints to a seven-hundred-foot drop-off, and they simply stopped at the edge. There was no place for him to go but up."

Susan thought for a moment. "Into the sky?" She had a look of stark disbelief on her face as she slowly walked to the liquor cabinet and took out a glass, came over to Max and said in a whisper, "Give me that bottle, I think I will have that drink now!"

Her hand was trembling as he poured her glass half full of the liquid courage. They both just sat there, mesmerized, nursing their Wild Turkey and listening to the quiet patter of the sleet on the roof.

After about five minutes of silence, Max, in an uncharacteristic revelation of his innermost thoughts, said, "Ya know, all my adult life, I have dreamed of finding life out there someplace. I have spent countless hours squinting through telescopes and looking at pixel scanners, looking for some minuscule evidence that someone, something, is out there — all with the unspoken hope that I would be the one to make the discovery. Now, as it happens, and if we are to believe our guest's tale at all, I am the one that has been discovered, analyzed, and catalogued. Then, as if that weren't enough, when it came to the moment of truth, I didn't do anything. I just sat there and let this incredible being walk out of my house and fly off without a word. How stupid! How unscientific! I can't believe I just sat there. I didn't even ask him where he was from, how he got here, how old he is, what he has for breakfast. I didn't ask a damn thing!"

Susan interrupted. "Wait a minute. We don't even know this guy is really who he says he is. He could be some high-tech magician, for all we know. He could have had a stealth helicopter snatch him off the cliff."

"Get serious, Susan. Have you had a look at the weather outside? No helicopter could fly tonight. Besides, who would want to pull a stunt like this? To what purpose?"

"Well, maybe you're right, but we still don't know he is an alien from outer space. God, that sounds like a line out of a comic book! Listen. What we need is some independent proof, or at least some evidence, some minimal data to support what we think we saw here tonight."

Max, exasperated that he seemed to be losing his well-trained objectivity, said, "Of course, you are right. Let's get a grip and try to do some checking. Maybe we can make some sense out of all of this."

"Okay, Max. Let's make a list of what we know for a fact." They returned to the table with a more business-like attitude, Max retrieving a yellow legal pad from the roll-top desk in the corner on the way. He handed the pad to Susan, and she began to make notes of what they knew.

"First and foremost, we have the crystals." As she said this, Max retrieved them from the coffee table and put them on the dining table in front of her. Although the crystals were inoperative at the moment, they were still extraordinarily beautiful.

"Next, and quite importantly, we met a man who claims to be an alien, and it appears that he is able to fly. Though both suppositions are unconfirmed. However, he has a remarkable grasp of history and puts on a great seminar and light show.

"Unless the crystals light up again," she continued, "there isn't much we can do about them tonight, right? So let's look at something we can check: the history. Do you have a terminal here at the cabin?"

"Yes," Max replied. "There is one in the roll-top desk." Susan moved to the terminal and began to type. She keyed commands with precision and blinding speed. The screen lit up and changed so fast Max was prompted to say, "Geez, Susan. Where did you learn to work that thing? It takes me three or four minutes to do what you just whizzed through in about fifteen seconds."

"Remember, Max. I do this for a living. Okay, let's see if I can access that big fat data bank at the office and see what they have on some of this so-called history Nute claims to have observed first-hand."

Max stood behind her and looked on as she continued to work her magic on the keyboard, quickly gaining access to Astrolabe's reference library. " Okay, let's start with Egypt. What was that guy's name he says was the first human he left the crystals with?"

"Narmer, I think. Yeah, that's right, the tribal chief who was in charge of the irrigation stuff at Memphis. Okay, let's see what we have on Narmer." A database on ancient Egypt appeared on the screen. Susan then did a search for Narmer. "Ah, here we are." Then she read the contents on the screen aloud. "NARMER: Thought by many historians and Egyptologists to be the founder of unified Egypt about 3200 BC. He is considered to be the predecessor of the first Pharaoh of record called Hor-Aha. Hor-Aha was also known as Men, or Min, and was credited with the founding of the ancient city of Memphis, the first capital of the new state of Egypt. Narmer was a fierce warrior, and his conquest of the Nile River culture set the stage for the development of the original kingdom of Egypt, known as the First Dynasty. Technology and sophisticated agriculture flourished during this period. Many scholars believe this was Egypt's most creative era.

"Look, Max. There's a picture. Do you have a high resolution printer?"

"Sure. It's in the bottom of the desk." Max opened the door on a custom-built cabinet that housed a thirty-mega-pixel color printer and turned it on.

Susan quickly entered a print document command and the printer began to scroll up a picture of the slate palette of Narmer, a photo of a relief sculpture dated circa 3200 BC. They both gasped in amazement as the printer began to reveal the carving. Narmer was depicted holding an enemy by the hair and wielding a mace in his right hand. The mace Narmer held was exactly like the crystals that lay on the table across the room.

"Max, my God, you don't think this could actually be a representation of Narmer clubbing his enemy with the crystals, do you?"

"This is really getting weird. How could anyone fake something like this, Susan?"

"Okay. Let's not over react here, Max. Let's look up something else. What was the other king he mentioned in Mesopotamia?"

Max pondered for a moment, brushing his hair back with his hand as he thought. "I have it: Hammurabi. He called Nute Shamash, the lawgiver, remember."

"All right, let's try that: H-a-m-m-u-r-a-b-i. I hope this is spelled right. Okay, here we are. HAMMURABI: Babylonian king who ruled an area of the Middle East in what is present-day Iraq from 1792–1750 BC, known principally for his attempt to establish a society ruled by law. He organized and recorded the first known code of written law called the Code of Hammurabi, which detailed a set of laws to govern many questions of criminal and civil behavior of his time.

"This written code was recorded on a large black basalt stele or pillar. His legal opinions were given credence among his subjects by his proclamation that they were given to him by the sun god, Shamash, who, along with Hammurabi, is depicted on the stone sculpture. The code of law recorded by the king was the first attempt in history to provide a judicial system for a kingdom as a whole through written laws. The inscription of laws on the stone pillar is written in cuneiform, the oldest known form of writing, which was invented in this same geographic region of Mesopotamia about 1,500 years earlier. Hammurabi recorded on the stele that the laws were to be used to decide future questions faced by his descendants and their people. This was the first use of the principle of precedence in legal matters. Shamash, the sun god, was supposed to have given the laws to Hammurabi, thereby making them more legitimate.

"This concept was common to many ancient cultures, many kings or other leaders claimed to be in communication with God or gods to give authority behind their commands and laws. Remember Moses and Ten Commandments."

"Quick, Susan. Print the picture."

Susan punched up the photo of the stone sculpture, and it began to slowly emerge from the printer. There it was, confirmation of both their worst fears and best hopes. Hammurabi was depicted standing in front of a seated figure holding a rod shaped exactly like Max's crystal. Could it be that they were looking at a stone carving of Nute and Hammurabi made 3,750 years ago?

"Holy cow, Susan. Nute's tall tale might not be so tall after all. Everything he said could be for real!"

"Just a minute. Just a minute! Let's check something else. Let's see if we can find something on Mr. Wise Guy himself, Nute."

"Okay. See what you can come up with."

Susan entered Nute's name. Nothing. But under a cross referenced alternate spelling, the following popped up on the screen: "Important deities in Egyptian mythology were Nut and Hathor, goddesses of the sky and of joy; Ptah, master artist and craftsman; Thoth, the moon god, who was also scribe of the gods and the inventor of writing. Some gods, such as Amen and Osiris, were always represented in purely human form. Others were pictured as animals or with human bodies and animal heads."

Susan only got to the first line when she stopped and looked at Max. "Oh my God. Nute is a woman! Or at least in Egypt, he was a woman. It says Nut was the Egyptian goddess of the sky. Well, the deity of the sky makes sense anyway, all except for the part about it being a goddess, female, instead of a male god. Look, Max. Here is a picture of some of their religious symbols. It says here they are called amulets. Look! Here is the symbol on the crystal's box, an ostrich feather that is said to signify truth, order, and right. Either Nute really knows his history, or the box could be a genuine five-thousand-year-old Egyptian artifact."

Max mumbled that he knew he had seen that amulet before. He slowly walked to the couch and plopped down with a blank stare on his face. Then, as if he had some instant inspiration, he blurted out, "Susan, do you remember how Nute said that he had given help to various civilizations? If that is true, it might explain how technological discoveries happened in different parts of the ancient world all at once and without any cultural evolution to suggest that a given discovery had been in the works for a while."

"Yeah, so what?"

"Here is so what. How do mathematicians in China and India and in the Middle East come up with the same discovery at nearly the same time without some kind of help? That help wouldn't need to be much, just a hint or an appropriately phrased question. What if Nute did act as a catalyst in the ancient world, traveling around from place to place, just hanging out and giving a little hint as to how to proceed when needed? This would sure answer a lot of questions about giant leaps in scientific technology. You and I both know how things generally get discovered. First there is an idea. Then each generation improves on it, and progress is made one step at a time, like the car evolved from a carriage or television from radio. But every so often, sometimes hundreds of years apart, wham! Somebody has a revolutionary idea and everything changes. Take the discoveries of Galileo, Newton, or Einstein for example. There was obviously some progress being made in their time, but these people changed everything. Without their contributions, we could very well be living with sixteenth century technology today."

"Come on, Max. You don't know it to be a fact that Nute intervened, however subtly, to get cultures across the world to progress at anything like the same rate. That is just wild speculation. I'll tell you what. Tomorrow I will go to Fayetteville and talk to someone in the Ancient History Department at the University to see if any of these connections make sense to them."

Max asked, "Do you know anyone there you could talk to without raising suspicion?"

"No, not really, but Marilyn did her undergrad work there. Let me give her a call and see if she knows someone." Susan went to the phone and called her assistant. "Hi, Marilyn. This is Susan. Do you know anyone in the Anthropology Department over at the University at Fayetteville? Never mind what for. I'm doing some research, that's all. . . . I know it's Friday night. Would you just give me a name and quit carping? Dr. Rosemary Higgins." Susan jotted down the information as she spoke. "Did her PhD with Glyn Daniel at Cambridge, right? Okay, great. Thanks, Marilyn. You have a great weekend too." She hung up.

"Max, I'm going to call this Dr. Higgins and make an appointment. Marilyn says she is really sharp, an expert on ancient cultures." Susan retrieved the number from her online directory and dialed it. "Dr. Higgins? Hi, I am Dr. Susan McKinney and I work for Astrolabe near Harrison. . . . Yes, I know. Not many people have heard of it. I would like to talk to you about a research project I am working on. I need some help. . . . Well, it is a classified project. I am doing some background work and need information on ancient cultures. I was wondering if I could speak to you this weekend, say sometime tomorrow? Great. What is your home address? Okay, then I will see you tomorrow, and I look forward to it. Thanks."

"Classified? That's a little dramatic, don't you think?" Max said with a quizzical look on his face.

"Well, what did you expect me to say, Hi, this is Susan and I'm checking out the story of a spaceman named Nute and wanted to know if you have ever heard of him?"

"Yeah, I guess you're right. That does sound pretty silly. Okay, let me call my buddy at Caltech who knows everything about the history of science and technology. It is two hours earlier in California, so he should still be up." Max dialed the number and asked for Ross. "Oh . . . when will he be back? Out to dinner? All right. Tell him Max Gibson called and that I'll call again tomorrow. Okay, thanks."

"There isn't much more we can do tonight, Susan," Max said as he hung up the receiver. "Why don't we get some sleep? I am exhausted."

"Yeah, me too." Susan got up and put on her coat. As she headed for the door, she said, "Thanks for a wonderful dinner, Max. I don't know when I have enjoyed watching anyone cook so much. With all that's happened tonight, it seems like a week since we ate, but I really did enjoy it. I will get in touch with you tomorrow after I talk to Dr. Higgins."

Max opened the door for her and said as she went out on the porch, "Remember, Susan. Don't breathe a word as to why you're interested."

"Right!"

Max watched as Susan started her Jeep, then let it warm up a moment before driving off into the winter night. The sleet and snow had just about stopped now, and the sky was beginning to clear in the west. He waved to her as she turned up the gravel road and toward the highway. He thought to himself that she was a lot different than he had expected, a lot more personable. And she was even better looking up close. "*And what a body!*" he heard himself say aloud. All in all, he thought she was pretty special.

What a night, he thought as he went back into the cabin. At four o'clock that afternoon he had been working on a rather mundane optics problem, and by ten o'clock that night he was contemplating the future of mankind and its possible demise. In his heart, Max wanted to believe he had met and talked to an honest-to-goodness alien. He was filled with both excitement and apprehension. Tomorrow he would find out if he was to be one of the two most important humans to ever have lived. As he walked by the crystals on the table, he picked them up and stretched out on the couch. He lay there fully clothed, holding the crystals like they were stuffed animals and he a child, and drifted off to sleep.

The Epiphany Crystals

CHAPTER 5

The early afternoon sky cleared, allowing a warming sun to begin melting the previous day's snow and ice. The streets were filled with runoff, and steam was beginning to rise from isolated spots of bare pavement as Max splatted his way along the road that led to his driveway. Making the familiar turn onto his muddy side road, he headed for the final three miles of his typical six-mile run that would take him back to his cabin. After a night on the couch, he had been a little stiff when he began his run, but now he was loose and beginning to hit his graceful athletic stride. He felt great as he effortlessly plugged along, only slightly irritated that his running clothes were soaked with slush. His mind wasn't on the joy of running, but rather on the conversation he had earlier that morning with his friend, Ross Templeton, at Caltech. He was anxious to confirm or deny his doubts concerning the revelations from the night before, and so he had called early and gotten Ross out of bed.

Without revealing his true reasons, Max had pelted Ross for over an hour with questions about the history of scientific discovery and the curious way discoveries seemed to come in clusters. They also discussed how different cultures often came up with the same advances almost simultaneously, apparently without any contact between those cultures. Many of these coincidences had been topics of debate for decades. As Max began the last mile of his jog, he stepped up his pace and began to wonder what Susan was learning at Fayetteville.

Max was running flat-out in his final kick to the cabin, causing his running shoes to kick up a cascade of mud and melted slush with each stride. As the cabin came into view, he saw Susan on the porch with a bundle of papers under her arm. As he got closer, he could see she had a look of anticipation.

Puzzled by her presence because he did not expect to hear from her at all until later, he continued his pace until he came up the paved portion of his driveway. He ended his run as if he had just finished a marathon, holding his arms up in triumph to break an imaginary tape.

He struggled up the steps, then leaned with his hands on his knees and tried to speak while breathing deeply to recover from the exertion. "Susan, what're you doing here? I thought you were going over to the University today."

"I couldn't sleep, so I drove over last night and was waiting for Professor Higgins when she got up this morning."

Max was still gasping as he said, "How did you get through the bad weather?"

"Hey, I drive a Jeep, and when I want to go, I go! Anyway, after she got over being mad at me for coming so early on a Saturday, we had a very productive talk. How did you make out with your source at Caltech?"

Max's labored breathing continued as he said with some difficulty, "Come on in and I'll tell you about it." Max retrieved a key from under the "high security doormat" and they both went into the cabin. "I am going to grab a quick shower, so make yourself at home and keep talking," he told her as he went into the downstairs bathroom and began peeling off his dirty jogging clothes. Susan began to relate what she had learned from Professor Higgins.

"First, I had no idea how many people have had theories about exactly what we are trying to confirm. There are so many clues that point to some extra-terrestrial influence that several books have been written about it. Some of these books were obviously science fiction, but many were inspired by real unanswered questions historians and archaeologists have speculated about for decades."

"Hold off a minute while I am in the shower." When Susan heard the shower start, she strolled out on the deck and occupied herself with her own thoughts while she looked out over the scenic but barren valley covered all in white from the previous night's storm. Max finished his shower and yelled through the closed door, "Okay, Susan. Go on."

"Well, it seems a lot of technology, especially in the ancient world, just appeared. Bronze just seemed to show up, for example. The human race seems to have existed for centuries in what Higgins called the late Neolithic stage, and then, all of a sudden, bronze was everywhere. The generally accepted theory is that traders spread this technology over Europe and Asia Minor about 3000 BC, but there's a catch. China's ancient culture was somewhat behind the West Asian and European cultures when it came to bronze, possibly two or three centuries. Then, like some kind of lightning bolt of innovation struck that land, they had a full-blown bronze industry. They started producing elaborate ornamental works that were far more advanced than anything the other cultures with bronze technology could make. The Chinese were using highly sophisticated metal-working techniques without any evolution of their previous bronze-working processes.

"The scholars argue that there must have been some intellectual diffusion from the West. I don't think so. I don't see how this diffusion could have escaped being included in the historical record, and moreover, the West was not even using these advanced techniques as far as anyone has yet discovered. I think it was really Nute, as he said.

"Have you ever heard of an anthropologist named Thor Heyerdahl?"

Max responded, "Isn't he the guy who sailed a reed boat from Africa to South America?"

"Exactly. He was trying to prove Egyptians sailed to Central America and taught the Mayans how to build pyramids. The problem is the Egyptians didn't know the western hemisphere existed, so why would they go there in the first place?

"Dr. Higgins said this was a problem that has perplexed historians for a long time. The similarities of the two cultures are striking. Here's just one example: The pyramid built for Menkure at Giza in Egypt is almost exactly the same size as the Pyramid of the Sun in Teotihuacan, Mexico. Both are a little less than sixty-six meters high, and the bases of these two structures vary by less than one meter. Both cultures revered cats, used false beards, and worshipped the sun. And get this. When Cortez came to Mexico, Montezuma thought he was the legendary god Quetzalcoatl that had been predicted to return at that time by their ancestors. What if it was really Nute they were expecting? After all, Quetzalcoatl was depicted as a flying serpent."

Max emerged from the shower in a terry cloth bathrobe and asked as he went into the bedroom to get dressed, "What do *you* make of all of this?"

"Well, it is all still speculation, but the evidence is sure beginning to pile up that what our visitor told us last night has merit."

"Ross gave me lots to think about too," Max called out from the bedroom. "He mentioned the same thing you did about bronze and its sudden appearance all over the 'civilized' world. He also mentioned a curious thing about the mace we originally saw in the picture of Narmer. It seems that a mace or club is a common symbol of authority in many ancient cultures. A ceremonial mace was one of the only artifacts found near Stonehenge in Britain, for example. I wonder if some of these leaders were trying to emulate Nute by making a crystal-like facsimile to control their subjects after he left. Another interesting thing is the use of a tall stone to record important information, like the Stele of Hammurabi and the obelisks in Egypt.

"The most convincing evidence for me, though, are the clusters of innovation that have occurred throughout history. The most obvious are the two big clusters in more modern scientific history, and I have been thinking about them a lot since I spoke to Ross.

"The first cluster was initiated by the work of Galileo and Kepler in the late 1500s and ended with Newton in the mid-1600s. In this mere one hundred year span, more was added to scientific knowledge than in the previous two thousand years. Then 350 years passed before Plank and Einstein provided an equally impressive addition to scientific knowledge, and in a span of less than five years.

"The case of Einstein is particularly curious because, after his brainstorm of 1903, he didn't contribute a single new idea the rest of his life. He just refined his 1903 epiphany. It makes me wonder if that epiphany wasn't initiated by Nute. The clincher for me is that these clusters, these explosions of knowledge in human civilization, seem to coincide with the levels of knowledge that Nute has been talking about."

Susan chimed in, "I also asked Dr. Higgins about Alexander the Great. She said he was considered a genius at military planning and used tactics never witnessed before his time. He used a special battle plan that. . . . Let me see. I have it here in my notes. Oh, yes, here it is. He used combined force of arms like we did in Desert Storm. His use of cavalry, archers, and foot soldiers in a combined force was brilliant. He was also especially skillful politically in that he respected native religions and encouraged his men to marry local women and settle down, which spread the cultural influence of the Greeks for centuries after his death.

"He also founded the library at Alexandria, thought to be the greatest in the ancient world. I hate to admit it, but it is all beginning to make sense. All these things are explainable by Nute's version of human history and his intervention he laid out for us last night."

Having donned his weekend uniform of jeans and sport shirt, the same clothes he wore to work, Max emerged from the bedroom and came into the great room. "You want some lunch? I made one of my specialties before I left for my run."

"Yeah? What's that?"

"Beanee-weenee, of course, one of my very favorite foods. It's easy to make too."

"Well, if you made it, I'm sure I will like it. I haven't had anything to eat since last night and I'm starved."

Max retrieved the concoction from the stove and took down a loaf of bread from the cabinet. He put four slices into the toaster. "Susan, why don't you get some dishes from that cabinet over there and I'll pop this in the microwave and warm it up"

As Susan took out the plates and silverware, Max continued. "You know, we need to do some thinking about what we are going to do tonight when Nute comes back to get our answer."

"I know. Why don't we decide what we are going to do while we eat. We need to take everything into account that he told us, both the task he is asking us to complete, to save mankind in a year, and the outcome if we fail. The whole 'taking us to someplace safe to be the seeds of a new civilization' thing is at least as daunting as saving civilization from itself."

"Okay, that sounds reasonable. We'll discuss our options over beanee-weenee."

Max dished up the stew of onions, mushrooms, pinto beans and a large proportion of diced franks. A side dish of piping hot buttered toast and homemade blackberry jelly rounded out the simple but delicious Ozark staple. When Max sat down, they dug in with ravenous appetites, only slowing briefly to continue their conversation. "Susan, let's say that Nute is completely for real. What do we do then?"

"I say we take him up on the idea and give it a shot," Susan replied, "saving civilization if we can. If he's right, and we only have twenty-five years or less, it would be more than an opportunity of a lifetime. It would be the opportunity of the millennia."

"All right, say we accept his challenge," Max said. "What could we do in one year that nobody has been able to do in the past five thousand years? I suppose you could say we have more motivation because we know what is going to happen, at least in general terms. But changing the world when there is such a well-entrenched, war-making capacity spread over the whole globe isn't going to be easy."

Susan's brow furrowed. "I would be just as worried about collecting enough genetic material to make a difference if we had to leave. How could you carry it all? If we were dealing only with seeds, eggs, or sperm, it might be possible, but it's still a monumental task, even if we had a year, Max.

"I think we should devise a plan and provide for both contingencies. What do you think?"

"That makes sense to me," Max replied. "It seems that the control of war will be the toughest part of this mandate he has given us to accomplish, because we would be dealing with people and humans are so unpredictable. At least genetic specimens won't fight back.

"My dad always used to say people only understand power. He is probably right; that's why the cold war ended in stalemate. Each side respected the other's military power. Maybe that's what we need, a type of deterrent that everyone respects and wouldn't dare provoke."

"You mean some kind of doomsday weapon?" Susan asked.

"Not necessarily. It could be a device, an army, or a person. It would have to be something that everyone feared and respected enough to keep the peace."

They both chewed in silence for a few minutes, the size of the task becoming more ominous by the minute.

"Let's get back to Nute," Susan said finally. "What are we going to do about him? Even though our evidence is persuasive, it's hardly definitive. When he gets here, why don't we ask him some questions that will establish his credibility once and for all?"

"That sounds good to me. How about if we ask him where he went last night after he left here? That ought to tell us a lot about his legitimacy."

"Max, are you expecting anyone? There is a pickup coming down the road toward the house."

"Oh, that must be Roger, my handyman. He comes by every day to take care of the greenhouse plants. Want to meet him? He is quite a character."

They watched out the window as the truck pulled into the drive and a man in overalls climbed out. Max greeted him from the front door as Roger made his way to the steps. Susan joined Max at the door.

"Hey, Roger. Come on in. I want you to meet someone." Susan noted that Roger was a pure Arkansan, wearing a plaid wool coat, a dirty baseball cap slightly back on his head, revealing a clump of dark greasy hair. It was almost a state uniform, she thought. He was affable and a "what-you-see-is-what-you-get" type person.

Max explained that Roger helped him with the small orchard and vegetable garden in the summer and did odd jobs like taking care of the greenhouse in the winter. Roger had also built the fence around Max's property and been kind of a liaison with the local population for him.

As Roger came up the steps, he blurted out, "How's it goin' Doc? Oh, excuse me, I didn't know ya had company, Doc."

Roger was obviously taken aback by Susan, perhaps not used to women in Max's house but perhaps also by her stunning appearance. He took off his hat and nervously twisted it as he approached her.

"Roger, I'd like you to meet a colleague of mine from work. This is Dr. Susan McKinney."

"It is my pleasure to meet ya, ma'am. Are you one of them stargazers like the doc here?"

"No, I work with computers mostly. I understand you work for Max sometimes."

"Yeah, me and the doc here try to take care of this place. He's got some real neat stuff here too. Did he show you the greenhouse? That's my favorite! I take care of the plants in the winter, ya know."

Max turned to Susan. "Would you like to see the garden area and the greenhouse?"

"Sure, that would be nice," she responded.

"Why don't you show Dr. McKinney the greenhouse while I clean up these dishes, Roger?" Roger and Susan proceeded out the back door of the cabin across a small breezeway to the greenhouse situated on the east side of the cabin. Roger jabbered all the way in his Ozark drawl, telling her how he had been a workman on the cabin when it was built and how Max had taken a liking to him and asked him to stay on and help with the yard and garden work. Susan could hardly manage a word before Roger took off again on his play-by-play of how the cabin had been built and his integral part in its completion.

Max was aware of Roger's propensity to talk, so he finished the household chores as soon as possible and went out to the greenhouse to rescue Susan from Roger's thorough but presumptive lecture on Max's house and grounds. He found them in the herb drying room at the east end of the greenhouse. Roger was telling her how he picks the herbs and puts them on the drying racks so Max can use them "in his fancy cooking." Roger grinned broadly as Max came into the greenhouse.

"Doc, I was just tellin' Susan here how you like your herbs dried and how good you can cook."

"Roger, Susan and I have some work to do inside, so we're going back in now."

"Dr. McKinney, it sure was nice getting to talk to you. Doc, I'll finish watering and pruning the plants and probably be back Monday."

"That'll be fine, Roger. See you Monday."

Susan preceded Max through the door, and Roger gave Max a high sign with his thumb indicating his approval. "Boy, Doc, she's a real looker."

To which Max quietly replied as he passed through the door, "She's smart too, Roger."

As Max and Susan walked back to the cabin she remarked, "Geez, can that Roger talk! He didn't stop the entire time we were looking at the greenhouse."

"Roger is quite a guy. He is from a long line of moonshiners. I bought this land from his cousin Clifford. The family used the spring over the hill to cool the condensing coil on their still for generations. His whole family was a little suspicious of me at first because they thought I worked for the Feds, revenuers as they used to call them.

Being an outsider here can be scary sometimes, but Roger would do anything I asked. I once joked that this would be a good place to grow marijuana, and the next day he showed up with twenty-five seedlings, ready to plant. After that, I was careful with what I say. He's actually the greatest help imaginable around here. All I have to do is tell him what I need and somehow he finds it for me."

Susan was preoccupied as Max talked about Roger. "Max, it is after 4:00," she said when he paused. "We better get ready for Nute. I am starting to get nervous."

"Yeah, I know what you mean. I can't get that little alien out of my mind. The more I think about all this, the more I think we should accept the fact that he is what he claims and go for it."

"You may be right. After all, what've we got to lose except our jobs, our reputations, and our careers?"

Max got the crystals out of their boxes and put them on the table. They sat down with their respective crystal in front of them.

"Okay, let's think of a couple of questions that will stump him if he's not who he says he is."

77

"You're right. If he can't give a satisfactory answer, we can tell him to have a nice day and ask him to leave. If he convinces us he is for real, we take the challenge and go for it," Susan said, exuding more confidence in her voice than she actually felt.

"Then it's settled. That's what we will do."

"Max, I'm starting to crash. Not sleeping last night is catching up with me. Do you think I could lie down for a while, then take a shower later?"

"Sure. You can use the guest bedroom, and I even cleaned up the bathroom and put my jogging clothes in the laundry hamper."

Susan went into the bedroom, closed the door, and took off her clothes down to her underwear. She was asleep in seconds after climbing into bed.

About 6:15, Max quietly knocked on the door. "Susan, it's time to get up. Use my robe in the closet. Everything you need should be in the bathroom, except makeup, of course. There are even some extra toothbrushes in the cabinet."

Susan was startled when she realized she wasn't in her own bed. But, after she became oriented to her surroundings, she slowly got up.

"Susan, did you hear me?"

"Yeah. I'm on the way. Max, could you bring me my purse? I think it's on the couch."

As she put on the robe and pulled her hair back, Max handed her the purse through a half open door.

"Feel better? I made some coffee and put a cup in the bathroom for you. Did you want any cream or sugar?"

"No, black is great." Susan proceeded into the bathroom to finish her waking up process. She found the coffee and thought to herself that Max would make someone a good wife. She opened the cabinet and found about three dozen bars of soap and six unopened boxes of toothbrushes. She chuckled and said to herself, "*Plenty of everything. Why am I not surprised?*"

After her shower and cup of Max's aromatic Columbian coffee, Susan emerged a new woman, refreshed and eager to deal with Nute. Max had made ham and Swiss cheese sandwiches on rye and had the table set for a light supper.

"Do you want some chips to go with your sandwich? I also have some blackberry pie I made the other day. How about a wedge?"

"Max, you are spoiling me with all of this food, but yes, I'd love some!"

"While you were resting, I thought a lot about the problem of global conflict. What we will need, I think, is a police force dedicated to that very purpose. This force would have to be independent and very strong, far beyond the strength of any individual country."

Susan listened intently as she ate her sandwich. Between bites, she asked, "Who would pay for this police force?"

"Well, if countries didn't have to spend so much money on their own defense, they would have plenty of money to pay for a global police force by way of some kind of tax. If the argument for such a force were strong enough, the force itself wouldn't cost much because it would be mostly a deterrent and the cost of actual wars would be avoided entirely. Such a force could work to control global conflict on the same principle as a nuclear arsenal. You would only have to demonstrate the power of that force a few times to show what it could do, and everyone would have to comply with global peace and harmony.

"Deterrence is the cheapest kind of defense. Instead of deterrence consisting of weapons of mass destruction, an unstoppable police force that all factions in the world knew, with absolutely certainty, would be deployed in response to any aggression would be sufficient."

"Yes, but who would decide how and when to use the weapon, this police force would have, acting in the name of deterrence?"

"That's the hard part. My only answer right now is possibly the United Nations or some alternative world government organization that could administer the police force and decide how it should be used. Anyway, all this is just speculation until we get the scoop from Nute. He should be here any minute, so let's clean up the table and get ready. You wash and I'll dry."

Susan, finishing her last bite of pie, said, "You got it!"

CHAPTER 6

Max and Susan felt as if they walked a razor's edge as they waited for Nute to arrive. They had all their questions ready and their contingencies well thought out, but what was at stake remained nearly overwhelming. Max sat quietly at the dining table drumming his fingers while Susan paced the floor. "What time is it?" she asked for the fourth time in five minutes.

"It's 7:23. Susan, asking me what time it is won't make the time go by any faster."

"I can't help it. This reminds me of my first date with Petie Snodgrass when we were going to the junior high dance at Brookside Country Club, my first real date. God, was I nervous. I was five-foot-eight and he was five-foot-two and had an eye level view of my newly acquired strapless bra. Actually, I didn't need one but I would never let him know that."

"Whatever happened to him?"

"Gosh, I don't know. The last time I knew anything about him he was selling shoes at the mall in Canton. What a little weasel. I can't believe I got so nervous for that little pimple face."

"Well, tonight should be worth this case of nerves. I can't think of anything we'll do our whole lives more important than what is about to happen here tonight."

Susan looked at Max, and without her asking, he said, "It's 7:26."

An unusually warm breeze from the southwest was gently blowing through the trees on Radford Mountain. The clear sky offered a backdrop of stars glistening in their midwinter glory. The calm evening was in stark contrast to the tension in the cabin, which grew even more taut as the appointed hour for Nute's arrival approached. Susan continued to pace in a half-circle around the great room as time seemed to stand still.

Max stood up abruptly as if he no longer could stand the waiting either. "It is 7:29. Just one more minute."

"Max, what do we do if he doesn't show up?"

"Don't worry. I have a feeling he'll be here."

The doorbell pierced the silence like a rifle shot. Susan jumped, startled even though the arrival was long awaited. Max tucked in his shirt as he started toward the front door. He glanced at Susan and acknowledged the hopeful sign she made by crossing her fingers on both hands. As he stood before the door momentarily, he said in a whisper to himself, "Well, here goes nothing." Then he confidently opened the door.

He was astonished to see a small attractive woman of about five foot one dressed in a well tailored navy blue coat with gold buttons. She had shoulder-length coal black hair cut in the style of the Egyptian women that he and Susan had seen in the many historical photos inspected in the past twenty-four hours. She wore heavy powder-blue eye makeup and dark red lipstick. Her hat was a wool beret worn on the side of her head, slightly to the right.

Max and Susan were speechless. After an awkward pause, she said, "Good evening, Doctors Gibson and McKinney."

As if he had been startled back to reality, Max said, "Who are you? I mean . . . I am sorry. We were expecting someone else."

"Oh really, Who?"

"A gentleman named Nute."

"I am Nute."

As the woman spoke, Susan gasped and covered her mouth with her hand and quietly said, "Oh my God! It *is* Nute, Goddess of the Sky."

After his brief lapse, Max regained his composure. "Won't you come in?"

When Nute came into the room, she smiled at Susan and commented, "Don't worry, Dr. McKinney. I am not a transvestite." She took off her coat and beret and handed them to Max, revealing a rather plain but perfectly tailored linen dress. The neckline was low-cut, and it was obvious she was very much a woman. Her skin was unblemished olive-tan and her perfect white teeth contrasted sharply with her dark red lipstick. The burgundy dress was gathered at the waist by a metallic belt similar to the one Nute had worn the night before. Her host and hostess were so awestruck they had nothing to say.

"What a lovely evening," she said. "The weather this time of year is so unpredictable. Last night rain and sleet, and tonight it's just beautiful."

"You were here last night?" Max asked.

"Of course. Let me put your minds at ease and dispel your doubts, which I know you have because I monitored your inquiry to the reference library at Astrolabe last night."

Max interrupted, and this time he would not be denied. "All right, where did you go last night and how did you get there?"

"Perhaps this will answer your question; it has always been quite effective in the past." As Nute spoke, she began to levitate over the dining table and around the room, without apparent effort and not even a whisper of sound. "I returned to the home I am using while on Earth by way of my customary means of travel, which you are witnessing now. I find flying not only prevents strain on the feet but is certainly faster." Just as easily as she had floated upward, she now settled down between Max and Susan. With a shy smile, Nute asked, "Convinced?"

Max stood by the dining table staring in total amazement. Susan took hold of the table to steady herself and said, "You have my vote." Then she slowly sat down.

Max followed her lead and sat down beside Susan. "Mine too."

Nute, with the utter calm of someone who had witnessed this reaction many times before, took her place across the table from them. Noting they both looked a little pale, she quietly asked, "Would either of you like a glass of water?"

"I am okay," Max said in a weak, tentative voice.

Susan replied, "No. Just give me a minute. I will be okay."

"Why don't you have some juice? It should help." Nute walked to the refrigerator, took out a plastic container of orange juice, and poured two glasses. She served her hosts, who were still in shock at the sight of this small woman floating about the room. When a little color began to come back to their faces, she sat down across the table from them and began to make her presentation.

"So you don't misunderstand, what you just saw isn't magic or some supernatural ability. I am able to move about without regard to the effects of gravity because of a device housed in my belt and controlled by a small computer that is tuned to my thought patterns. In your ancient world, it would have been impossible for me to even make an attempt to explain such a concept. However, I think you can now envision at least the possibility of such technology. I am not a god or a mystic. My abilities and your future abilities are nothing more than the products of technology. The magic comes from your ability to think and create, not to fly.

"Last night, I explained the reason for my visit and why you were selected to try to stop the progression of events that will otherwise lead to the elimination of your species on this planet. Are we clear up to this point?"

Max and Susan nodded yes as Susan took another drink of the orange juice.

"Very well. Do you have an answer for the Council? Do you agree to our proposal?" Max was finally able to reply with a little more confidence. "Susan and I have discussed this at length, and we agree to your proposal."

"Excellent. Then we can begin. One year from today, I will return and we will assess your progress. If I feel the situation is hopeless, I will transport you, along with the genetic material, to the Council for assignment to another environment. From that time forward, the Earth will take its own course. Level Eight is the last level of help that will be authorized for your species. You must understand. If we leave, you will never see your present Earth again. It takes at least fifteen Earth years just to make the round trip where we will be going."

"Won't we be too old to start a new civilization?" Max asked.

"No. We will suspend your aging process indefinitely if this becomes necessary. If, on the other hand, you are successful in curbing the threat of war and manage to bring some order to the world political system, you will begin a process that will lead to your civilization joining the Council. The criteria for joining the Council are as follows: The ability to live in peace for at least two generations without war, a unified world government with broad political support that shows justice and compassion for all, the complete disarmament of individual nations.

"This may seem simple, but if you can meet these conditions, you will be the first K-10 culture to be admitted to the Council. The first one in my sector as well, I might add."

Nute folded her small hands in her lap.

"Now, the first order of business is to fit you with a transceiver to allow you to communicate with the crystals."

Susan interrupted with apprehension in her voice. "What do you mean, 'fit us'?"

Nute retrieved two small objects about the size of a medicine capsule and a small leather pouch from her coat and returned to the table. She held them up for Max and Susan to see. They were miniature crystals. Max and Susan each took one from her and instinctively held them up to the light and watched them sparkle. Nute told them the pouch contained a device to implant the micro crystals.

"I will insert these just under the skin on the back of your necks. There will be no pain, by the way. This implant will allow you to direct your thoughts through the crystals to communicate with each other. After a short programming time, the micro crystal will be able to emulate your thought patterns and you will be able to use the processor to translate all known languages on your planet. You will also be able to speak and understand any language."

"You mean we will be able to speak French, German, Urdu, or whatever?" Max asked.

"Fluently. Your most valuable asset, however, will be the ability to communicate with the main crystal. You can do this verbally, if you wish, or simply with internal dialogue, in your heads as it were. If you are within about two hundred meters, the main crystal will receive your signal and understand your thoughts.

"So, if you are both ready, who wants to be first?" Max and Susan were both a little reluctant, so neither volunteered immediately.

Nute then said, "Why don't we start with you, Dr. Gibson? Come with me and we will do this as quickly as possible." Nute picked up the crystals and the pouch, and started toward the bedroom; Max followed with some reservation.

When the door was closed, Nute said, "Please take off your shirt and remove all metal objects from your body. Now, face the window please." Max was a little hesitant but complied.

"Yes. That's fine."

As Max stood patiently waiting, Nute walked around behind him. "Close your eyes, please." Nute levitated to Max's level and used a small device she had in the pouch to place the microcrystal under his skin. The crystal immediately began to glow, indicating it was functional. "The transceiver will begin to emulate your brain patterns now. It should only take a few minutes. While you are getting dressed, I will complete the procedure for Dr. McKinney. We will use the upstairs bedroom, if it's all right with you."

"Okay. I'll wait for you in the dining room." Within a few minutes, Nute and Susan came down the stairs. Nute asked Susan and Max to be seated on the couch, and she put the crystal on the dining table and pointed it toward the front wall. "I thought you might be interested in the results of the examination we did Thursday night"

"What do you mean, Thursday night?" Max interjected. "I don't remember any examination."

"Oh yes, I forgot to mention it. We did a full body scan of both of you Thursday night, to check your DNA and do blood work and such. You were both asleep." As Nute spoke, the crystals projected the results on the front wall. Blood chemistry, IQ, liver function, and a list of every disease they ever had was displayed. Additionally, their anatomically correct mannequins were projected, leaving nothing to the imagination.

Max and Susan were both a little embarrassed but fascinated at the same time with the display of themselves in the nude, or rather, each was fascinated with the display of the other. Neither said a word, of course.

A picture of their individual family trees then lit up. After about twenty-five generations, the names were replaced by small lights on a world map showing where their ancestors had lived. Each generation was indicated by a pinpoint of light. Max's ancestors began in England, moved to France after a time, then to Eastern Europe, and then down through Turkey. A number of lights representing generations came on in the Middle Eastern region, and then they began to light up in northern Africa. When the total of Max's ancestors had been fully displayed, there were more than twenty-three hundred generations represented by lights. The original forefathers of his line were displayed in green and began to blink near what is now Al-Ubayyid in central Sudan in Africa. Susan's display lit up in Scotland, then moved to Scandinavia, and then central Russia. The generation lights then proceeded to the Caspian Sea and into Iraq. There was a cluster in Mesopotamia and several along the Nile River. The display finally stopped near Lake Rukwa in what is now Tanzania.

Nute said with pride, "There you have it. This is your complete genetic history since our original genome was taken forty thousand years ago."

Susan was fascinated. "Does this actually show our ancestors back to forty thousand years ago and where they lived?"

Nute smiled. "Yes, it does. This profile follows the descendents that have come through the blood line that we originally catalogued. Actually, everyone on Earth now living is descended from a handful of these nomadic tribes we found in northern Africa. Would you like to see them?"

Susan was ecstatic. "Of course! How can you do that?"

Nute replied, "When we did the original inventory, we recorded each person's DNA of your species. Actually, there weren't that many then. We are able to look at a representative family of the hundreds of individuals who have contributed to your genetic makeup over the generations."

Two sets of holograms appeared in the room, each one showing a set of ancestors. Max and Susan were clearly moved by the chance to see their forbearers. Even more spectacular was seeing the thousands of unions that had produced their personal genetic blueprints.

Nute then quietly said, "You see, this is why the Council feels it is important not to let your species be lost to the cosmos forever. The two of you do truly represent a wealth of diversity, adaptation, and evolution that could be snuffed out in a millisecond. We have seen it happen before, and it is sad to see such potential wasted."

The two of them were still focused on the four people shown in the hologram. Then Max said, "What language did they speak?"

"They would not have been able to understand each other, but you could understand each and every one of them now with the crystal translator."

"You mean we could talk to them?"

"No, but you can listen to the recording I made when I was there and you will understand them. Want to listen in on the camp-fire conversation?"

Max eagerly said, "You bet!" Susan also agreed enthusiastically.

Two pictures were projected simultaneously, each showing Max and Susan's respective ancestors. Max and Susan understood the conversations that accompanied the pictures. The people in Susan's frame were talking about the day's hunt for antelope, and in Max's, they were talking about chasing off a hyena. Susan's family was talking about the new tooth coming in for their youngest daughter, who was still nursing at her mother's breast. Max and Susan were spellbound listening to the conversations of their primitive ancestors. The recording was over in three minutes.

Susan immediately said, "Is that all there is to it?"

Nute replied, "Yes. You may entertain yourselves with this later. It will be in the permanent memory of the crystals. Just ask for the genome history. Right now, unfortunately, I must leave." Nute made preparations to leave, picking up the leather pouch from the table and returning it to her coat pocket in the other room. Then she started her final instructions. The crystal projected a map of north central Arkansas, near Harrison.

"I will need to leave shortly, so we must discuss the details of our rendezvous. Do you know the area around Wollum?" As Nute spoke, the map lit up, and the area southeast of Max's cabin, about four miles by air and eight miles by river from his home, was highlighted.

Max walked over to the map to get a closer look. "Oh, yes. Roger and I have floated this part of the river several times and we camped there once. There is a large gravel bar and a small road fords the river."

"That's right. I will meet you there at 3:30 a.m. on December 10, 2023. Meanwhile, the crystals will keep me informed of your progress. I know you have innumerable questions right now, and I would like to stay and answer them all. But I must leave on other business. The crystals will be your reference library. One other thing: Not far from here is a spare parts depot built several thousand years ago on another trip. We always have pre-positioned supplies at all of the places we visit. The crystals have a full inventory of the supplies and equipment there in case you need anything."

Nute stood up and put on her coat. "I truly hope you are successful, and I look forward to my return trip to check on your progress," she said. Nute shook Max and Susan's hands and left.

Max turned to Susan. "Well, I have done it again. I let her walk out of here without a single intelligent question. After all of this, though, I don't think my mind could assimilate any more information anyway."

"Max, do you have any more of that Wild Turkey?"

CHAPTER 7

Shell-shocked by the events of the last twenty-four hours, Max and Susan sat at the dining table with glasses of Wild Turkey over ice, quietly reflecting on their new adventure. Their best-laid plans to challenge Nute were instantly shattered by Nute's transformation into a woman and their bombardment with one scientific revelation after another. They had been humbled, even embarrassed, by their intellectual impotence in the face of such a superior mind. They were only now beginning to realize the scope of the proposal they had accepted. In the span of one day, they had met an alien, watched her or him fly, and agreed to make an effort to extricate mankind from its collision course with otherwise inevitable self-destruction. What a day!

"Max, do you really think we can pull this off? I mean, can we stop warfare, or failing that, go with Nute and start a new civilization?"

"No to the first question, for certain, but what choice do we have? How could we not try, knowing what we know now? Who knows what we can do with Nute's Level-Eight technology? Look what Narmer and Imhotep did in their relatively primitive culture in Egypt with Level Four. Narmer started the first dynasty of Egypt's civilization and Imhotep built the great pyramids. And what about Einstein? Look how his brief exposure to Nute changed our fundamental notions of physics by a quantum leap — no pun intended. If we can make these crystals really work for us, I think we might do wonders. By the way, Nute's Owner's manual is a little thin on how to operate the crystals. I wonder how we get them to come on."

The instant Max finished saying that, the crystal lit up and a voice filled the room, startling them both: "All that is necessary for you to use me is to think about it."

"Oh my God! Max, did the crystal say that?"

"Yes, I did," the voice replied. "Generally it is better for humans to interface with me by giving me a name so I may respond when needed. Would you like to give me a name for this purpose?"

Susan asked, "Is this like a user-defined protocol on a new program?"

"Exactly right, Dr. McKinney."

"Okay. Let's think of a name. How about Joe or Karen?"

"No, said Max, surely we can come up with something better than that, something more appropriate. . . . Say, something like uh . . . I know, Watson, Sherlock Holmes' famous assistant."

"No, he was too stupid. He never knew what Holmes was up to. How about Genie, like letting one out of a bottle that is able to grant any wish."

"That's it! Perfect. We will call you Genie. How's that?" Max exclaimed.

"Very well. Would you like my voice to be masculine or feminine?"

They answered in unison, "Feminine."

"Okay, Genie. Let's try a few questions," Max said with newly found enthusiasm.

"How did Nute fly?"

Genie's voice took on the rich character and flavor of a southern belle, gracious and calm, as she answered Max's question. "The device, held in place by Nute's belt, is a small refluxing gravity field generator. It is capable of lifting and propelling a mass of up to

94

five-hundred kilograms at speeds of up to two-hundred meters per second. The device is powered by two energy modules and has an operational life of two hundred years.

"Please direct your attention to the schematic diagram I am projecting on the west wall. As you can see, the generator produces the antigravity field by refluxing gravity field particles and directing them by way of a diffusion torque converter to develop axial and horizontal thrust . . ."

Max spoke up. "I don't mean to interrupt, but that will be enough right now, Genie. Let's try something a little more simple. How do you work, Genie?"

"Dr. Gibson, my technology is quite complex. My design and construction are far more advanced than a simple antigravity device. My two main components are housed in the bar and the globe. Although capable of independent operation for short periods, the two components are complementary: The bar houses the memory and power supply and the globe contains the higher functions of intelligence for the device."

"Are you saying you can think?" Max inquired in a puzzled tone.

"Yes, of course. I have cognitive and logical reasoning ability, but my chief benefit to you is to be a storehouse of information. I am constructed of the crystalline form of a metal unknown to you which, when grown in a controlled environment, makes it possible to store unimaginable amounts of data. The circuit pathways are grown on a crystal lattice on a molecular level, making my memory extremely efficient, durable and, needless to say, very compact. My power supply will last for 750 of your years before I need a new power source. So, how may I be of help to you?"

Max hesitated for a moment, and then he asked, "Okay, then. How did Nute change into a woman?"

"He didn't change at all. He just decided to use his female body, for effect, I suppose. Nute is able to use a body that is familiar to you by a process that involves genetic engineering from samples obtained from people he has known in the past. This may be a little hard for you to understand, but Nute is able to be that person temporarily by creating them from their genetic pattern. I believe you might call this a clone. His life force, or energy, is able to use their form by creating their body and using it for relatively short periods whenever he needs it."

"Yes, but what is his natural form?" Susan interjected.

"I am unable to answer that question. That is a Level-Nine inquiry."

"What do you mean, Genie, a Level-Nine inquiry?" Max asked with some irritation.

"I mean that I am not authorized to respond to a Level-Nine inquiry."

"Okay, how about this? Can you help us make a weapon that could defeat anyone in the world?"

"Of course. It would be quite simple actually. First, you would . . ."

Max abruptly interrupted. "You don't have to tell us right now. All I need to know is if you have this knowledge."

"The answer to that question is yes, Dr. Gibson."

"Could you also then make this weapon impervious to any attack made by humans?"

"Yes."

"Max, what are you driving at?" Susan asked.

"Well, if Genie can help us build such a weapon, we might be able to have our own global law and order by the principle of assured destruction, which seems to be the only system that has ever maintained any form of peace for mankind.

"There have always been people who recognized the futility of war. History is full of such people, but sooner or later, someone somewhere gets the idea to dominate someone else and the conflict starts. Religion, wealth, natural resources, have been the reasons for huge wars in the past. Or all it takes is sociopaths like Hitler or any one of a number of other petty tyrants to decide he wants to rule some portion of the planet he does not now rule. If we had a world policeman with absolute power to enforce the law, we might just make peace work. The prerequisite, of course, is the wise use of this absolute power. It seems that Nute has laid this 'opportunity' in our laps with his gift of Level-Eight technology.

"Genie, do you think we could build a weapons system within a year that could fit the description I have just made?"

"Yes. If you wanted it to fly, however, I don't think you would have time to build a gravity reflux generator. Your technology isn't quite ready for that particular piece of hardware. The materials needed aren't available on Earth at this time. As an alternative, we could use one of the spares in the bunker. As you may remember, Nute said you are cleared to use some of this equipment, if needed."

"Okay, now that we know that we can build some kind of a weapon, how do we go about using it?"

"That would be for you and Dr. McKinney to decide. Remember, my job is to provide information, not to give advice on how to proceed."

"What do you think, Susan?"

"I don't think we should rush into this. We need to give this strategy more thought. I'm worried about how we get ready for Plan B too. If I'm in charge of coming up with how we collect the genomic material, we had better do some planning for what takes place if Nute returns and we have not been successful at achieving peace."

"You're right." Max looked pensive, as if lost in thought for a moment. "The first thing we need to do is get a little breathing room at work. Do you have any vacation time coming?"

"Yes, but I have to finish the Mars landing project. I couldn't just walk away from that. It is already two months behind schedule."

"Perhaps I could be of help," Genie said with a quiet confidence. "Just take me to the terminal and let me clear up your project. They won't be able to refuse your vacation after they see what *you* have been able to do this weekend."

Max and Susan walked to the terminal, and Susan set the crystal on the desk and hit the on switch. As soon as the terminal came on line, the screens flew by so fast that neither Max nor Susan could see what was happening. In a few seconds, Genie said, "I think you will find the software for the Mars landing site is satisfactory."

"What about the site plan?" ask Susan, " I was waiting for that before I could finish the program."

"I used a plan I already had in my databank. I think you will find it is more accurate than Wilson's. Now, Dr. Gibson, would you like me to complete your Keck project?"

"Can you do that?" Max asked in disbelief.

"Don't be intimidated, Dr. Gibson. This is like asking an NBA player if he can make a lay-up."

Max was a little embarrassed by his question as he watched Genie blow through months of work in seconds. The lines of programming data scrolled by so fast they were illegible.

When the screens finally stopped, Genie said, "This program will keep your colleagues busy for several weeks. You can tell them you were inspired this weekend. This is what all the other people I have helped usually say."

Max and Susan stood at the desk with blank looks that gradually turned into sly smiles, as if their mothers had just done their homework and they knew they were going to get an "A."

Susan, who considered her problem the more complex of the two, thought out loud as she turned and slowly paced across the living room. "I need to devise a way to get research funding for some type of genetic project that will allow me to collect genetic samples from all types of species. I would not want to attract too much attention to the project, and so it would need to sound legitimate and have a high profit motive so that Astrolabe won't hesitate to fund it. Let me see. What would be the most valuable thing a geneticist would want? Of course! What they need is a way to read the genome of a particular organism without chemistry, enzymes, or electrophoresis. Genie, can you read the DNA sequence of any organism?"

"Yes, the evaluation conducted on you and Dr. Gibson earlier was just such a scan. It is accomplished with a powerful type of magnetic resonance that precisely evaluates tissue on a molecular level. It produces a great deal of information, including the DNA sequencing, cell chemistry, and the status of the various biochemical processes of the tissue being studied."

"Great. Gilroy will be having wet dreams at the mere mention that something like this is possible! I'll tell him that I need more specimens to try out the new *Genome Reader*. He will pressure Clark for me, and I'm sure he'll get all the money and travel vouchers we need.

"All I need to say are the magic words: Joint Publication. Gilroy will be putty in my hands. First, I need to set up a demonstration to show Gilroy I have the goods. Then I'll simply let his greed and lust for power take over, a piece of cake."

"Okay, Susan. You follow up on this, and I'll take a few days off to visit my dad in Colorado. I need to talk to him about a strategic military plan. I'm sure he'll have some ideas about how to go about creating a super weapon. I think I have about three weeks vacation coming, so this should give me some time to think."

"Why don't you take Genie with you to Colorado and I'll work on the genome project here," Susan suggested.

"That sounds fine to me," Max replied.

"I'd like to get home to visit my family in Ohio too. I think you're right. We both need some time to think."

Then Genie quietly said, "If I might make another suggestion. Why don't you leave me here for the time being? You can communicate with me as long as you are near a phone or cell tower, and this way you can avoid a lot of questions and your objectives will be more secure until we are ready to go to Colorado."

"Of course, that would be better," Max said, and Susan nodded her head in agreement.

"Max, I am heading for home." Susan sighed. "I am exhausted. If I don't get some rest, I'm going to fall over. I'll work on the bait for Gilroy and Clark on Monday. I'll touch base with you before you leave for Colorado."

Max helped Susan with her coat and saw her to the door. When they got to the door, Susan gently slipped her arm around him and said, "I am so nervous about all of this. I am really glad we are working on this together." She gave him a prolonged hug and whispered in his ear, "I like your style, too."

He gave her a thumbs up sign as she sped away in her Jeep. He carefully placed Genie near the phone and put a heavy bath towel over the crystal to hide it. As if speaking to an old friend, he asked, "Is this okay, Genie?"

Genie replied, "Yes, Dr. Gibson. You need to rest. I sense lactic acid buildup in your system. Don't worry. I will monitor the premises and tell you if there is anything you should know about."

"Thanks, Genie. I'm exhausted."

Max slowly unbuttoned his shirt as he walked up the stairs. He plopped down on his bed without even taking off his jeans. He was asleep within seconds.

CHAPTER 8

During the night, Max had rolled up in the bedspread. He awoke bound up like a mummy on top of his blanket and sheets. The early morning sun dimly lit his bedroom as he unwound himself and made his way into the bathroom to begin his daily hygiene ritual. After his shower and a little trim-up on his beard, Max dressed, came downstairs, and started the coffee. As the coffee machine began to perk, Max took the towel off Genie and said, "Good morning, Genie."

"Good morning, Dr. Gibson," the crystal replied.

"Genie, you should call me Max. After all, you know more about me than anyone. Please call me Max."

"Very well. Did you sleep well, Max?"

"Yes, as a matter of fact. I slept like a log. How about you?"

"Thank you for asking, but I don't sleep, as you know. I just go on monitor mode and gather data until I am needed. I have been communicating with Susan this morning. She has been thinking about the demonstration for Dr. Gilroy. She has some questions for you. Shall I contact her for you?"

"Yes, but what did she want?"

"I will let her explain. Are you there, Susan?"

"Yes, Genie. Is Max up yet?"

"Yes, Susan. I can hear you, although I don't know how. The phone is still on the hook. How does that work, Genie?"

"Your communicator sends a signal to me and I relay it over the phone lines to her communicator. It's quite simple, actually.

Sometimes I use cell phone towers or a communication satellite. It just depends on the situation"

"Okay, Susan. What is the question?"

"Genie tells me we don't have time to build a real magnetic resonator by Monday. I am wondering if you could help me make a box of some kind to hide Genie in for the demonstration. I will give Gilroy a snow job so he will start paving the way for our project."

"That should be simple enough," Max replied. "We have a lot of equipment cabinets and the like down at the lab. There should be something to impress Gilroy. We could even have it blink and make noise if you want."

"Great! I've been doing some research on what outcomes would be the most impressive. I should be done in a couple of hours. What do you say we meet at the lab about ten o'clock?"

"That would be fine. I'll bring Genie with me, and we'll plan our show. See you then."

Max was thoughtful for a moment. "Genie, let's talk about the equipment I need for the weapon system. Where did you say I could find it?"

"Nute placed a number of supply bunkers on your planet, one on each continent. The largest and oldest is in Africa, near Lake Victoria, and the bunker in North America is about 150 miles from here, in Kansas."

"I don't understand. What do you mean by 'bunkers'?"

"On our first few visits, we were able to travel in large freight-type craft without bringing attention to ourselves. The Earth was very sparsely populated then. We took the opportunity to bring supplies and spare parts with us in case we had some type of malfunction so far from home. Consequently, we could come in smaller vessels on subsequent visits and go largely undetected. The bunkers also serve as a home for Nute and a base of operation when he or she, as the case may be, comes to visit."

"Nute has been staying at the bunker in Kansas?"

"Yes."

"Genie, I am going to have breakfast and then we can go to the lab."

Max finished a quick meal of cereal and toast before heading for the lab with Genie safely tucked away in his briefcase. Max was deep in thought, occasionally asking Genie questions, as he drove his customary route to the Astrolabe complex. After the normal clearance routine, he opened the lab and put Genie on his desk. The place was deserted on a Sunday, and Max had some time to get ready before Susan arrived. He poked around in the storeroom and found an obsolete PC housing. He was able to pry out the old CD drive housing and fit an obsolete eye piece from a telescope in it. The result was an impressive looking but worthless box in which to hide Genie for the demonstration. The idea was to have some type of legitimate looking hardware to scan a sample of some kind. For effect, he attached an input/output cable to the back of the housing to make it look like the machine could transfer data to the mainframe. He realized, of course, that Genie would do all the work and provide just enough data to make Gilroy's mouth water.

Max just about had the equipment ready for the dog and pony show when Susan quietly knocked on the door. Max cautiously asked in a muted tone as if he were the door man at a cocaine party, "Who is it?"

"It's me," Susan whispered. Max opened the door just wide enough for her to enter and then shut it immediately. "Did you get the stuff we need ready?"

"I have it over here on the bench. I think this should look good enough for Gilroy. What do you think?"

"Max, this looks very impressive. All I have to do now is decide what we want the bogus box to do to get Todd's juices flowing. I looked over the current publications and didn't find much. Unfortunately, most of his research is under high security, and since I didn't have sufficient clearance codes, I couldn't access the material about the most recent research. He's usually working on protein synthesis having to do with direct gene encoding these days, but I don't know what he is up to specifically."

As she spoke, Susan laid out the papers she had removed from her briefcase and pointed out Todd's published research to Max. "Other than that, I can't get access to what he's working on now. Genie, can you access Todd's work on the mainframe?"

"Yes."

"Why didn't you say so?"

"I'm sorry, Susan, but you didn't ask. Would you like me to get that information? I could summarize the achievements in his field and give you the background for his current research, if it would help."

"Boy, you are sure spoiling me, Genie. I would have made it through grad school in half the time if I had a research librarian like you." Susan laughed.

Max and Susan made themselves comfortable and watched as Genie projected a lifelike hologram on the lab wall. Each scientific discovery was documented by the real people as they worked in their labs. Max and Susan were awestruck as the scientific history lesson was unfolded in front of them. It made them both a little uneasy to realize that Nute or Genie must have been there at each discovery to "capture the moment."

Genie began the briefing. "The first important work in genetics was done by the Brno monk, Gregor Mendel, from 1854 through 1866. He discovered that individual characteristics in plants do not mix in hybrids but are transmitted in discrete quantities to their offspring in a packet of information, which was named a "gene" by Johannsen in 1909. Flemming and Van Beneden discovered cell division in the 1880s, and Waldeyer established that genes resided on the chromosomes in 1888. The concept of evolution via mutation was discovered by De Vries in 1901. Ephrussi, Beadle, and Tatum revealed that the principle function of genes was to produce enzymes that control cell function in 1946. In 1953, Watson and Crick discovered the chemical make-up of the genetic material and coined the term DNA, which gave humans their first insights into the true function of chromosomes and the chemical nature of heredity."

Genie went on with a detailed chronology of the history of genetics for about ten minutes. Each discovery, she noted, brought the science of genetics closer to the state of present day knowledge and closer to the dilemma facing Todd.

"In the early 1980s, a number of companies began to experiment with alterations in the genetic code by introducing foreign instructions to the DNA via the naturally occurring mechanism of a virus. By their nature, viruses are designed to enter the cell and take over the manufacture of specific types of molecules. These new molecules originally produced new viruses, but after modification, they could be made to produce other types of beneficial chemicals. One of the first and most famous was accomplished by researchers at the pharmaceutical giant Eli Lilly Company when they modified the bacterium E. coli to produce insulin. Astrolabe Systems became interested in this area because anyone with a vision could see that this was the lucrative future solution to many of the problems facing the human race. Agriculture, medicine, and especially genetic diseases all could be dealt with through this new science.

"In 1986, Dr. Hugo Kaplan was hired to head up the Pharmaceutical division of Astrolabe in Baltimore, and Dr. Todd Gilroy was named to direct the Agricultural section here at Harrison. Thus far, Dr. Gilroy's work has produced a new strain of rice that is both highly productive and disease resistant. It is being field tested near Stuttgart, Arkansas, on a number of large plots along the Mississippi River. At the moment, Gilroy is working on a recombinant DNA process to increase wheat production by adding two more rows of grain to a head of wheat. He is having problems with the gene splicing enzyme needed to insert the gene splice into the wheat cell nucleus."

Susan stood and began to pace around the lab as she spoke. "Okay, Genie. What has been giving Todd the most trouble?"

"Dr. Gilroy is on the wrong track. He is trying to use an enzyme that is not the right shape for the specific gene he is trying to open. He will get it eventually, but right now he is stumped."

"Can you identify the enzyme?"

"Yes, the yet unnamed enzyme is displayed on the wall. You can see the chemical components are right but the spatial arrangement is incorrect. As you know, most biological mechanisms operate on a system of spatial relationships much like a lock and key. The shape of the molecule is more important than the compounds composition chemically. This is how they work as an enzyme. They unlock the other compound and let the reaction go forward."

"Okay. Suppose we tell Todd that we have discovered a way to identify the enzymes needed by optically scanning the compounds on a molecular level," Susan responded.

"Actually, Susan, that is exactly what I can do."

"Great! Then, that's what we'll do. If I tell Todd we have a way to identify lock and key mechanisms between peptides and enzymes, that'll get his attention, right?"

"If you provide such information, you most certainly will be a candidate for a Nobel even one such enzyme. You see, each peptide is formed in the shape of a circle while it circulates in the cytoplasm, and especially in the ribosomes. Before genes can be spliced, the circle must be broken so the new splice or gene can be added, and so, without such an enzyme, the peptide continues to be intact and no splice can be made."

"All right, let's say we list enzyme-peptide pairs that control the genetic information of an organism with which Todd is familiar, E. coli, for example. We'll also say that we stumbled onto the technique while we were looking for a way to analyze blood samples from the astronauts or something. Does that make sense, Max?"

"Not to me, but I am an astronomer. It just has to make sense to Todd."

"Well, it should make sense to him because he knows that one of my projects is to develop a remote means to analyze astronauts' blood samples while they are in deep space and transmit the findings to Earth. This is part of the telemetry work I have been doing since I came to Astrolabe. We could tell Todd I was fooling around with a magnetic resonator to analyze blood samples and found that it could be tuned in to look at much smaller particles in the cytoplasm of the cell, even the molecular structure of the chromosomes and other components. Our analysis would be based on the shape and optical properties of the molecules rather than their chemistry. It would just be a matter of using a super computer to catalog and do a paring analysis of the various molecules floating around in the cell. We could identify anything we wanted. Right?"

"Actually, Susan, that is exactly what I have done. The technology to do this is very advanced, but you have described the principle well enough."

"What do you think, Max?"

"Susan, if you showed this to me, I certainly would be impressed, and probably intimidated by your discovery."

"That's what we're hoping for. If Todd buys this little show we're going to put on for him, we could tell Clark that I'm going to work on a joint venture with him and I need to collect samples of genetic material to read and compare in my new machine."

"You mean, Astrolabe Systems will develop a database of genetic material?"

"Yes, and this will give me an excuse to gather all the genetic samples in the world. I can feed Todd a few scraps of new knowledge to keep him interested and the funds flowing. This will work!"

Susan was obviously becoming enamored with Max as they worked together with Genie. She had that "look" that betrayed her feelings, and Max had noted that she turned the demonstration into a competition between her and Todd, as if she wanted to show off for Max. Max could tell she thought it "five-love in the final set," and Todd was about to be toast on her next serve.

"Now that we have a handle on how we are going to take care of my half of this project, what do we do about your half, Max?"

"Genie and I were discussing that on the way to the lab. She says the bunker in Kansas has all the equipment I'll need to make a super weapon that is indestructible. I think I'll take a detour on my way to my parents' house to look over the bunker and see what's actually there. When I get to my dad's, I should be able to come up with some kind of plan and get started on the device. Why don't you take Genie with you tonight and get ready for your presentation to Todd tomorrow. I'll checkout with Steve Clark and get ready for my trip to Colorado Springs."

Max and Susan took all of the equipment for Todd's show up to her office on the third floor where they set up the demonstration to look like it was part of her work on deep space physiology. When everything was ready, Max and Susan left for home.

CHAPTER 9

Susan was wide awake at 5:30 the next morning and thinking about the details of her upcoming encounter with Todd, ready to implement her game plan to secure her funding and travel allowances for the next twelve months. She hurriedly showered, then stood in her fanciest lace panties and push-up bra in front of her dressing mirror like a medieval knight preparing for battle with her armaments arrayed in front of her, pondering the effect she wanted to make on Todd. Her plan was to be seductive yet business like, so she methodically brought different clothing combinations out of the closet and stood in front of her mirror evaluating each one's merits. She settled on a dark blue two-piece suit cut just above the knee and a white silk blouse that revealed just enough cleavage to be enticing. Normally, she wore a brightly colored scarf to protect her modesty, but in this case, she decided to be a little more revealing and left the scarf in the closet.

Having made her selection, she laid the garments on the bed and went to work on her hair and makeup. She decided on the carefree business look so she selected the large hot rollers for a full-bodied casual curl for her hair. Since she had been impressed by Nute's dark red lipstick, she opted for a more theatrical makeup motif than she normally wore at work, or anywhere else for that matter. Then, for the final and no doubt most devastating selection, she opened a perfume called Raw Sex that she kept on the back of her dresser. The scent was judiciously applied to her earlobes and cleavage.

When her outfit and other packaging was judged to be just right, she carefully placed Genie into Max's briefcase, gathered up her other papers, and got ready to leave. When she passed by the mirror in the hallway by the back door, she stopped and said out loud to her image, "You are mine, Todd." As she headed for the door, she grabbed a stale Danish off the top of the refrigerator and stuffed it into her mouth. She unlocked the door to her Jeep and got behind the wheel. Then, Danish in mouth, she sped off with Genie to the Astrolabe complex.

As Susan drove, trying to eat her sweet roll without getting crumbs all over her painstakingly chosen outfit, Genie quietly asked, "Susan, do you think it is wise to involve Dr. Gilroy in your plan at this stage?"

Susan still wasn't used to Genie talking in her head, and was startled momentarily, dropping a batch of crumbs into her artificially pumped-up cleavage. Brushing herself off, she asked, "What do you mean, Genie? We need his support to get funding to collect the genetic samples. I don't have enough clout with the company to get that kind of research funding. Besides, I think I can handle Todd."

"I don't think you understand, Susan. The technology you are about to reveal to Dr. Gilroy is far beyond any technology that now exists. If applied properly, it could quickly become the basis for solutions to many of the problems that face your civilization. The ability to directly read the molecular lock and key mechanisms of cell physiology and biochemistry would make it possible to read all genomes, cure cancer, and solve most viral and genetic diseases. The technology will have the ability to identify cell components that control aging, normal cell function, even heredity itself. This is much too important a concept to discuss in a technological vacuum. You are about to hand over technology that is at least fifty years in the future for your civilization if it were to survive that long. Are you sure Dr. Gilroy, or Astrolabe Systems, for that matter, is ready to manage this type of innovation without it becoming the proverbial *runaway train?*"

As Susan finished the last dry crust of her pastry roll, she thought for a moment, then said, "I guess I hadn't thought about this plan in those terms. I've been so preoccupied with fooling, or I should say, vanquishing Todd, that I didn't analyze what we're actually doing. Do you have any suggestions?"

"I think it would be wise to limit your discussion to the smallest parameters possible, perhaps a single peptide or enzyme. You could say that the system has been tuned to a specific configuration and then give the demonstration, which should satisfy Dr. Gilroy."

"Genie, you are right, as usual."

Susan pulled up to the gate, gave her thumb imprint, and then drove to her normal parking spot without notice. She gathered up her books and carefully carried the briefcase containing Genie into the building. As planned, she had arrived well before any of her staff and began to set up the PC cabinet for Genie. With the physical layout set and her game face on, she rehearsed how she was going to handle Todd in her mind. Then as she paced in her inner office, she played her part out loud and even gave Todd's probable replies.

About 8:15, Max phoned Steve Clark, the administrator of the Harrison division. "Hi, Steve, this is Max. I wanted to touch base before I leave for the holidays. I finished the Keck project over the weekend, so I thought I'd get a head start on the traffic to visit my parents in Colorado Springs. . . . Yes, I entered all my data into the mainframe and left instructions with the guys in the lab on the needed hardware. I'll talk to Frank before I leave and get him up to speed on the Keck deal. The home office should be happy too because they'll be able to make a few bucks on this one. Well, anyway, I'll be leaving sometime today. I'll be back about the tenth, give or take a day or two. Okay.... A Merry Christmas to you too. See ya soon."

Max hung up and immediately punched-up Frank in the lab. "Hi, Frank. I'm goin' to take off for my folks' place in Colorado and won't be comin' in today. Don't worry. I finished the Keck project this weekend, and you'll find all the info in the computer. Just open the Keck file — it's all there.... Yeah. Hardware configuration, software, the works. How was the casino boat in Branson? ... What do you mean, loan you some money? All right. Look in the top drawer of my desk. There is the twenty-five bucks I won on that bet with Bradley on the Cowboys and Chief's game. You can pay me when I get back. See ya in a couple of weeks."

Max had one last call to make before the decks were clear. He gave Roger instructions on how to take care of the cabin in his absence. He also told him how to get in touch with him in case of an emergency. Max then began to pack for his trip to Colorado. He even dug out his skis, hoping he might get in some time on the slopes while he was there.

As he continued to load the car, he couldn't help thinking about Susan's quest to convince Todd to back her efforts to collect the genetic samples. Then it occurred to him he might be able to listen in on the conversation. He quickly went into the house and sat down by the phone and thought Genie's name in his head as Nute had instructed. "*Genie, are you there?*"

"Yes, Max. What can I do for you?"

"Has Susan talked to Todd yet?"

"She is about to phone him now. Why do you ask?"

"I was wondering if I could listen in on the presentation."

"Of course, Max. All you have to do is stay by the phone."

Max was startled when the TV suddenly came on, offering a bird's eye view of Susan's office on the screen. He could hear her talking in his head too. He watched and listened in awe as the drama unfolded.

"Hi, Todd. This is Susan down in the physiology lab. I was fooling around with a gadget to scan white blood cells this weekend, and I may've come across something that might interest you. . . . Well, I was working on a way to identify surface antigen-antibody architecture on white blood cells when it occurred to me that you might be able to use my new scanner in your work. I came up with a way to optically scan molecular configurations, perhaps even some of your peptide-enzyme links. Why don't you bring up one of your samples and let me see if I can make any sense of it. Haven't you been working on wheat or something? . . .Oh, you know this place; there aren't many secrets in here. Never mind that. Bring up something you have been working on and let's give it a shot. All right. See ya soon."

When Susan hung up the phone, Max said via Genie, "Well done. If you don't mind, I've been listening in, and I'd like to listen to the whole spiel."

Susan was startled by Max's comments and jumped slightly. "Okay, but just don't say anything. It will probably make me laugh right in Todd's face!"

It seemed like only a few seconds and Todd was at Susan's office door. Marilyn greeted him in the outer office with a skeptical glare and said, "What are you doing here, Dr. Gilroy?"

Susan stepped into the outer office. "It's all right, Marilyn. Todd is here to see me." Todd marched into Susan's office, a proud grin on his face like he had just been chosen by his teacher to lead his first grade class to the cafeteria for lunch. Todd was wearing his usual bow tie with a pastel green shirt and carried a small vial of liquid that was pale yellow in color. A black stopper prevented spillage.

As soon as the door was closed behind them, Todd began the conversation. "Gosh, Susan, I was surprised to get your phone call. I didn't think we would ever get to work together."

As Todd spoke, Susan motioned for him to take a seat in front of her desk. "Won't you sit down, Todd?" Susan slid back slightly on her desk and let her legs separate just enough to give Todd a peak at her hem line as it crept up. Todd's eyes wandered to her creamy white skin as she revealed the above-the-knee portion of her legs. He was noticeably agitated by Susan's demeanor and tugged at his shirt collar as if it were getting hotter in the room.

He stammered and cleared this throat and finally managed to get out, "Uh . . . I like the dress, Susan. I mean, it looks good on you. Well, ya know what I mean."

"Why, thank you, Todd. I get tired of the same old things, and since this was a special occasion, I thought something new might be appropriate for our new collaboration."

"What collaboration is that, Susan?"

"Let me tell you what I came across this last weekend."

Todd was now breaking out in a cold sweat, his pulse rate obviously climbing, and he seemed uncomfortably hot. His right hand trembled as he fidgeted with his sport coat buttons, trying to keep his composure while Susan continued to explain.

"Over the past few weeks, I've been working on a way to detect viral attachments on the surface of white blood cells. This is a project to help identify possible illnesses encountered on deep space voyages. We had to develop a way to examine astronauts' blood samples while they were in quarantine, and do it remotely by telemetry.

"Anyway, we modified a type of magnetic resonance imaging technology to scan very small samples. After I wrote a program to interpret the data, I came up with a three-dimensional way to scan the various optical landmarks on the surface of the cell. Actually, the program worked a lot better than I expected. We were able to identify various landmarks that seemed to coincide with enzyme-peptide couplings."

For the first time, Todd's interest in Susan's legs seemed to wane slightly and he actually began to listen to what she was saying.

She continued. "As I fine-tuned the scanner I was able to get more and more resolution to the surface architecture. Then, last weekend, it occurred to me that you might be interested in the scanner to help identify some of your enzyme-peptide pairs in your gene splicing project."

"How do you mean, Susan?"

"Well, I know you've been working with various enzyme-peptide pairs to help make the gene splice for your wheat experiment."

Todd immediately interrupted. "How do you know about that? My research is supposed to be top secret."

"Never mind that. Why don't we see if I can scan your sample and identify anything? Did you bring something to examine?"

"Yes, but be careful. This is a purified sample of a peptide ring we have been trying to crack for weeks. It has taken us two weeks just to get it purified. It has been through seventeen steps, including electrophoresis. Let's see if your scanner can tell me what it is."

Todd gave the tube to Susan, and as she took it, she made eye contact and gently touched him on the shoulder. She then gracefully nudged him as she slid between him and the desk, forcing an almost face-to-face encounter. She had intentionally placed his chair close to her desk to allow for this well choreographed maneuver. As she slowly passed him, she quietly said, "Just watch this, Todd."

Susan took the sample to the phony scanner and intentionally obscured Todd's view of the keyboard as she rapidly tapped meaningless keystrokes for several seconds. Then, after a dramatic pause and with flair, she struck the enter key. The printer immediately began to print the data Genie had gleaned from Todd's sample. Not only did the printout show the contents of the vial but the structure and all the possible enzymes that would fit the architecture of the molecule — twenty-seven in all. Todd stood in front of the printer in amazement, unable to speak. After carefully examining the printout and realizing the scanner had solved a problem he and his entire department had been working on for over a year, Todd awkwardly sank into the chair and continued to intensely scrutinize the printout. Without lifting his eyes from the page, he asked, "Who knows about this?"

"Just you and me, Todd."

"I think we should keep it that way for now, don't you?"

"Absolutely, Todd. I don't think anyone else should know, not even Clark. If we quietly gather genetic samples and analyze them, we could build a library of genomes we can use for years to develop any project we want."

"You're right, Susan. This technology has unlimited potential. We could do this together and be rich as well as famous. Mostly rich!" Todd's greed had obviously overtaken his lust. He was no longer interested in Susan's legs but consumed by the printout and what it meant for him and his program at Astrolabe. Susan's plan had worked to perfection. Now she maneuvered for the coup de grâce.

"Todd, do you think you can get funding to collect samples for such a project?"

"Are you kidding? I can get all the money we need for this. No problem. Just give me time to clean up this mundane wheat project with some positive results and Clark will give us a green light. The wheat deal is chicken feed, literally. The sky is the limit for this kind of technology. We can call our own shots. Susan, we could even start our own company!"

"Then do we have a deal, Todd? I will continue to perfect the scanner and collect the samples. You keep the money flowing and we will do a joint publication. Okay? Let's get together after the holidays and work on a plan."

Susan put her arm around Todd as she ushered him to the door. In spite of her proximity, the smell of her perfume and the warmth exuding from her body, he scarcely took his eyes off the printout as he left her office. At the door, he turned and said, "Susan, not only do we have a deal, but I hope this is the start of a great relationship."

Susan gave him her most seductive and alluring smile. "Me too, Todd."

Todd quickly stuffed the printout in his coat when he went into the outer office and made for the door as if he suddenly had a case of diarrhea. She knew he simply couldn't wait to get back to his lab and show off the data, intending to take most, if not all, of the credit himself, of course.

Susan said, "See you later, Todd," as he made his exit.

"What was that all about?" inquired Marilyn.

"Oh, nothing," Susan said in a matter-of-fact way as she closed her office door behind her. When she was safely in her office, she clinched her fist, pumped it in the air and uttered an enthusiastic, self-congratulatory, "YES!"

"Nice work, Susan!" Max interjected as she plopped down at her desk, put her feet up, and reclined in her swivel chair.

"It was pretty good, wasn't it? Todd was easier than I thought. You don't think I led him on too much do you?"

"Nah, I don't think so. But you did pour it on a little when you rubbed on him as you moved past him at the desk."

"How did you know about that?" Susan blushed a little.

"Genie, of course. She patched in a video of the office while Todd was there."

"You could see all of that?"

"Yes, I could. I might say you had me convinced that you were flashing 'come and get it' to ol' Todd. You're a little too good with your feminine wiles, if you ask me, a little too seductive to be a rank amateur, as you claim."

"Why, Max. If I didn't know better, I would think you are jealous!"

"I am not! All I am saying is you were very skillful at showing your breasts to Todd, especially when he is someone you supposedly can't stand."

"That does it. You are jealous. I don't know if I like Genie being able to transmit my private conversations let alone video."

"Well, you better get used to it because I think I'm going to keep an eye on you and good ol' Todd."

"Don't be ridiculous! Todd is about as obnoxious as they come, and a buffoon. I only enticed him because we need him for the funding. Okay?"

"Okay, but you sure seemed to enjoy doing it."

"I said, okay?"

"All right." Max gave in but his resignation was involuntary and he was surprised by his more-than-passing interest in Susan's ability to manipulate Todd. Although he hated to admit it, a slight hint of jealous rivalry came to the surface when he saw Susan brush up against Todd and give him that alluring look. He found himself reacting with emotion rather than his usual dispassionate logic. For Max, jealousy was a new feeling, and he didn't like it. He was beginning to realize that Susan was becoming more than a collaborator. She was beginning to push his alpha-male button a little more than he was used to.

"Now that we have that settled, I need to get started for Colorado to see my folks. I was planning to go by the bunker in Kansas on the way. Don't ya think I should take Genie with me?"

"Yeah. Why don't I bring Genie by your place on the way home?"

"Okay, see ya soon," he said with a bit more pique in his voice than he intended.

"I should be there in about twenty minutes."

Max continued to load his car and make final preparations for his trip west to Kansas and then on to Colorado. He had all his winter gear loaded and his skies tied on top of his luggage rack. Just as he made his last tie to his skis, Susan's Jeep splashed through the mud and turned onto his driveway.

"Have you cooled off about Todd yet?" She teased.

"Yeah, a little, I guess."

"Looks like you're all set to make your trip."

"Yeah, all I need now is Genie for some company."

"Well, here she is. She certainly did her job for me with Todd. I hope Todd doesn't want a repeat performance while you're away. It might be a little difficult to make that old PC cabinet do as well without Genie."

Genie interrupted. "You can reach me by phone. Just call me."

Max and Susan both chuckled as Susan put both of Genie's wooden boxes on the front floorboard on the passenger's side.

"Well, Max. I guess this is it until we get back together next month. I think I'll probably leave tomorrow. I'll tie up the loose ends on the Mars project before I leave. I don't want to scare them all too much with Genie's homework. You know I'm really going to miss your cooking. I can't imagine doing it for myself again."

"Master Wong can't be that bad," Max said with a boyish chuckle.

Max and Susan stood awkwardly beside his car, like a couple of teenagers unsure of how intimate to be, as they tried to say their farewells. Susan finally just grabbed Max in a big bear hug. "You take care of yourself, and take care of Genie too. I don't want anything to happen to either of you!"

"What could anyone do to me as long as Genie is with me. I feel like Buck Rogers with my ray gun at the ready. Right, Genie?"

"Of course, Max. I will zap anyone you tell me to."

Max and Susan laughed. Then Max got in the car and slowly drove off. He looked in the rearview mirror and saw Susan give a pathetic little wave as he turned down the highway. "*God, I miss her already*," he thought to himself as he bounced along the muddy road. "Genie, remind me to have Roger fix this road when I get back."

"Does Roger have that capability?"

"No, but I'm sure he has a cousin or somebody else he knows who can do it."

CHAPTER 10

Max remained thoughtful and with little to say as he and Genie cruised through the rolling hills of eastern Kansas. Genie gave explicit directions as they navigated through the small towns and back roads, each turn calculated to be the shortest possible route to the bunker. Genie also took into account the traffic and possible interference by the local population. Max then began a long and specific series of questions that he had been formulating in his mind.

"Genie, what exactly is the mode of transportation between your home planet and Earth?"

"Do you mean what propulsion is used, Max?"

"Yes!"

"A form of ion particle engine coupled with an antigravity generator, the latter used when the craft is under the influence of a large mass, such as a star or black matter. The generator actually produces a counter flux that compensates for gravity in the space-time fabric of the universe. The way this is done is beyond your capacity to understand, but the technology enables us to travel at .9836 the speed of light without distortion or damage. As you may have guessed, travel beyond the speed of light is impossible in your time reference."

"What do you mean, in my time reference?"

"The universe as you can observe it, including time, space, velocity, and so on. There are other dimensions of which you are not aware, and these are useful when you approach the speed of light. The concept of other dimensions will take your civilization many centuries to grasp. Had Steven Hawking lived longer, he surely would have been a pioneer in this area of technology. As you may have guessed, the technology I have described is Level-Nine technology, and I can't make the concept available to you."

"Well, I guess it really doesn't matter much anyway. What I really need to know now, Genie, is how're we goin' to build a device that can essentially rule the Earth in less than twelve months? I need to know how we propel this thing and make it impervious to all weapons that might confront us."

"Don't worry, Max. Everything you need will be in the bunker. I have several plans in my databanks that will work nicely. If history is any indication, your problems will come from your own people."

"Do you mean my own government?"

"As is always the case with new weapons, every government and every faction will want to have it. You will be wise to keep this weapon a secret as long as possible."

"I still don't believe my own government would hurt me or take an invention of any kind away from me."

"Let me put it this way: if anyone finds out what your new capabilities are, including your access to me and to the bunker, you will be in danger. The technology will be forcibly taken from you and used to their advantage, and your current plans will be ruined. This is the way it has always been in the past on Earth."

"I guess I seem pretty naïve about all of this, Genie."

"Actually, Max. You are quite intelligent, but yes, naïve would be a good word to describe you. You just don't have the thousands of years of experience in your memory that I do. Many times, almost without exception, I have seen how new technologies affect your species. Something as revolutionary as the device you have in mind will be especially disruptive. Your enemies, and even some of your friends, will show little restraint in stealing the hardware and adopting the concept to achieve their own agenda. The temptation will simply be too great. If you resist, you will be eliminated by any means they see fit."

"What about law and order?"

"Now you are definitely being naïve."

Genie interrupted their conversation to give more directions. "Turn left here, Max."

Max turned west onto a two-track section line road, the winter-killed grass between the tire tracks indicating it was seldom traveled. The overcast night sky shrouded the Kansas hill country in complete darkness. The car's headlights produced a harsh contrast as Max penetrated what seemed like an endless undulating prairie.

"Are we getting close, Genie?"

"We will be there in approximately 2.6 minutes."

"Good!"

In what Max assumed was the predicted 2.6 minutes, Genie interrupted the silence. "Stop here." Max abruptly stopped the car, causing gravel to spray out in front his car. Max got his jacket from the backseat, pulled a flashlight from the glove box, and opened the door into the brisk twenty-degree night. He quickly zipped up his jacket to shield himself from the relentless Kansas wind. He flipped on the flashlight, and wielding it like a saber, looked in all directions for the bunker.

"Genie, I don't see anything!"

"Relax, Max. Did you expect a sign? If you take me with you, we can go inside. The entrance is straight in front of you on the left side of the car." Max opened the door and retrieved Genie from his briefcase. He headed toward the hillside, but then a low rumble in the ground made Max stop dead in his tracks. Two metallic cleavers sliced up through the hillside about thirty yards in front of him. Max heard the muted tearing of the buffalo grass as the cleavers unfolded like a flower bud to expose the entryway to the bunker, a fortress-like opening that looked like a bank vault. There was a swish of air when a door opened and broke the vacuum seal. The door slowly opened into a metallic hallway that sloped down slightly into the gentle elevation of the hillside.

Genie prompted Max. "Do you want to go in now?"

Max was startled by Genie's inquiry. "Yes, of course." Then he slowly made his way toward the opening, unsure of what to expect.

The footing was not easy in the buffalo grass, which was matted down by the winter weather, and so Max had to walk raising his knees high to maneuver in the thick grass. As Max approached the opening, the lights came on inside, revealing a long, glistening hallway that penetrated the hillside. When Max finally reached the door, he entered the hallway and began his descent. After walking twenty-five feet, Max turned at the sound of the door closing behind him.

Genie, sensing his concern, said, "Don't worry, Max. It opens from this side too."

The walls, floor, and ceiling were covered by a metal casing that Max thought looked like brushed stainless steel. Lighting was provided by square panels that appeared to glow with a low-level, slightly pink light. After a hundred meters, the hall leveled off, and a bit further, it opened into a gigantic cavern with containers of all sizes stacked in orderly rows. The interior was covered by the same metallic surface and automatically illuminated by the same type of lights that came on in the hallway. There was no visible means of support for the roof. To the left Max saw what appeared to be an administrative office with several levels of windows that overlooked the massive storage facility.

Max felt dwarfed by the enormous underground structure. Finally he asked Genie, "What is all of this stuff?"

"A complete inventory of all the material needed to assist any travelers to this sector, whether it is Nute or any of his people, should it become necessary to make repairs or do routine maintenance."

"You mean this is like an auto parts store but for spacecraft?"

"Yes, something like that. However, there is other specialized equipment here."

"What do you mean?

"This place is also a power generating station as well as a navigation beacon for our spacecraft. This is essentially an unmanned port of call and residence for visitors when they come to your planet on business."

"How big is this place anyway, Genie?"

"The dimensions are 126.2 meters high, 200.6 meters wide, and 542.3 meters long. It was constructed when the Council took a more serious interest in this planet, in the year 152,460 BC. There are storage facilities, living quarters, a communication station and power plant, repair equipment, and a docking station."

"Man, when you guys plan ahead, you *really* plan ahead. What else is stored here, Genie?"

Genie flashed a complete inventory of equipment and supplies via hologram in the area just in front of Max, who gazed at it wide-eyed. The green glow reflected off his face as he got closer to what seemed like an interminable list of high tech supplies and equipment.

"Do you have one of those belts Nute wore to my house?"

"Yes, of course. Do you want to try it on?"

"Sure, why not."

"Take me to row 62, section BB."

Although Max was aware that the symbols were in Nute's language, he was able to read them with the help of his communicator and went right to the spot, where he found a stack of metal boxes that were arranged by sizes. He removed one of the belts from one of the storage containers and tried it on — it fit perfectly.

"How do I make it work, Genie?"

"Just to your right, there is a section of power supplies. Those on the top left should fit the belt. Snap one in, and then you just need to think which way you want to go. The belt will take you there."

He took the small belt buckle power supply and snapped it in place. Then Max began to levitate. He then glided around the building, tentatively at first, but after a few minutes, he was swishing around like a professional.

"Wow, I could get used to this. No wonder Nute likes to travel this way." Max swooped down and picked up the briefcase with Genie and zoomed down the aisle toward the administrative office. When he turned the corner in front of the glass opening, he lost control and plowed into the wall. He was only about three feet off the ground, so no harm was done, but the reason for his mishap nearly caused his heart to stop. Max leaped to his feet gasping for breath. He stood before a room of twenty-five or thirty people, all in manikin-like poses.

"Genie!" he screamed. "What the hell is this!"

"Relax, Max. Your heart rate is elevated to an extreme level. This is a storage room for Nute's bodies. They aren't alive. Think of them as clothing, Nute's wardrobe, if you will. These guises help him blend in with the various indigenous people with whom he has lived."

Regaining his composure, Max slowly walked toward the group of lifelike people. He recognized the two Nutes he had met last weekend, but a host of other men and women were also standing before him with blank stares as if waiting to be placed in a store window for a display. When Max finally conjured the nerve to touch them, they felt cold but otherwise like flesh over bone. Completely naked, the bodies stood in a long single file line against the wall. There were groups of blond men and women, Blacks, Asians, and aboriginal types as well. Max realized that this was a display of the human race, all races and ethnicities, lifelike and perfect in every detail.

Max walked slowly among them, examining each one. He resisted the temptation to touch the women's breasts, but he did touch each one's face, fascinated by their beauty. Toward the end of the line was a husky man of about five foot two covered with hair. His heavy features and low forehead, coupled with his massive musculature, belied his prehistoric origins. Max reached out and grasped his upper arm and said to himself, "*Wouldn't want to meet this guy in a dark alley.*"

"Genie, has Nute been all of these people? I mean, has he used their bodies?"

"Yes, Max. Nute found it useful to be able to blend in with each of the cultures he has helped."

"So, what you're saying is that these 'people' have been manufactured by Nute to use as real people?"

"Not exactly. These *are* real people. Nute merely made a copy to use as a type of disguise, similar to a costume. Only in this case, the costume is an entire person. Nute selected someone who was typical of the culture and made a copy. The person he copied then became a container for Nute. I know this seems a little frightening to you, and that it is hard to understand, but Nute can do this quite easily. There is also an extensive wardrobe in the next room that you might find interesting."

Max walked into the next room and found the mother of all closets, about one hundred feet long filled with clothes of every description hanging down both sides, all historically arranged. Ancient animal skins gradually gave way to Elizabethan silks of the eighteenth century. Toward the back, modern worsted wool and synthetic suits of various sizes for both men and women were hung neatly, ready to be plucked off the rack and put on. Additionally, a full array of shirts and blouses and casual wear lined the walls in stacks behind the clothes on hangers. Max thought Nute's wardrobe looked like a clothing store with an inventory that spanned about ten thousand years of fashion, a place ready to dress-out a Neanderthal or a Wall Street banker, whichever was necessary, from head to toe.

Max walked slowly, fingering the fabrics. He definitely was not a fashion maven, but he truly appreciated the depth, variety, and completeness of the garment entrepôt.

"Would you like something to eat, Max?"

"You have food here?"

"A full kitchen is behind the storage area. The bodies need food when they are being used, and so we have a complete stock of everything."

"Don't you have to worry about spoilage or deterioration? I'm sorry. What am I thinking? Of course, you don't. I keep thinking like an Earth person."

"The kitchen is equipped with a device that prevents deterioration. It is the same device that keeps our spacecraft free of organic breakdown, employing a type of molecular stabilization that is a Level-Nine technology. I think you will find the produce and meat selections quite fresh."

After Max had prepared a steak with all the trimmings and finished a rich cup of what he judged to be pure Colombian Arabica coffee, he gave his compliments to the owner of the establishment and decided to spend the night. He told Genie to wake him at six o'clock the next morning. Genie directed him to the sleeping quarters, and soon he was asleep in this well stocked, even luxuriant, hotel for star travelers.

CHAPTER 11

Max was awakened precisely at six o'clock and stumbled half asleep into the shower, where he found a complete array of toiletries, including shaving cream and a razor. He spoke to Genie as he stepped out of the shower and buried his face in a fluffy cotton towel.

"Do you think I could use some of the clothes, Genie?"

"Of course. I am sure Nute would consider you his guest. You may have anything you would like, perhaps some underwear and clean socks."

After Max had selected a new shirt and a new properly seasoned pair of Levi's, he went into the kitchen and poured a cup of the freshly brewed coffee. As he helped himself to the Wheaties, he got down to the business at hand and the reason for his visit.

"Okay, Genie. Let's see what we might be able to use from the military hardware department."

"That would be in section Q toward the back. I believe we need an antigravity unit for propulsion and a harmonic wave generator as a weapon. If we could build a suitable container for these devices, it would be unstoppable by the current level of military technology available to the nations of the Earth."

As Max and Genie were gliding along with his new flying belt toward section Q, he asked, " How would this weapon work?"

"Ah, yes. Here we are, Max. Let's find the harmonic wave generator and I will show you how it works. Do you see the circular device on the second level? That is the antigravity generator. This particular model can lift and propel about one-hundred tons, a little more weight than a main battle tank like the old Abrams M1 A1. That should be more than enough to house all the other equipment we need."

Genie then projected the plans of a flying tank-like device. Max thought it spooky. It looked a lot like those old grainy black and white photos of UFOs. Genie explained that the shape was determined by the antigravity generator, which looked like a large flat doughnut. The generator was housed in several inches of armor with concealed bays for weapons deployment and room for a pilot in the middle of the craft. The device was twenty-two feet in diameter and the center section was dome-shaped, eight and a half feet high with a three foot tapered bevel all the way around

Genie explained how the harmonic generator selectively disrupted matter by focusing a powerful microwave signal that could be tuned to the specific material you wanted to destroy.

"Specifically Max, the harmonic generator can be tuned to identify weapons and cause vibration in the metal parts, generating heat and warping the metal, thus making these implements useless as weapons. This could be done in a matter of seconds with rifles or heavy artillery. The clever thing about this weapon is that it does not hurt people or other property. For example, the device can be tuned to distort bullets or other projectiles, even a missile that might be aimed at it."

Max said, "In other words, Genie, this is a schematic for a totally indestructible aircraft that could disable all current weapons and just keep flying to do whatever damage needs to be done to convince any adversary to cease and desist."

"Yes."

Max was fascinated by the plan. He looked at each detail, asking questions and becoming familiar with the inner workings. After an hour of questions about the weapon, he asked, "Okay, Genie, exactly how does the antigravity generator work?"

"Similar to a helicopter, except instead of air, the antigravity generator balances the flow of gravity flux particles and is able to move about with ease. You don't have to know more about how it works, Max. In fact, you will have to take my word for it because this knowledge is beyond your comprehension at this point in your civilization's development. Let it suffice to say that it works just like the belt you have on right now, only it is stronger."

"How fast will it go?"

"As fast as you need it to, Max. Just push the stick forward and it will go faster and faster until it reaches its maximum velocity, which is a level 9 inquiry."

"I'm a little concerned I might have to explain how it works to get the funding to build a complete craft."

"Don't worry, Max. The military will be eager to fund this without much explanation. All you have to say is that the plans are classified after delineating a fraction of what the device will do. That designation always works with military types and government bureaucrats. Besides, the actual theory of the generator is Level-Nine technology, and as you know, I can't share that with you anyway. Let's go over two rows and look at the harmonic disrupter."

Max carried Genie the requested two rows. "Yes, here we are — the K-50. This is a fifty gigawatt power source and should be more than enough to take care of any contingency, certainly sufficient to provide for a small array of directional disrupter pods, which are far less complex and could be manufactured here on Earth."

"Genie, how are we going to get this stuff back to my house? I think it might be a little obvious to just fly it over there, don't you?"

"Actually, this particular model will require that a ship be built for it since it is only a spare replacement part."

"If we could disguise it somehow," Max said, "we could probably get all of it on a flatbed truck. I think we could hire a truck in Fredonia and say we are hauling oil well rigging equipment or something like that. It isn't far to the oil fields near El Dorado Springs so that wouldn't sound out of place at all."

"That sounds like a good idea, Max. The gravity generator will come apart in the middle, so I am sure the two halves will fit on the truck. I will have the terminal robots crate the generator and disrupter and have the cargo ready for our return trip. We will also need a power plant and a crystal control unit, but they are quite small and should not be any problem to load."

"What was that you just said? The terminal what?"

"There are six robots stationed here for heavy work, unless you would like to crate the equipment yourself."

"No, that'll be just fine. I was just surprised to learn that there are robots here, that's all. Where are they?"

"They should be coming down the aisle just about now." When Max turned to look behind him, he saw two spheres, each about the size of a large beach ball with four appendages, one in each direction at 90 degrees. A claw type device at the end of each arm appeared to function like a hand.

"Are you sure this little ball can lift the generator and build a crate for it?"

"Oh yes, Max. The R-92 units are quite capable. They will have the crates ready for our return trip."

"Well, I guess that just about does it. If we start now, don't you think we could be in Colorado Springs by nightfall, Genie?"

"Yes, the sun will be up soon, so let's get started. I am looking forward to meeting your family, Max. When are they expecting you?"

"I haven't talked to them, so I guess I should call them. Genie, do you have a telephone handy?"

"Of course. Would you like to place a call to your parents' house? Just speak normally. I will patch you through the bunker's communication system."

Max's mom said hello. "Hi, Mom. I wanted to let you know that I'm on my way home for a few days. I should be there sometime tonight. What's for supper? . . . Roast beef. That's great. . . . No, there won't be any female companions with me this time. I did meet someone, though. I'll have to tell you all about her when I get there. Is everyone else going to be home? . . . Good. It will be nice to see everyone again. See ya soon."

Max and Genie spent the day driving across Kansas and eastern Colorado. They passed the time discussing military history. Max was particularly interested in strategy and a historical perspective on how politics influenced the way wars had been started in the past. Genie's rich embellishment of history with anecdotes made their conversation both fascinating and insightful for Max. For a time, Max discovered, Nute had been a maid servant for Alexander the Great, and Genie was able to share much of the behind-the-scenes plotting and military strategy, even events that eventually led to Alexander's illness and death. Max also gained insight into Sun Tzu, the famous Chinese General and revered philosopher of warfare. Max had even heard his dad quote Sun Tzu when he talked about military strategy.

By the time they arrived in Colorado Springs, Max had a much greater understanding of Nute's view of the human species. However, each episode Genie described seemed to also reinforce the idea that what Max was trying to do would be impossible. His mission would be Man's last chance to overcome the highly evolved, selfish, territorial, and aggressive nature of his species. A battle with sticks and rocks over a choice waterhole had evolved into the present thermonuclear capability to wipe out everything and everyone on the planet. How was he supposed to not only overcome such might but such a proclivity for violence?

When Genie spoke of Nute's many travels and experiences, it was clear that there had been a personal relationship for Nute with his human companions. Genie described them more like old friends, and her stories had the flavor of reminiscences instead of just observed facts. Max came to realize that Genie was more than just a reference library, but that she was also becoming his friend. He was even coming to appreciate her subtle personality and beginning to understand how incredibly fortunate he was to have her as his mentor and confidante. The fact she was a seemingly inanimate information storage device had long ago become irrelevant.

CHAPTER 12

They arrived at Max's parents' house just after 6:30 that evening, in time for dinner. Curtis and Gloria Gibson had lived in Colorado Springs since Curtis retired from the Air Force and took a teaching position at the Academy. His son's Steve's death in a flight test mishap for a new fighter had affected Curtis deeply, but he still loved the Air Force and was a good teacher for the cadets. Max's mother, Gloria, a consummate housewife in the June Cleaver tradition, had been a guiding influence in all of her children's lives. She had encouraged Max's early development by making sure he was challenged intellectually. Steve's death was hard on everyone, and it had been up to Gloria to keep the family from falling apart.

Max, who idolized his older brother, was only fourteen when Steve was killed and always blamed the Air Force for taking his brother because the crash had been caused by a classified weapons system failure on the experimental plane. This blame was a big factor in Max's aversion to the military in his career choices. Although Max's sister Kate was a very grown-up sixteen, he still considered her his little sister.

Max was looking forward to being close to his family for the holidays, but he also felt this might be the last time he would be with them without a lot of complications associated with his new life as a peace maker and savior of humanity. Max didn't feel quite so alone in his mission as he turned into the family driveway and saw his mother through the window as she scurried around the kitchen.

"Genie, I'm going to leave you under the seat for now, if it is all right with you."

"Yes, I think that would be wise. I will be able to communicate with you if necessary, and the fewer people who know about me the better."

Max had no sooner gotten out of the car than his mother was out of the house and clamping a big hug around her baby boy. She exclaimed, pushing him to arm's length, "My God, let me look at you! Have you been eating enough? You are so thin."

"I've been running a lot, Mom, that's all. You look great!"

Max's sister also ran out to greet him.

"Can this be little Katie? Boy, have you grown up."

Kate did not jump on him and lock her legs around his waist like when she was eight, but she did give him a big hug. Then she reminded him that she was sixteen now and her name was Kate not "little Katie."

Max's father, Curtis, who had watched from the porch as the women in his life greeted his son, now walked to the car and offered a strong handshake and a hearty, "Welcome home, son."

The family quickly moved out of the cold wind and into the house. During dinner, everyone brought Max up to date on their various activities, each giving a synopsis of their life during the year since they had all been together. Then everyone wanted to hear what Max had been doing, especially his mother, who wanted to know all about his new romantic interest. Max gave all the details he dared give his mother and sister about Susan. Finally he said, "You will just have to meet her."

Gloria quickly retorted, "When *will* we get to meet her?"

"Yeah," said Kate. "You seem to be pretty interested in her. Is she good looking?"

"Well, I think she is, and I think you will too. But you will have to judge her virtues for yourself."

Gloria modestly began serving her special holiday dessert, pecan pie. She knew this was her family's favorite, but she said as she dished it up, "This probably isn't very good. I think it may be overdone." The pie was perfect, as was everything about Max's homecoming. After dessert, Gloria and Kate cleared the table and Max and his dad moved into the family room to let a great meal settle a bit.

"Dad, I was wondering if we could get in some skiing while I am here?"

"Sure. They have plenty of snow at Keystone and Vail. We could be over there in a couple of hours. Did you bring your skis?"

"Yeah, I did. I even thought to bring my ski pants and parka too."

After a quiet evening of family chitchat, Max unloaded the car and turned in for a restful night's sleep. He felt cozy in his childhood bed, secure in that way that only comes from being with your family in a loving home. As he drifted off, he thought of the thousands of generations he had seen at Nute's demonstration and wondered if they had the same secure family environment he enjoyed as a child.

The next morning, Max and the whole family drove to Keystone Resort, a family favorite ever since Curt retired. Gloria and Kate restricted themselves to the medium difficulty hills, and Curt and Max went for the expert downhill racer type challenge. About noon, Max and Curtis found themselves totally alone at the top of a seldom used run, which gave Max the opportunity he had been waiting for to talk to his dad privately.

"Dad, I need to talk to you about a military matter."

"What do you mean? Son, that isn't a subject you've ever given much thought."

"I haven't until now, but I've developed a new concept at work that definitely has military applications."

"Something to do with optics?"

"No. It's a revolutionary idea that has weapons applications and will be far superior to anything currently available."

Curtis instantly and instinctively scanned their immediate area to see if anyone was near. Then he said, "Let's go down the mountain and get more in the open so I can see if anyone is around."

They skied about a quarter of a mile downhill and east to a bald crest that had a clear view of about four-hundred yards in all directions.

"Max, I'm assuming that what you're talking about is highly classified, right?"

"Right."

"Then don't tell me anymore about it. If you have developed some kind of new weapons system, you need to be careful, son."

"What I really need to know, Dad, is how to apply the new technology to modern warfare."

"Jesus, Max. The last I knew, you were so pissed off at the military you didn't ever want to have anything to do with the 'soldier boys,' as you called them. Now, you spring on me that you have an idea for a new weapons system. Where the hell did this come from?"

"I know, Dad. This concept just fell into my lap."

"That's a pretty big thing to fall into one's lap, son!" Curtis took a sidelong look at his son, as if he was not sure that his motives in asking the questions were being stated. After a long pause Curtis said, "Actual warfare hasn't changed much since the days of the

Roman legions. The basic fire-and-maneuver offensive and defensive tactics are still about the same."

"What if I were to tell you I could produce a weapon that was indestructible and capable of defeating any other weapon. What would be the best way to use such a weapon?"

His father now looked at his son as if he has told him the moon is sitting on his head. "Hell, that's easy. All you'd have to do is deploy the weapon and use it to enforce whatever doctrine you deem worthy of enforcement, the old *might-is-right* theory. Look, if you don't have any fear of reprisal, you don't have to worry about defensive tactics at all. Most military strategy is based on survival. You protect your military assets, and you use those assets to inflict as much damage on the enemy as possible; but you use your assets without expending them. If you are successful, your side, though diminished, will still be standing at the end of the conflict — the winner by default.

If you can attack with impunity, all of the normal defensive tactics go out the window. Since Alexander's time, the scenario has been the same: the powerful simply wipe out their enemies and enjoy the spoils of war, whatever the spoils might be. They rape the women, seize anything of value, then rule over and dominate the remaining population."

"So, what you are saying is that, to conduct operations with such a weapon, no special consideration would be necessary as regards to tactics?"

"Hell no! You just kick ass and take names. The big problem with the kind of weapons system you described, if it's actually possible, isn't the tactics but the politics. The wise use of such a system would be the problem. If such a weapons system fell into the wrong hands, it would be a disaster, maybe the end of the civilized world if some despotic regime got their hands on it. Son, I can't emphasize enough that you must really be careful with stuff like this. How big is the team that knows about this weapon?"

"Just me and my colleague, Susan. I told you about her last night."

"Well, that's good. Remember, Max. Don't trust anyone you don't absolutely have to with this. I don't even want to know about it. It makes me nervous just talking about it, even out here on the side of this snow-covered mountain. And just so I am clear, this warning includes our side as well."

"What do you mean?"

"I mean there are people in our government, especially in the military, who would snuff you out like a candle in the wind and never give it a second thought to get their hands on something like this. Is it operational yet?"

"No. It hasn't been built yet."

"Do you think anyone else could build it without you?"

"No way. No one would have a clue unless I show them."

"In that case, don't show anybody. The military will probably want what is called a liaison officer to work with you. Do not accept this because their real purpose, of course, is to let the brass know the moment the system is operational. You will then be unceremoniously dropped from the project. If you make too much of a fuss, you will have a CIA heart attack and be dropped from life on this Earth."

"Do you really mean that?"

"You bet your ass, I do!"

"They don't show you this kind of stuff on the recruiting posters do they, Dad?"

"Don't get me wrong, son. I love this country and respect the mission of the military. God knows there are people in this world who would take us out in a heartbeat if they could. Our military strength is the only thing standing between us and speaking Chinese or Russian or saying compulsory Muslim prayers five times a day. An absolutely unstoppable strategic weapon like you describe is a wholly different matter than our collective security. Something like you describe will bring out the worst in everyone."

Max respected his dad's advice concerning military matters, but it was more convincing since this was exactly what Genie had told him on the trip from Arkansas. Now, however, after Curt had laid out for him in such stark and pragmatic terms how things would go if he let the military know his secret, he had gained more clarity on the subject. It also made him recognize his own naiveté when it came to real-world strategic power politics, and that made him all the more nervous. He now understood what Genie meant when she said that the politics are much harder than achieving the technology.

Max and Curt raced down the hill to meet the women for lunch and continued to enjoy their family outing for the rest of the day, like they had done so many times in the past. None of Max's family fully understood how special this holiday season would be. Max kept up a good front, but he knew this was the last time they would enjoy each other's company with such carefree innocence.

When the family returned home, Max and his sister started a playful snowball fight with the new snow that was now falling with intensity. They reverted to their roles of big brother and little sister from years earlier. Max would get the best of Kate and let her go. Then she would immediately attack and pretend that she had actually gotten away on her own. They had not enjoyed this playful give and take for so long that it proved to be a delightful pastime. Even though they had grown into adulthood, Max and Kate really enjoyed being just kids again, if only for a half hour.

The rest of the weekend Max and his family spent enjoying the pleasures of each other's company, and Max scarcely thought of his problems. His mother kept trying to find out about Susan, and his sister wanted to hear anything her big brother had to say. Max's father, however, was very pensive and didn't talk much. He was clearly worried about Max's safety because of his years of experience in the military establishment. He knew his son would be like a babe in the woods if he got mixed up with Pentagon types, who were piranhas when it came to new weapons systems. He had known some who would stop at nothing to get what they wanted, some who had even taken bribes from the private sector to get some big-time system approved by the government. They weren't called bribes, of course, but took the form of a cozy job after retirement from the military at four or five times what the military paid. Curtis feared what they might do to get control of the system in the first place. This was the truly dangerous part of the scenario and what really had him worried.

CHAPTER 13

The day after Christmas, Max and his family said tearful good-byes, and he headed back to Kansas to go over the equipment checklist and to get a truck to haul his cargo to Harrison. His mother was always emotional to see him leave, but his dad was far more troubled than usual to see him drive off this time. He was certain in his heart that he would never see Max again. Kate, his newly grown-up sister, was like any teenage girl with a hero fixation on her older brother, and given that girls her age seem to have more intense emotions than anyone, it was a sad sight. Curtis did his best to console the women when Max made the turn at the end of the block. He slowly turned them, an arm around each, and they headed back into the house to gain refuge from the snow shower now coming down with vigor.

As Max got out of sight of the house, he asked Genie if everything was all right.

"Max, it has been quiet while you were with your family, but I sense a pattern of stress in your breathing. Are you all right?"

"Yes, I am just a little sad to leave my family. It was really nice to be in familiar surroundings with people I love and trust. My dad agrees with you, by the way. He gave me the don't-trust-anyone speech when we were on the mountain skiing."

"I am sure your father knows a lot about the military and how those who run it think."

"He made a believer out of me. In my work, it never occurs to me to be suspicious of anyone. I just never think about it. In his line of work, suspicion is how they operate and they plan for the worst, always."

He paused for a moment, then added, "Let's call Susan and see what she's doing."

"Go ahead, Max. She is on her communicator."

"Hey, Susan. How's the vacation with your family?"

"Great, Max. How's yours goin'?"

"I had a very informative talk with my dad and a great time visiting my mom and sister. After speakin' to my dad, I think I have in mind exactly what we need for the deterrent weapon system. All we need are a few armored aircraft with severe destructive capabilities that are also impregnable. Genie and I looked at the basics of such an aircraft in the bunker and will be bringing some of the parts back with us. We'll need to ask your dad if he can make a casting of the airframe at the vault company."

"I was going down to the plant with him this afternoon to see some old friends. I could talk to him about it then."

"Susan, tell him it needs to be about twenty-two feet across and about nine feet high. I estimate it will weigh thirty to forty tons with Genie's alloy. It needs to be cast in one piece with several openings for the pilot's hatch and weapons. I'm sure he understands this kind of stuff. The main thing is having the foundry capacity to make the casting in one piece."

"That should work. I think some of the vault doors they make are nearly that big. I'll ask him this afternoon. Well, gotta go. My sister and I are going to fix lunch."

"Oh yeah? What are you having?"

"That's none of your business! The way you cook, I don't want you making fun of our culinary adventure." Then he heard her call, "I'll be right there, Rachael." She again addressed him. "My sister is hounding me to help her. Some things never change. Now get off the phone, Max! I'll call you later. I miss you."

"I miss you too. Enjoy your lunch. Bye, bye!"

Genie continued to answer Max's questions about the aircraft and its capabilities as they traveled to Kansas. He also asked her questions on other, far-ranging topics of military history and physics. Max had never had access to such plain-spoken answers to all his questions. Occasionally, Max did venture into Level Nine, and even into Level Ten, territory and had to be reminded of his place at Level Eight. Overall, he and Genie continued to develop a close and friendly relationship.

Late that afternoon, they stopped for gas in the little town of Winfield, Kansas, just south of Wichita. They had been traveling on Highway 160 for the past couple of hours and were about forty-five minutes from the bunker. While Max was pumping gas, he asked a trucker if there was a nearby load agent where he could book a flatbed for a load of freight.

The trucker replied, "There's a large terminal over at El Dorado. There is a refinery there and they haul a lot of oil-well drilling equipment on flatbeds. The terminal is called Mother's Truck Stop. An ornery old bitch runs it. If you can stand to deal with her, she could probably book you a truck and driver — they specialize in independents."

When Max inquired if they could keep quiet about the freight they wanted hauled, the trucker said, "If the money is right, they would be deaf, dumb, and blind."

When Max finished pumping, he handed a couple of twenty dollar bills to the trucker and asked if the trucker might forget their conversation. The trucker replied with a sly grin as he climbed into his truck, "What conversation would that be?" Then he drove off.

After a short drive to El Dorado Springs, Max spotted the infamous Mother's Truck Stop. Max left Genie in the car and walked inside, where he realized he was a little out of place. Everyone else was wearing cowboy boots, hats, and western shirts. He made his way through the clanging, buzzing, and dinging cacophony of the arcade games to what looked like an office in the back, noting that the massive establishment catered to every need of the cowboy truckers: lots of greasy fried food, coffee, showers, and sleeping rooms.

When Max stepped around a rack of pornographic calendars he found himself standing in the doorway of the office and looking at what he thought must be Mother herself, all three hundred plus pounds of her. Mother was sitting behind an old wooden desk in a ten-by-twelve-foot room enclosed by glass. A couple of chairs were situated just inside the door, and the rest of the room was chock-full of papers, old magazines, empty coffee cups, and other litter. She alternated between chomping on the biggest cheeseburger Max had ever seen and long drags on a Pall Mall king-size straight. She was wearing a loosely knit sweater that was open about halfway down the front. The two buttons that were intended to allow easier donning were stretched to the limit by her massive breasts, which were straining toward her armpits. She wore no bra, of course, revealing to Max for the first time in his life the true meaning of the word *jugs*. Her Pomeranian dog was sitting on the desk and nibbled on Mother's fries whenever she took a drag on the cigarette. The whole room reeked of stale smoke and dog shit, the antithesis of a Norman Rockwell scene.

She looked up briefly and said, "Come on in, honey. What can I do for you? Boy, you're kind of skinny. You want something to eat?"

"No, thank you, ma'am. I was looking for someone to haul a load of freight for me. I was wondering if you could find a driver and a flatbed rig to take a load to Harrison, Arkansas tonight."

"Tonight? What the hell ya haulin' that you need it loaded tonight?"

"Six wellhead shut-off valves, two-hundred feet of nine-inch casing pipe, and part of a platform. I think we can get it all on one forty-foot flatbed."

"Well, let me see, if you are in that damn big of a hurry." She picked up a well worn spiral notebook, took a drag on her cigarette, and flipped through the pages, almost knocking over her drink.

She picked up the phone, punched intercom, and said, "Gilbert to the office." In about a minute a young man appeared at her door.

"What do ya want, Mother?"

"Gilbert, go up to the second floor dorm and see if Ray Carson is up there. I got a load for him."

"Mother, his truck is in the shop. He broke an axle trying to haul that 763 track loader yesterday. I tried to tell him it was too damned heavy but he . . ."

Mother interrupted, "I don't give a shit about that! Who else is out there with a forty-foot flatbed?"

"Joe Russo is back there playing pool. He's got a flatbed."

"Well, don't just stand there. Go get his scrawny little ass."

After Mother had smoked two more cigarettes and got her paperwork finished, they had a deal. Joe would haul the equipment and pipe to Harrison. He would not be responsible for loading or unloading and would get $4.67 per loaded mile. They were to load and travel tonight. Max gave Mother a little bonus of five hundred dollars cash to make the deal go a little smoother. She agreed to keep the whole deal quiet, which seemed to be no problem for her. Max noted, as advertised, money talks in this neck of the woods. Max told her that they had a lead on a new oil field and wanted to keep it quiet. She didn't seem to care much as long as she got the extra money.

When Max got back into the car, Genie inquired if everything went well. He replied, "It went great!"

Joe followed them to the bunker in his Kenworth sleeper pulling a forty-foot flatbed trailer. When they neared the site, Genie quietly asked, "How are you going to explain the robots gliding around lifting all of the heavy equipment on to the truck?"

Max realized that it might be a little awkward to explain that to Joe, so he asked, "Is there any way we can divert his attention or put him to sleep or something like that?"

Genie replied, "Of course. I have excellent hypnosis capabilities. Just have him look at me for about thirty seconds, and then tell him what you want him to do. He won't remember a thing."

They pulled up in front of the bunker at about 9:40. Max got Genie out of the box and took her back to Joe's truck. Max climbed into the cab on the passenger side and told Joe he had something to show him before they loaded. Joe shrugged. "Sure."

Max held the crystals up in front of him and they began to glow and sparkle. Joe didn't say a word, but a blank stare came over his face after twenty or thirty seconds. Genie silently communicated to Max that Joe was ready.

Max quietly said, "Joe, you will climb into your sleeper and take a nap while we load the trailer. When I wake you, we will drive to Harrison, Arkansas. When we reach my house, you will take no note of where you are or what roads we took to get there. You will take another nap in your truck while we unload. I will pay you, and then you will drive back to El Dorado with no recall of anything that has happened tonight. Do you understand?"

Joe answered, "Yes," and promptly climbed into the sleeper and went to sleep.

By then Genie had the robots loading the trailer. Max had the parts list and checked each item off as it went on the truck. It took about an hour to get everything loaded and secured with tarps and tie-down straps. When all was secured to Genie's satisfaction, Max woke Joe and they headed to Harrison. The 150-mile trip to Max's house was uneventful and they made it in about three hours, putting them in Jasper just after 2:00 in the morning, which meant they would arrive unnoticed.

Max had Joe back up to the storage barn, where the robots unloaded the equipment. Max retrieved cash from the house and paid Joe for the bill of lading and a couple of hundred extra for his trouble. Joe seemed eager to get back to El Dorado Springs, so he left as soon as Max paid him.

Max commented that Genie's hypnosis was a great tool and that it had worked well on Joe. Genie said, "Thank you, Max. It is always a pleasure to impress you."

Susan's time off with her family had gone well. She spoke to her dad about the casting, and he said it could be done but he wondered who would pay for such a large hunk of metal. Susan assured him that Astrolabe could afford it. All she needed to know now was if the Diebold Safe Company could cast a thirty to forty ton billet of special alloy. Her dad assured her they could.

The biggest news at her house was her romantic interest in Max. Her dad, especially, wanted to meet the guy who could keep up with his genius super-jock daughter. No man yet had been able to come even close. All had fallen by the wayside just like Petie Snodgrass when she was twelve. Max was about all her sister Rachael wanted to talk about too. She had to have every detail: where did he go to school, was he really so smart he could have earned a PhD at nineteen, and on and on. Susan surprised herself a little when she found herself bragging about Max to her sister. She didn't realize she had become so close to him in just a few days. She wasn't accustomed to that at all. Normally, men were so intimidated by her that, after a date or two, they realized how inadequate they were and simply faded away.

Finally, when her mother started in on her, she decided to call Max and see if he could come to Canton for a few days before they went back to work at Harrison. She knew Max had taken the bunker equipment to his place the day after Christmas, and she decided to extend her invitation. She also thought it might be a good idea for Max to talk to the plant manager about the casting. So, with great fanfare, she called Max by conventional phone around 9:00 on the morning of the 27th.

"Hi, Max. I hope I didn't wake you. I know you got in rather late last night."

"Oh, that's okay. I was already up and making coffee. Why are you calling me on a regular phone? Is everything all right?"

"Well, my family really wants to meet you, and we were all wondering if you might fly into Canton for a day or two."

Max detected a little stress in her voice. "Well, let me see. Genie, could you show an airline schedule?"

She said, "Of course," and displayed three flights to Canton from Springfield, Missouri, and one from Little Rock.

"I suppose, if you think it is important, I could catch the flight out of Little Rock and be there this evening, about 7:30. I wasn't planning to go back to work until about the third or fourth of January anyway, so that should work."

"Max, that would be great! I really appreciate this." As soon as she hung up, Susan told her mother she was going to take a shower and do some shopping.

Actually, she wanted to explain to Max via private conversation what had just happened. When the bathroom door was closed, she called Max via the communicator. "Max? Gee, I am so sorry to put you on the spot like that. Can you really come?"

Max, having endured the same third degree at his house about Susan, understood completely. So he teased her. "Yeah, I really wanted to meet your sister. I hear she is pretty hot. Everyone says she is better looking than you, and I was just trying to find an easy way to tell you."

"You devil! That isn't funny. Can't you be serious for one minute?"

"Yes, of course. I understand because my family is the same way. They can't wait to meet you either. Maybe we could go out to Colorado Springs for a few days later. Deal?"

"Okay, it's a deal."

"Max, my family really is excited to meet you, and I do hope a visit here, and now, when there is so much to do, isn't too bad for you. I kinda want to see you too. Seems like I have been missing you more than I expected. Do you miss me"?

"Of course, I do. It would be nice to talk to someone who knows what's going on with all this stuff. Ya know?"

"I know what you mean," Susan replied. "I'm always nervous I'll say the wrong thing and get us in trouble somehow. My family has no idea about all of this, but they know something has changed about me. They think it's you, and I'm letting them think that. Okay?"

"Sure, I understand. I had to tell my dad some of our plans to get his take on the military perspective. So, I know he's worried about my safety now. Things sure do get complicated in a hurry, don't they? It really will be good to see you."

"I guess I better go. I'm supposed to be taking a shower. Bye, Max. See you tonight."

"See you tonight, Susan."

CHAPTER 14

Max's flight from Little Rock arrived in Canton on time, at 7:30. He had been to the barber shop for a haircut and beard trim before he left. In honor of the occasion, he had actually bought a couple of new shirts and some plain cotton slacks in blue, black, and khaki. This was about as fashionable as Max was going to get.

Susan and Rachael were waiting for Max when he came out of the walkway from the plane. Susan gave him the I-haven't-seen-you-for-a-week hug and introduced Max to her sister.

"Max, I'd like you to meet my older sister, Rachael. Rachael, this's Max."

"Rachael, I'm so happy to meet you. Susan tells me you live in New York."

"Yes, in Manhattan, actually. My husband works in the theater district and I'm a literary agent.

"Oh, really, what kind of writers do you represent?"

"Mostly nonfiction authors who produce how-to and self-improvement titles, but also some authors of historical works."

"And what does your husband do in the theater?"

"Oh, he's a writer and sometimes producer of Broadway plays. He mostly does rewrites and polishes up new work for the stage."

"I guess that keeps you pretty busy."

"Not as busy as you and Susan seem to be. What's this classified stuff? What's that all about?"

"Well, just what it says. *It is classified*, but it *is* fun. Right,

Susan?" Susan rolled her eyes when her sister couldn't see her and gave Max a little affectionate jab in the ribs when they were getting in the car. As they were driving home, Max and Susan carried on a conversation with their communicators.

"How did it go in Colorado, Max?"

"Good. I got the scoop on military strategy and what kind of weapons we need from my dad. We picked up all the equipment to complete the aircraft from the bunker. I brought a piece of the finished cast metal to show the engineers at the plant, and I also brought a piece of the mineral additive Nute had at the bunker. A small amount will need to be added to the alloy when they cast it."

"Sounds like you've been getting a lot done. I hope you aren't too mad at me for having you make this trip. It is mostly social you know," she apologized.

"Not at all, Susan. We can get a lot done. I have a schematic for the airframe so your dad and I can get started on that."

About that time Rachael, who was driving, turned into the driveway and said, "For friends, you guys don't say much. Do you?"

That made them realize they hadn't said a word out loud since they got into the car.

"I guess we better stop the private conversations, Susan."

"Right."

Max retrieved his travel bag and they entered the house. Susan introduced Max to her parents. "Dr. Max Gibson, I'd like you to meet my parents, Dr. Albert McKinney and my mother Nancy. This is Rachael's husband, Tom."

When the introductory small talk was complete, Nancy took over as hostess and grabbed Max's coat. "You must be starved and worn out, Dr. Gibson."

Max interrupted, "Please call me Max, and yes, I could eat."

"Mother, I warn you that Max is a real chef and knows what he's doing in the kitchen."

"Nonsense, Susan," Max said, blushing a bit. "I'm sure I will love whatever you have, Nancy."

"Well, it's just an ordinary old pot roast with glazed carrots, wild rice casserole and some homemade bread."

"Sure sounds great to me!" Max smiled broadly.

The next two hours were spent in fascinating table conversation. Max told them what he did at Astrolabe, and Albert explained his high tech metallurgy lab experiments. Rachael and her husband were so awestruck by the scientific conversation that they didn't even try to participate. Susan didn't have much to say either. She just reveled in the show Max was putting on for her parents, watching him with quiet pride as if he were her best student at a piano recital.

Max picked up on the fact that he and Susan's father were the only ones talking and finally asked Tom, "How is show business anyway?"

"Well, after all the exciting stuff you guys are doing, my world seems a little mundane."

"Not so," exclaimed Max. "When I told my little sister I was going to meet you, she squealed and told me to get your autograph for her. She's sixteen and thinks Broadway is the coolest. If she had any talent, I am sure she would want to be in the business."

"Actually, I get to meet a lot of interesting people, but my job is rather dull. I just clean up dialogue and dangling plot details. I'm kind of a literary janitor."

Rachael piped in, "That is not true. If it weren't for you, they would never get a show produced and on the stage."

The conversation continued until well after eleven o'clock when Max realized it was getting late. He wanted to firm up his plans with Albert before heading to bed.

"Albert, Do you think we could go down to the plant tomorrow? I would like to talk to your engineer about my other project."

"Sure, Max. What time do you want to go?"

"I'd like to take a run in the morning. It is daylight about seven o'clock and it takes me about forty-five minutes to do my usual five miles," he calculated aloud. "So let's say we leave around nine, Okay?"

"Nine o'clock it is. See you then!"

Nancy took Max upstairs to the guest bedroom and got him settled. She got out the extra towels and showed him the shower. Tom and Rachael's room was between Max and Susan's. When the doors were all closed, Susan called Max via the communicator.

"Max, are you awake?"

"Yes, of course I am."

"I wanted you to know how proud I am of you. I have never seen anyone handle my dad like that. I can tell he is impressed and has genuine respect for you and your intellect. I have never seen him act like that. He is usually the smartest person in the room, and he knows it. It is obvious he knows you are the smartest person around, except for his baby daughter of course. That would be me, Bub, and don't you forget it."

"How could I forget it? You keep reminding me."

"I'm kidding, Max. I think you're pretty smart too. It's so good to see you. I really missed you — a lot! Good night, my sweet."

Max was a little surprised by the term of endearment that slipped in her conversation, but managed to respond with, "Good night, my dear."

CHAPTER 15

Max was up to begin his run at his usual 5:30, which was 6:30 in Canton. The McKinney home was located in northwest Canton in an exclusive subdivision called Hills and Dale. It was a brisk twenty degrees that morning as Max started his run down Glenmont Drive and headed west. Most of the homes on his route were on estates of two or three acres and had been built in the glory days when Canton was an industrial and manufacturing powerhouse. Hills and Dale had been the exclusive neighborhood for executives and owners of the various factories located in Canton.

The area around Canton was rich in a type of clay suitable for making kilns and casting molds for metal as well as fine porcelain. Coal was plentiful in nearby West Virginia, and Cleveland supplied iron ore by the millions of tons, which made the area a pivotal part of the "Rust Belt" economy during the twentieth century. This created immense wealth for the industrial elite. However, many of the plants are closed now for various reasons. Only a few of the strongest remained, like Hoover Vacuum Sweepers and Diebold Safe and Lock.

While Max was running, Susan and her mom had some time alone in the kitchen as they prepared breakfast. Susan made sure they were alone and started a serious mother-daughter talk. "Mom, what is it like to be in love? I mean, the real thing. . . . Oh, you know what I mean."

"Of course I do, dear. It's the most wonderful thing ever. It just takes over everything and there isn't much you can do about it."

"I know, I think about it all the time. Max is just so . . .so different than anyone I've ever met. We're working on this important project together, and I'm sure that has something to do with my feelings for him, but I just can't get him off my mind. Since I left Harrison, I have felt a little unsettled . . . you know, emotionally. Thinking about Max makes me feel better somehow. I don't understand it completely. They didn't teach us anything about this in medical school Mom. What do I do?"

"That's easy, honey. Tell him how you feel and let nature take its course. If he loves you too, that's simply the best feeling in the world. If he doesn't . . ."

"Don't even say it, Mom! I just couldn't stand it if he doesn't feel the same way. I can't believe how fast this happened. I've only really known Max for a couple of weeks, but just listen to me — I sound like I am fourteen again. I feel like those girls we used to call boy crazy and say they had juicy panties."

"Juicy panties, huh? Well, I'm not sure that part is something your mother needs to talk to you about, but I think the relationship will be all right, sweetheart. You could look a lifetime and not find anyone better than Max."

"I don't think it would matter, Mom. I'm pretty sure I have stopped looking. I just hope Max is feeling the same way about me right now"

Daylight was approaching as Susan and her mother continued to prepare a breakfast fit for a king.

Max jogged by Brookside Country Club, and as he plodded along, he remembered Susan's story about going to a dance there with Petie Snodgrass when she was twelve. The stately clubhouse reeked of old money and looked like it should be in England or Scotland. His path wound around the battery of tennis courts where Susan had started her remarkable tennis career. He could just imagine her zinging her serve past lesser opponents and trying to be humble as she approached the net to accept the loser's congratulations.

He also thought about the centuries of technology that would be lost all over the world if he and Susan were not successful; the millions of man-hours invested in civilization in places like Canton, wasted in some unknown conflagration that lay in wait sometime in the near future. The factories, smelters, kilns, even the country clubs, libraries, and art museums, all snuffed out by human doing.

By the time he was approaching Susan's parents' block, he was more determined than ever to be successful with his new "enforcer." He had definitely decided to make the new enforcement weapon a part of the United Nations, a kind of super policeman that no one nation would control. The weapon would enforce the laws against aggression and injustice wherever it found them, without regard to national borders or the strategic weapons that advanced countries might have. Although his concept was sound, even Max knew the chances of success were small.

Susan's folks' house came into view as he rounded the corner on Glenwood again, and Max picked up the pace to his customary sprint at the end of his five-mile run. When he came up the driveway, he could see Susan and her mother looking out the kitchen window and getting breakfast on the table.

When he entered the door, he was out of breath, as usual, but he was able to say, "What's to eat?"

Susan replied, "My mother's Belgian super-duper waffles. Think you could eat one?"

Max took a deep breath and said, "Give me time for a shower and I can eat three of those. They sound great."

Susan's Dad came down the hallway and said that he was going on to the plant and would meet them there. There had been some trouble with the night casting, and he had to go down early. Nancy gave him a cup of coffee and a kiss on the cheek as he headed out the door. "Have a good day, dear."

In a few minutes, Max came down for breakfast all cleaned up and ready for the day. He took note of Susan as she bent over the table setting down his plate of waffles. He had never seen her in tight blue jeans before, and the sight was impressive. He thought, "*Man, she looks even better from this angle.*"

Susan playfully said via her communicator, "What are you looking at?"

"Oh, I was admiring your mother's china," he replied via his communicator.

"This is really nice china, Mrs. McKinney," Max said aloud.

"Oh, it's just ordinary stuff, made here in Canton. The plant is closed now, but it was a big operation at one time. My friend Ruth's husband was the CEO there. It was real hard on their family when they had to close the plant. Foreign competition and labor costs got them. By the way, Max, call me Nancy."

Susan said via communicator, "You are an insufferable liar. You were checking me out, weren't you?"

"Okay, maybe a little. Your backside does look pretty good in those jeans, you know."

"Nancy, the waffles are great," Max said aloud, looking up from his plate. "The raspberry sauce and whipped cream are an especially nice touch. I believe you could fatten me up if I ate here all the time."

Susan said via communicator, "You better quit flirting with my mother."

"Max, I'll get the car out and warm it up while you finish," Susan added out loud. "I don't guess Rachael and Tom are going to get down in time to eat with you. They're late risers from New York, you know."

Soon Max and Susan were on their way to the Diebold plant in north Canton, and alone for the first time since Harrison. It felt good for both of them to just be together.

Susan, with a melancholy tone in her voice, started a serious conversation. "Max, I want you to know that I really appreciate you coming up here to meet my parents. I'm a little jealous because they all adore you. I feel so lucky, though. Not only has Nute brought us together, but I feel he made a perfect match."

As soon as Susan spoke, Max noticed she was getting nervous and beginning to tremble a bit, small beads of perspiration collecting on her upper lip. "Susan, are you all right?" he asked.

"Yes. Of course I am. I just want to tell you how I feel right now, that's all. Do you think it's getting hot in here?" Susan leaned over and turned the heater off.

She began again: "What I'm trying to say is . . . Wow, I haven't ever felt like this before."

"I know, Susan. It happened to me when I was fourteen. I had a music teacher who worked with me on the piano. She smelled so good that I finally had to quit the lessons because she made me so nervous I couldn't play anything around her. Don't worry, though. Feeling like this now is a good thing. That is, if we are a perfect match. And by the way, I believe Nute has made a perfect match too. Remember how you made me nervous at the breakfast table? That wasn't just idle voyeurism. I feel just like you do right now."

At the next red light, Susan took Max's jacket collar and pulled him towards her. She gave him a kiss like he had never received before, long and wet with her mouth open. She kept on until a guy in the car behind them honked, pulled around, and yelled, "Get a room for crying out loud! It's 8:45 in the morning."

After that kiss, Max and Susan both knew that they were not only partners in an epic task to save civilization but falling hopelessly in love as well. As she drove away from the light, neither of them had anything else to say, but they both had a satisfied and self assured look that spoke volumes.

Susan turned on to the 6000 block of Mayfair Road in north Canton and proceeded to the security check point. As she pulled up to the guard shack, a familiar face greeted her. "Boy, are you a sight for sore eyes," the middle-aged man said. "Your dad said you'd be in today, so I came down to check you in personally. It sure is good to see you, Susan. Is that Dr. Gibson with you?"

"Yes, Mr. Snodgrass. We're here to visit the foundry."

"Yes, I know. Your dad left VIP visitor tags and these hard hats for you." Clifford Snodgrass was chief of security and the father of Petie, Susan's childhood friend. He had worked for Diebold for more than thirty years. Clifford handed Susan her name tag and hat and walked around the car to the passenger side to let Max have his. When Max rolled down the window, Clifford passed the name tag and hat in to him and quietly said in a near whisper, "You might like to wipe the lipstick off before you go in to see her father."

Max quietly said thanks and quickly wiped the lipstick off his face and mouth.

Susan, mumbled under her breath, "Oh, jeez." And just to change the subject and make conversation she asked, "What is Petie doing?"

"Well, he started out working in that shoe store, you know, and he got to be the manager. Then, to everyone's surprise, he up and bought the place. That was eight years ago. Now he owns thirteen shoe stores in Canton and over in Mansfield. The boy seems to have a head for business and is doing quite well. He married Jessie Cockran and they have two kids. And I sure enjoy my grandkids."

As he mentioned their names, Kyle and Megan, he showed Susan a recent photo of the entire family. Susan took the photo and showed it to Max. Petie wasn't anything like what he'd expected from Susan's description. He, his wife Jessie, and their kids made a handsome family. He didn't look much like the twelve-year-old pimple-faced weasel she had described.

"Susan, it was sure nice to visit with you; and Dr. Gibson, it was nice to meet you."

The security chief then took his leave and Susan and Max made their way into the foundry at the back of the complex. This was the oldest part of the company, which had been producing safes and vaults since 1915. Susan told Max to go on because she was going to visit with some friends. She needed to catch up and also brag about Max to her old girlfriends. He went on into Albert's office that overlooked the foundry. Albert introduced him to everyone as Susan's friend, Dr. Max Gibson. When all of the pleasantries were over, Albert called in Joe Giblonski, the chief engineer of the foundry.

"Joe, is Giblonski a Polish name?", Max inquired.

Joe replied, "It sure is, and proud of it."

Max began to speak to Joe in perfect Polish. Albert was astonished and listened as Max continued. "Joe, are both your parents Polish?"

"Yes," Joe said with a broad grin. "My grandfather and grandmother still live in Poland. We spoke Polish at home until I went to grade school. Our Catholic Mass is celebrated in Polish here in Canton because so many of us Polacks attend St. Joseph's. Are you Polish, Dr. Gibson?"

"Please call me Max, and no. I just have a knack for languages. They seem to come easily to me for some reason."

After this exchange, Joe and Max had a great rapport, and the conversation became like one between two old Polish friends ready to talk business.

"So, Joe. Do you have top secret clearance?"

"Yes, both Dr. McKinney and I have top secret clearance because of the armor plate we make for the Army."

"Well, I've been working on a project for some time that will require a large casting out of a new alloy. Here's a rough drawing of the casting. If you have a CAD machine, we could clean this up so it will probably make more sense to you."

They were speaking in English now, and so Albert piped up, "Sure we can! I will get that transferred in a jiffy."

He punched the intercom and a draftsman entered the room. "Did you buzz, Dr. McKinney?"

"Yeah, Steve. Could you transfer Dr. Gibson's schematic to our computer aided drafting machine?"

"Sure. I'll have it back to you in a few minutes."

"Great, Steve. We'll be here when you get it done."

Max had purposely drawn the schematics in paper and ink freehand so it would look like a new invention.

Max then pulled a rectangular piece of metal that looked like stainless steel out of his briefcase. The metal measured about four by six inches and was one thirty-second of an inch thick. Holding the metal up in front of Albert and Joe, he said, "This is the alloy I want to make the casting out of. It's similar in hardness and strength to 401 stainless. However, with the small amount of the mineral added and after being tempered with a certain frequency of direct current, it becomes the hardest metal I know of. Even a diamond drill will not penetrate it."

Albert and Joe stood speechless as Max held their undivided attention. "Joe, do you have an electroplating device here at the foundry?"

"Sure. We chrome plate stuff all the time. It's down on the main floor in the back."

Albert, Joe and Max walked down to the plating room. Max hooked up the transformer leads to the piece of metal.

Max explained, "This won't give us the maximum effect because the exact frequency is much higher than what you have, but I think you will get the idea. Let's give it about 40 volts and about 200 amps of direct current rectified to 120 cycles for a few minutes. That should be enough to show you how the crystalline lattice starts to form under the right conditions."

Before he started the transformer, Max took a piece of metal from the bench and made a deep scratch in his test piece to show how soft it was. He flipped the switch and the characteristic low-pitched hum of the plating machine began. Max hooked up the test piece and turned up the amperage.

After ten minutes, the metal was red hot, but it began to cool as soon as the current was turned off. Max picked it up with a pair of pliers and dipped it in the water bath nearby. The metal cooled with a plume of steam and bubbling sound as it was totally quenched. When he removed the metal from the water, it looked like chrome and rang like a bell when struck from the side. He tried to scratch it with the same metal piece, and the metal simply slid across the surface without leaving behind a scratch or blemish. This simple demonstration made a believer out of one of America's top metallurgists and a foundry engineer of thirty-five years. Albert and Joe simply could not believe the hardness and strength of the flimsy metal they had handled a few minutes ago.

About that time, Susan came in. "Have you boys been playing with Max's wonder metal? What do you think?"

Albert responded with the excitement of a high school kid. "What do I think? Wow! This is the coolest stuff I have ever seen. We could make millions with this metal. This is what every metallurgist has always wanted. Right, Joe?"

Joe explained in Polish, "This is wonderful, fantastic, and it was so quick!"

Susan was now fluent in Polish via her communicator as well, so she followed up with, "Did you think I would bring you a dummy to play with?"

Albert, surprised by her sudden use of another language, asked his daughter, "What did you say?"

"I asked Joe if he thought I would bring home a dummy to meet my dad."

"Joe exclaimed, "I should say not. What a demonstration. Susan, you should have seen it. It was wonderful."

The group slowly walked back to Albert's office where Steve had the CAD drawings ready. Steve had embellished the drawings into 3D and added all the dimensions taken from Max's preliminary schematic. For the next two hours, the four of them pored over the CAD drawings and made estimates based on their years of experience with large castings. The plan was to make the castings out of the enhanced alloy of iron, nickel, beryllium, chrome, and Max's classified mineral, which was of course, Nute's mineral. All the machine work would be done on the casting while the material was still relatively soft and flexible. Their timetable allowed for two months to complete a clay mock-up of the ship, another month to build a ceramic mold, a complete night shift to cast the ship, and three months to drill and tap all of the fittings for the accessories, the power plant, and the antigravity device. In about six months, they could have the shell, or airframe, ready for the ship.

Max thought to himself, *first things first. They would need a set of working drawings and security clearance for the craftsmen, and that process would give him time to get Clark and Astrolabe on board with the money so they could start production.*

Max and Albert had their heads together all that day. They even had lunch brought in. That night, Max and Susan rode home together in quiet confidence about the project and the great progress they had accomplished.

Finally, Susan said, "I don't know when I've seen my father get so excited about a project. He seems so young and energetic. For the past few years he has been suffering from burnout, especially since a lot of his friends have lost their jobs and the manufacturing segment in this area has declined so badly. Today, he has that sparkle of creativity that I haven't seen for a long time. I owe all this to you and Nute. I just hope all our efforts aren't wasted."

"Yeah, I know what ya mean. Your dad sees this as a scientific breakthrough and sees himself on the cutting edge — pretty heady stuff. I even feel that way sometimes. Then, when I think about what we are really doing and how bad the odds are against us, I'm back to reality in a heartbeat."

Susan convinced Max on the way to her parents' home to spend one more day sightseeing around Canton. The next day they visited the Pro Football Hall of Fame, President McKinley's memorial, and the usual highlights. They had lunch at Susan's favorite little cafe on the edge of the downtown district. Everyone in the family knew they were really spending some one-on-one time with each other before they had to go back to Harrison. Susan's family was so taken with Max they would have had him marry her that week if possible.

After lunch, they were headed for home when Susan took an unexpected turn into a residential area. After driving a few blocks in a very nice neighborhood, Max finally asked, "Where are we going?"

"Oh, I have a little surprise. We're going by my best friend's house. Her name is Kathy Sloan, and I spoke to her yesterday at Diebold. They turned in the driveway of a mammoth three-story house with a side portico and a two-acre yard with mature oak trees much higher than the house.

Obviously, the Sloan's were old money, thought Max. He had visions of an awkward social situation and being paraded about like a show pony in front of Susan's old friends, and for the first time since he had known her, he felt uncomfortable in their budding relationship. When they got out of the car and approached the door, Susan pulled out a set of keys and proceeded to open the door without ringing the doorbell.

"Don't you think we ought to let them know we're coming into their house, Susan?"

"It's all right, Max. They're in Florida for the winter."

Kathy was Susan's absolute best friend and confidant, and she was delighted to be a party to a clandestine romantic interlude. As teenagers, they had used her bedroom to listen to music, talk for hours on the phone, and conjure up their romantic fantasies. This inner sanctum was used to compare notes on the relative merits of their classmates and especially to develop strategies for the conquest of all the cute boys. They tried unsuccessfully to fix Susan up with any number of boyfriends, their plans always failing miserably when it actually came to the date and Susan intimidated the boys to the point of embarrassment with her brains and jock status. Kathy was more than happy to see Susan have the real thing happen in her bedroom after all those years of talking and dreaming about it. She was nearly as excited as Susan and made her promise to give her every last detail of their encounter in exchange for the private use of a secure rendezvous at her parents' house.

As Susan closed the door behind them, she said, "There's no one here except us."

The remark had scarcely come out of her mouth when she pinned Max against the inside of the door and kissed him in her own special way. Her heart pounded as they both hurriedly took off their winter coats and let them fall to the floor in the entryway. Susan could hardly speak from the excitement of the moment but managed to explain that she had made the arrangements with Kathy at the Diebold office yesterday when Max and her dad were working in the foundry.

As Max flung his scarf on the floor, he slid his hands over Susan's bottom and gently lifted her cheeks, pulling her so close to him that he could feel her heart pound and her abdominal muscles quiver. Her back arched as she gushed with receptive sexual energy that had been building since Max came to Canton.

Max had some experience with boyhood infatuations, but nothing like this. Susan had never had anything hit her so hard and was a rank amateur. She was well versed in the mechanics from medical school, of course, but nothing had prepared her for the rush of sexual ecstasy that came over her when Max touched her and pulled her close to him.

They left a trail of clothing down the hall to their private sanctuary. When they arrived at the edge of the bed, Susan was only in her panties and fancy lace bra and Max only in his boxers. He gently pushed her back on the bed, and she firmly brought him over her and smothered him with a kiss. Her well exercised leg muscles fell limp as dish rags as she prepared to accept him.

The afternoon was spent in Kathy's bedroom, exploring their sensuality, which in turn built a profound commitment between them that neither had expected. Max completely spent his manhood fulfilling every teenage fantasy that Susan and Kathy had ever had in that room. As with all lovers, they felt as though they were the only ones to ever have felt the emotional satisfaction and contentment of true love. After the vigorous and repeated consummation of their love that afternoon, it was clear they were mates for life.

After reaching exhaustion, they lay entwined, Max's arm around Susan with her head on his chest. Susan whispered, "Max, I think I'm really in love with you. You'll *never* get rid of me now."

"I love you, Susan. I can't believe it, but I do. There isn't anything I can say except I love you. There is no explaining it. It just is — that's all. As improbable as it is that any of this is happening to us, being in love with you is the most important part of it to me right now. Being with you like this has pushed so many buttons in me that I don't understand. I just have to give in and go along for the ride."

"I know what you mean. I never understood all the comparisons to music, poetry, and art when someone tries to explain what it's like to be in love. Not until now, anyway. No wonder the creative people get so productive after feeling like this. All I can say is that it feels great!"

Susan rolled over on top of Max and began to kiss him gently, and they once again drifted into a blissful union that seemed perfect in every way.

The winter sun was beginning to set when Susan advised Max that they needed to go. She changed the sheets, tidied up the room, and they headed for her parents' house. They anticipated that her family might notice they had spent the afternoon enraptured and tease her about the *glow* she seemed to have. When Max mentioned this to her, she confidently said, "I don't care — I love it! I wouldn't trade the feeling I have right now for anything. Let them say whatever they want!"

Max was exhausted, but Susan remained invigorated and seemed to emit a radiance that Max could see. When they arrived at the house, everyone else did in fact notice her glow too, especially her mother. Contrary to what Susan expected, however, no one said a word. Her mother just smiled and gave her hand a squeeze as she passed by, intuitively knowing what had taken place that afternoon. Her daughter was in love.

CHAPTER 16

Max and Susan accomplished a lot while they were in Canton. The preliminary work on the airframe was well underway, and they had consummated their romantic feelings for each other. They both declared it a great trip and agreed they were in absolute and total love, but they both also knew they had to get back to reality in Harrison. Steve Clark didn't know about Max's airship yet, and Albert was spending Diebold money at a fever pitch. So, while Susan finished packing, Max called Frank to see if the workplace was still standing.

"Hi, Frank. How is everything going at Astrolabe? I want you to clear the decks of all projects and get ready for a new venture. I'm going to talk to Clark about it when I get back this afternoon. Yeah, I had a great time in Colorado. I even got to ski a little. I'll see you this afternoon."

Then he dialed again. "Hi, Glenda. This is Dr. Gibson. Could you schedule an appointment for me with Mr. Clark this afternoon about four o'clock? Tell him I have an idea for a new project that I'm sure he'll like. I've been working on it over the holidays. . . . Okay, great. Bye.

Susan finally got all her stuff packed and deposited by the front door as the family gathered to say goodbye. Albert brought the car around and loaded the luggage while Tom, Rachael, and Nancy all said their farewells. Nancy gave Max a long hug and said, "I think you're just about the nicest young man I ever met. I hope to see you again soon."

Rachael was equally gushy and told him she was happy for her sister's good luck in finding him. Tom, on the other hand, was much more formal. He shook Max's hand and told him how nice it was to meet him, even though Max had replaced him as the nicest young man Nancy had ever met. Everyone laughed.

Their flight to Little Rock was uneventful, and they arrived on time at eleven a.m. Because they both had driven separately to Little Rock, each had a vehicle in long-term parking. After paying the ransom to get their cars out, they headed back to Harrison, Max following Susan. About forty miles north of Little Rock, they stopped for lunch. Max called Genie via communicator and a cell tower.

"Genie, how's it going at the home place?"

"Excellent, Max. Roger has been here every day to water the plants and check on everything. He certainly is methodical. He came at the same time every day and went through his routine exactly the same way every time. Was everything in order in Canton?"

"Yes, everything went very well. The casting for the ship is well underway at Diebold, and Susan's family was great."

"I gather they approve of your friendship with Susan?"

"Yes. They seem to be happy about everything. Genie, I was wondering if you could prepare a summary of the device for presentation to Steve Clark this afternoon, just the basics. I wouldn't dwell too much on the antigravity part of the propulsion system, but you need to prepare a generic drawing of the ship and the weapons systems.

"I'm going to try to get some money from him this afternoon. I estimate we will need about fifteen million dollars to get the prototype flying and another five million dollars to get the pods for the harmonic disrupter fabricated. Do you have anyone in your files who could make the pods for us?"

"Yes, of course. Raytheon would be the company with the closest technology. They did some secret work on the "Star Wars" defence project under President Reagan but abandoned it after funding ran out. Actually, they are not too far from a breakthrough and could have a pod ready in about a year with a nudge here and there. With more help from us than nudging, they could have it ready in six months."

"That would be great. I'll mention that to Clark. Have you picked up on anything from Todd Gilroy?"

"He has been very busy. The information Susan gave him enabled him to complete the wheat experiment, and now he has convinced Clark to fund his project with Susan completely. Todd, I must say, has become quite the Astrolabe celebrity. The office computers are full of interoffice e-mails about his new project. That's right, *his project*. That transformation took place while you were away. He started calling it his project as soon as Susan left the building. Clark thinks it's all Todd's idea and Susan merely gave him some technical help."

"I will let Susan deal with him when we get back this afternoon. She'll be able to cool his jets enough to keep him under control. I'll see you this afternoon around one o'clock."

Did you get all that Susan?" Max asked.

"Yes. I was listening. I'll take care of Todd, don't worry."

The two wayward travelers continued their mini-convoy toward Harrison on Highway 65 until they reached Highway 412 at Bellfonte, where Max turned off to his cabin and Susan continued on to her apartment in Harrison. They agreed to keep their distance at work and keep their relationship quiet for the time being because the news would complicate Todd's project and might suggest collusion on their part. Although it was unclear what difference their collusion might make, it seemed more fun to keep their relationship a secret anyway.

That afternoon, Max met with Astrolabe Director Steve Clark. He laid out the plan Genie had prepared and discussed its potential and the need for security. Although Clark was not a scientist, his MBA from Harvard business school belied his brilliant entrepreneurial skills and he immediately grasped the enormous value of this breakthrough. He agreed that the first application of antigravity should be a military one, but he also said he could not help but think of the thousands and thousands of devices this technology would instantly make obsolete — and Astrolabe would have the patent.

Clark could envision aircraft, construction cranes, and automobiles supplied with an Astrolabe antigravity generator. They would have no competition at all and could charge whatever the market would tolerate. They would be rich beyond belief, even world dominant

"Max, tell me exactly what it is you need to make this project work?"

"Well, in a word, money."

"No, no, no. I mean, besides money. For something like this, money is not a problem."

"Okay," said Max. "I have a list here. We'll need additional security; top secret clearance for our workers; rail siding to bring in some heavy equipment; a more secluded place to work with a machine shop and full aircraft capabilities and workmen, including ten to twelve aircraft machinists and a complete machine shop; 5,000 amp, three-phase electrical service to the facility. We also need clearance to talk to Raytheon about building the weapons system.

"That should be all for now. I estimate about twenty million dollars to achieve the weapons system. I spoke to a friend of mine at Diebold Safe and Lock. They can cast anything we need."

Steve's interest had obviously continued to build as Max spoke. "Let me call a friend over at Raytheon, Chet Miller, the head of R&D, and see if they are interested in working with us on this. Let's see, I have his number right here.

Hi, Chet, this is Steve Clark over at Astrolabe. How is Mary? . . . And the kids? . . .Great. Say, I'm wondering if you would be interested in a co-op on a new military project? Well, it is brand new stuff, cutting edge. We're looking for someone to help with the weapons system fabrication. Interested? . . . Okay, our lead guy is Dr. Max Gibson. He can fill your guys in on what he needs. I think you will be impressed. . . . Yes, that's right. He will be calling you."

Hanging up the phone, Steve turned to Max, "I think they'll be very cooperative. He nearly swallowed his tongue at the prospect of some new work. They must be really slow over there. Here's his name and number; call him when you get ready. When do you think you could have a mock-up ready to fly?"

"We could probably have something in a couple of weeks," Max replied.

Steve's jaw dropped, "Really?

That would be great. I'll have the bankers in for a demo, which should sew up the production funding. Max, you don't know how excited I am to see you take an interest in a commercial project like this. This will put Astrolabe, and you, on the map. Our little company will be the King Kong of the high technology industry. I will get to work on that list of yours and start the ball rolling. Concentrate on the project and I'll take care of everything else."

Steve, true to his word, provided what good administrators do best. Before the day was out, he had scheduled an emergency meeting with the architect and the railroad for 8:00 the next morning. A call to Wells Fargo security division provided six new security people at Max's house that evening. By week's end they had built a new twelve-foot electrified fence around Max's house and set up a guard tower with patrols, security cameras, the works.

Work continued on Max's new fabrication facility twenty-four hours a day, seven days a week. The dozers built a road to the extreme back of the Astrolabe property, out of sight from the rest of the facility and much more secure. By Monday, just one week after Max's return, the footings had been poured and the outline of a building was taking shape. A week later, and it was done. The White River electric cooperative was the only snag, as they had to build a new substation just for Max's building, which took an additional week. Meanwhile, Max and Genie had built a small prototype of the ship from some models of alien spacecraft they found at Walmart, which had been developed for a movie called *Space Invaders*. Max loved the irony.

Steve Clark scheduled the demonstration in Max's old optic office just two weeks after his initial meeting with Max about the project. This would be the first time Frank had seen any of the stuff that Max had been working on at home with Genie. Max and Susan, on the other hand, had been communicating about each other's progress on their secure communicators every night at bedtime. Their interest and enthusiasm for each other had not diminished, and they ended each conversation with "I love you and miss you."

When Frank saw them drive up in a small truck with security vehicles in front and in back, he knew something big was up. Max got out of the small truck carrying the toy space ship in a box marked "SPACE INVADERS." When he reached the optics lab, Frank asked with some annoyance, "What's going on, Max?"

"We are going to have a small demonstration this afternoon for some banker types so we can get this new project financed."

"Since I hadn't heard from you, I was worried you weren't going ahead with the project."

"I've been pretty busy, that's all. I needed to work at home due to new security concerns."

"What do you mean, security concerns?"

"I think you'll understand once you see the demonstration." Just then Steve Clark, obviously upset, came in. "Max, I need to talk to you."

They retired to Max's old office and Max asked, "What's up? You look like a cat that just had its tail stepped on."

Indeed, Steve had lost his usual cool disposition and was clearly agitated about something.

"Well, you know the bankers we invited? They wanted to know what they were getting for twenty million dollars, so I told them we were going to demonstrate a new weapons system that would revolutionize military hardware. Well, being bankers, they called the Pentagon and asked the procurement officer for the Joint Chiefs of Staff if he knew anything about it. Naturally, he said, 'No.' This prompted General Bernard Potter to call me and chew my ass out because he hadn't been informed about the demonstration. To make a long story short, he'll arrive by military chopper from Washington, DC at 1400 to see the demonstration. Are you ready?"

"Yes, of course I'm ready. Why are you so nervous about this guy?"

"He's a notorious hard-ass who gives all government contractors a rough time. I was hoping we wouldn't have to deal with him, but something this big had to involve him eventually, I suppose. He has four stars and he knows how to use them. He reports to the Chairmen of the Joint Chiefs, and frequently, he reports directly to the President."

Max finished unpacking the space invader toy and placed it on the table in front of about ten chairs set out for the guests. The bankers started to arrive about 1:45 and a muted murmur filled the room as the money men waited. Even a few jokes were floated about when they recognized the toy on the table in front of them. The faint whop, whop, whop of the General's chopper grew louder until wind started to kick up dust against the lab. Shortly, Potter and his entourage came into the room. He asked in a booming and authoritative voice, "Who is in charge here?"

"That would be me, General. Steve Clark, administrator of this facility for Astrolabe. Won't you sit down? Dr. Max Gibson, our project director, will proceed with the demonstration."

Max stood up and gave a few details about his new invention, telling them this was nothing less than a device that can defy gravity, move about and lift weight, such as a tank or personnel carrier, without any visible or audible means of propulsion, without disturbing the air. As Max talked, the toy began to levitate. The group instinctively gasped and moved back. The toy continued to float around the room, hover, and then move rapidly from corner to corner. Max brought it back to the table and asked General Potter to inspect the toy. When the general picked it up, he found it to be quite heavy and not the plastic toy they all thought it was. Max asked General Potter to place it under the table near the middle. As he did so, the toy levitated the table and moved it to the other end of the room.

"Okay," blurted the General. "How does it work?"

"The physics gets pretty complicated, General. But, basically, it's a dispersed phase antigravity particle generator."

"Anyone else know about this?" the General asked. "You didn't publish any of this in some bullshit journal or anything like that, did you?"

"No. I discovered it and built it into this toy, and I did this quite recently."

"Clark, this is officially a government project as of right now."

Max stepped between the two men and said, "This is not a government project! I won't allow it."

"You have nothing to say about it, son. I'm in charge now." The General's tone was dismissive.

Max bristled. "First, I am not your son, and you are the one with nothing to say about this project. This entire project is right here in my head, and I am the only one in charge of that! You are definitely not in charge of me or my invention, General."

General Potter, showing his frustration, turned to Steve. "That right, Clark? There are no schematics or other plans from which someone could work?"

"I am afraid not, General. Max is the only person who knows anything about this project. He made the prototype at his home in his own workshop. I saw some plans once, but they all look the same to me. It could have been the plans for a hot tub for all I know."

"At the very least, I am placing a liaison officer here to help out."

Max remembered his father's warning that liaison officers are merely spies and as soon as the equipment is functional they will get rid of you—that the function of the liaison is to report back to HQ when they think they know enough to dump you.

Max replied vigorously, "There will be no new liaison officers in this lab." The General gathered up his coat and assorted junior officers and headed out the door to the waiting helicopter. The bankers left in the room were falling all over themselves to fund the project now that they knew the military was demanding to take over.

As Max and the others walked to the door, Steve said, "Max, you made a powerful enemy today."

"I *am* sorry, but I was not going to let him bully his way into running this project. It's too important for that."

"That's why he wants in so bad. Max, don't put anything about this project on our computers. I think you'd better get the plans you left in my office too. We don't want any loose ends. I'm assigning some of our private security as bodyguards for you. I don't trust Potter one little bit."

CHAPTER 17

Over the next few weeks, Max and Frank moved their operation into the hyper-secure new building that they simply called the "new office." While the airframe was being built in Canton, they readied the conventional aircraft equipment like radar and communications gear to install in the ship. When Frank wasn't looking, Max would slip in modifications that Genie made so that the equipment was at least a generation ahead of any currently available technology.

Genie suggested they include a small crystal processor to allow communications with all of the hardware that Nute had and which would be compatible for the foreseeable future. This also made the craft fully capable of operating by remote signals from Max, Susan, or Genie. Genie also programmed a doomsday scenario into the crystal that would take over if anything happened to them.

The Raytheon group was making good progress on the microwave phased disruptors from the plans that Max had sent them. In fact, they thought the small one might be ready about the same time the airframe was delivered in June.

Max and Susan continued their habit of talking to each other every night before they went to sleep—their way of keeping in touch and nurturing their relationship. Susan was traveling all over the planet now collecting genetic samples. First, she collected the obvious samples from sperm and egg banks in the U.S. and Europe. Then she moved on to research banks at universities and medical schools worldwide.

After three months of travel, she returned from her final human sample collection trip in China, which completed the sample collection of all genetic, racial and ethnic types of the human genome.

Susan then switched to the plant kingdom and continued her work in South America because it contained the largest diversity of plants and animals on the planet. She was helped by the many university projects being conducted there in hopes of cataloging as much of the genetic diversity of Earth as possible before extinctions due to pesticides and pollution became a problem. This strategy made it much easier to collect the samples since most of the work had already been done.

When Susan had enough samples for a shipment, she packed them in one of Nute's special suspended animation storage boxes and shipped them to Roger, who then took it to the rendezvous place at Wollum and hid it. Roger was getting a big kick out of all of this. Since the security guards had moved in at Max's cabin, Roger was the only secure way of handling the samples. Roger came and went with impunity at Max's cabin and the United Parcel Service depot. Max had arranged for him to receive the boxes at the terminal, and he felt very important in this role. He didn't understand it, but he knew that Max had trusted him with a very important job. Max bought him the little Toyota pickup and gave him a raise to be the guardian of the sum total of Earth's genetic diversity. If Roger only knew!

Roger selected a wooded area near the ford on the Buffalo River at Wollum to hide the boxes. He was able to get to the spot by taking the back roads, which allowed him to look back at the road as he came down the mountain to see if anyone was following him. He would then bury the boxes and cover the area with natural vegetation. No one was the wiser.

On Easter weekend, Max convinced Susan to come back from a sample gathering trip in Sao Palo, Brazil to visit his family for a few days. His mother, especially, had been after him to bring Susan for a visit. They arrived by plane on Thursday, and Susan was an immediate hit with everyone, especially Gloria and Kate. Gloria had to know everything about Susan and her family. Kate wanted to know about her clothes, makeup, and all the girl stuff she missed out on by not having an older sister.

On Saturday afternoon, Max, Susan, and Curt went to the grocery store and were in the car alone, away from Max's bodyguard for the first time. Max immediately seized the opportunity, "Dad, I am so glad we can finally talk . They have a guard with me all the time now, and I assume my phones are bugged too.

"You were right. We had a General over procurement show up at a project demonstration and he wanted to immediately make it his project."

"What's his name?"

"Potter."

"Barney Potter?"

"The very same. I told him that, under no circumstances, would I turn the project over to the military. He then insisted on a liaison officer to stay with me. I turned that down, too."

"Barney Potter is your worst enemy right now, Max. He is absolutely ruthless. He made his way to the top of the Pentagon with bribes and other corrupt practices. He'll do anything to get at that project. Be careful!"

Susan, who was taking all this in, interjected, "You don't think he'd hurt Max or anything like that do you?"

"I think he'd avoid that if he could, but he'll do whatever he thinks is necessary, believe me. I've known him for more than thirty years. He loves power. If your project would provide that for him, he'll stop at nothing to get it." Max's dad was adamant.

Max continued. "Well, we have pretty good security at the office now, and the project is a closely held secret within Astrolabe. I have bodyguards with me all the time, Dad, even at home. How could he get at the project? I'm the only one who knows anything about it."

"That's probably your only protection right now. How soon before you're operational?"

"Eight or nine months."

"That will be your critical time. When the project is finished and works without you is the time you trust no one except Susan — not even your security guards."

Max pulled into the grocery store lot, and the three of them dutifully tracked down everything on Gloria's shopping list. When they were in the car again and it was a little more private, Max began a serious talk with his dad about contingencies. Being a military man, he understood the need completely and grasped the significance of Max's comments.

"Dad, there may be a time when you will need to be able to protect yourself and the family from radiation and fallout. I think you know what to do. Things could get pretty dicey with this new system and you should be prepared."

"I understand, Max. What do you think the time frame will be for deployment?"

"I still think deployment will be in December. If there's going to be a problem, it'll be after that. I have my cabin in Harrison completely ready so you could communicate with me there via short wave. Here are the frequencies and times I'll monitor on this sheet."

"Is your communications gear protected against electromagnetic pulse?"

"Yes. I'm completely hardened at the cabin and have at least a one year supply of food and water for about ten people."

"I guess being around the military *has* taught you a few things, son." Susan was struck by the matter of fact way Max and his father talked about Armageddon. They discussed it like it was a bad storm or something. This was somehow shocking and reassuring at the same time. It was nice to know they could survive, even if the worst happened.

When they returned to the house, the bodyguard was fit to be tied. He immediately chided Max for leaving without him and made him promise not to do it again. The rest of the weekend was spent enjoying the bliss of family life. Gloria and Max provided a spectacular array of meals, and everyone, even the bodyguard, ate until they could eat no more. However, there was a drawback to the confines of family happiness: it was pure torture for Susan and Max to be around each other and not be able to be "together." Their sexual energy level was off the chart and it took all their composure to keep their hands off each other in front of the bodyguard and Max's family. They were delighted to see each other over the holiday, but they maintained a kind of lovers' abstinence heartache most of the time they were in Colorado Springs.

Max, Susan, and the bodyguard returned to Harrison. Max was ready to work on the ship the Monday after Easter, and Susan caught a flight back to Sao Paulo. Although the security people laughed off Roger as the village idiot, he did stir some curiosity from his own family. Most of his cousins were unemployed and more than a little jealous of Roger's steady income. When they asked him about all the freight he got at the UPS terminal in Harrison, he told them that it was high performance car parts. He and Dr. Gibson were building a hot rod car to run moonshine over into Newton County. This being a plausible explanation as far as Roger's family was concerned, it stopped all questions about his comings and goings. They even forgave him for his high income because they knew moonshine was a high risk business and he would eventually end up in jail and they would have the last laugh.

As the weeks and months passed, work steadily progressed. Soon Diebold would be ready to cast the airframe, and Max decided to go to Canton to give them the mystery mineral personally and to watch the casting process, which was set for Thursday, June 8, 2023. The casting would be done at night because heating the massive electrical furnace drew too much current from the electrical grid. Every light in Canton would dim if they fired it up during the day. It took several hours to melt all the component metals, so it was a slow process.

It was the afternoon of June 7 when Max arrived at the Canton airport with a small cardboard box containing the mineral. A taxi took him directly to the foundry. When he arrived, all his Polish buddies and Albert were there to greet him.

"Dr. Gibson, how are you, you old Polack?" asked Joe. When they saw him, the entire Polish crew came over to greet him in Polish. Then Joe Giblonski took Max around to meet the rest of the casting crew.

"This is Prusak, Drake — his mother is Polish — and my son Joey. We also have a couple of misfit Greeks here — Pappas and Agnew."

When Max turned to meet Pappas and Agnew, he said in fluent Greek, "Don't let this guy call you misfits. I love Greeks, too!"

They were all astounded and broke into broad grins and then a belly laugh, ending in a bear hug like he was a long lost friend.

Albert just stood back and thought to himself, "*Is there no end to this guy's talent? He even speaks Greek!*"

Max, now speaking English, said, "So, guys. Here's what we need to do." They all listened intently as the professor gave the old hands a seminar on metallurgy.

"First, start a pot of standard 316 stainless: 67.9 percent iron, 0.1 percent carbon, 17 percent chromium, 3 percent molybdenum, 12 percent nickel. Dr. McKinney and I estimate it will take 31.6 tons of metal to cast the mold and have 1 percent excess for the sprue. You will need to bring this up to 1,425 degrees Celsius.

We will then add the mineral I have in this box. There is exactly 67.56 grams of powder, and it all must go into the alloy. After the mineral is added, the pot needs to come up to 1,560 degrees Celsius. The mold temperature needs to be 1,160. Then we can cast."

Dr. McKinney took over. "Men, because of the mass of this casting, we are approaching the limit of our ladle and we had to ask special permission to start our furnace early. Ohio Power and Light has agreed to let us start at about 7:45 instead of the usual 10:00. This should give us enough time to cast at about 4:30 a.m. Joe, have you got the metal ready?"

"Yes, sir. We have the scrap iron in the yard, and the other ingots are ready to be loaded on the forklift in the back of the shop."

"Okay, guys. Are there any questions? All right, then. Let's get to it. This is a big one. Let's make it count."

It was obvious that the entire casting crew was very proud to be a part of the project. Their faces showed that "made-in-America" pride and the quiet confidence that comes from knowing that you are working on something really important. They lined up and, one by one, came by to shake Max's hand and tell him how much they appreciated the chance to work on something so historic. Max was becoming a charismatic figure to these men and stirred a sense of pride not seen since they built parts for NASA's mission to the moon. Max was visibly moved when Joe Giblonski came by last and spoke to him softly in Polish.

"Max, I am so proud to know you and work with you on this. You've brought something to this company that I haven't seen since I've been here, a kind of enthusiasm and pride that is a wonder to behold and even more amazing to feel. For that, I thank you and hope this monster casts perfectly."

He shook Max's hand firmly and then turned to his crew and said in a loud, booming voice, "All right, let's get moving! This ship isn't going to cast itself."

Albert then turned to Max and said, "It'll be several hours before anything happens. Let's go out to the house and get some supper. Nancy can hardly wait to see you."

When they were in the car—with bodyguard in tow—Albert said, "The guys who made the clay pattern for the casting all think this thing looks like a flying saucer they used to see back in the '50s, Max."

"Well, that's classified, but I suppose it does. Since I haven't ever seen a flying saucer, I couldn't say for sure." They all laughed, even the bodyguard too, as they continued on to Albert's house. Albert called Nancy on his cell phone and told her he and Max were on the way home and to set another place for Max's companion.

Nancy had prepared a scrumptious meal of baked ham and sweet potatoes with homemade rolls and sweet and sour green beans seasoned with bacon. They rounded off the meal with apple pie and ice cream.

Max was lavish in his praise about the meal and continued to solidify his position as her most favorite young man. Nancy inquired about how Susan was holding up under all the traveling, and Max confirmed she was getting tired of it and was eager to get home for awhile. Max even admitted to Nancy that he really missed Susan and was ready for her to be home too, which brought an all-knowing smile to Nancy's face as she cleared the dishes.

Albert, feeling the pressure of the moment regarding the casting said, "We'd better get back to the foundry and keep an eye on the gang down there. Honey, the meal was great. Max, we better get going."

Back at the foundry, everything was going well. The crew was working especially hard because they wanted to impress Max and return the favor of the trust he'd placed in them by performing like professionals to produce a perfect casting for him. They considered him one of their own. When Max and Albert arrived, they had added all the metal they could get in the furnace and were waiting for the ingots to melt down so they could add the rest of the components of the alloy. At 4:10, the casting alarm sounded, and the massive ladle on the sky-crane slowly traversed the foundry toward the mold that was waiting hot and ready. With great fanfare and sparks galore, the metal alloy was poured into the mold. When the last few dribbles exactly topped off the sprue, the crew cheered as everyone knew the casting would be perfect. Max gave everyone a thumbs up and congratulated them in three languages.

Relieved that this step was finally completed, Max caught the early-bird flight to Little Rock and headed for home and some sleep. His bodyguard, Russell, took care of all the arrangements, and Max collapsed in a deep sleep on the plane. When they arrived in Arkansas, Russell retrieved their car and drove them to Max's cabin, Max asleep in the backseat for the entire ride.

CHAPTER 18

The airframe casting was complete and all the fittings for the top machined and the turret-like covering for the pilot was assembled and ready. Max told Albert to have it shipped by rail and have the airframe covered by tarpaulin. So as not to cause attention, they scheduled the arrival at Astrolabe for 3:30 in the morning. During the intervening months, Raytheon had finished the disrupters and had test fired them on an impromptu firing range at the new office. Frank had been in charge of that and enjoyed the power of being able to destroy almost anything by just pointing the disrupter at it. Anything organic caught on fire and anything metal got hot and melted. "What a weapon," he had told Max, saying it reminded him of a Buck Rogers ray gun only silent and much more powerful. The disrupters were obviously ready to install, and Max had been busy with the antigravity device and the power plant, which were transported from his storage building at home on successive weekends and ready to install in the airframe.

All the accessory equipment was ready to install when the airframe arrived quietly on the night of August 1, 2023. Max supervised the unloading, placing the ship on four large pylons with gigantic insulators of a type used on high tension electrical wires. The next day, Frank was astounded when he saw the real thing. They spent the rest of that day making sure all of the drilled and tapped holes were in the right place because, after they applied the current to the casting, it would be too hard to drill again. All of the internal parts were attached to soft metal brackets that would be attached to the airframe. These were all checked. When Max and, especially, Genie were satisfied, they arranged to do the current pass through that night after midnight.

After everyone was gone except Max and the security guys, Max hooked up the special rheostat and began to apply the current. Genie looked on as Max listened to her instructions, gradually increasing the frequency and wattage applied to the casting. He started with sixty cycles per second and twenty amperes at one hundred twenty volts, then gradually increased the power to 1,500 amps at 200 megahertz and 5,000 volts. The metal glowed a dull purplish red as the rheostat was increased to 3.2 gigahertz, left there for eight minutes, and abruptly turned off. Even with the windows open, the temperature in the room was over a hundred degrees when the current was finally shut down. The wisdom of placing the casting on the insulated pylons was obvious by the end of the process. Everyone was happy to see the process end, the temperature in the room reaching a level Russell declared nearly unbearable.

The next day, the ship was cooled off. It now had the characteristic chrome appearance, and as advertised, it was harder than a diamond. The workmen now began to install the components in the craft. Max relayed directions from Genie, and the work went well for the next several weeks. By the end of November, they were ready for a test flight.

The computer system, about the size of a pack of cigarettes, was the real advantage of the ship. It controlled navigation, flight control, communications, the electromagnetic pulse weapon, and all other combat systems. The computer also had reasoning capabilities and was able to make logical decisions during combat, making the system self-reliant and a formidable adversary for any enemy. The pilot's seat was in the middle of the craft, and the pilot could turn

360 degrees, if necessary, and look out of a special type of hardened glass that Max had custom made in Pittsburgh. During combat, this glass would close and digital display monitors would give a three-dimensional view of the world outside. In combat mode, the craft's only exposed areas were the disruptor pods and the electromagnetic pulse apparatus, which were retracted during routine flight. Max had built the EMP device himself, with Genie's help, of course.

They'd made the controls much like a helicopter's, which meant that anyone who could fly a chopper could fly the new craft. The stick and pedal controls were fly by wire and seemed well suited to the up, down, back and forth flying capability of the craft. Max decided to have the test flight on a Saturday with just Frank present so as not to cause a sensation on the Astrolabe campus. Everyone knew there was something special happening on the back lot, however. The increased security confirmed that. They waited for an announcement of what was going on, or perhaps some slip-up that let the cat out of the proverbial bag. Such a slip was not very likely to come from Max.

Max and Frank met on Saturday, November 17 for the test flight. Max climbed into the pilot's seat and strapped in as the turret began to close. He was suddenly overcome with panic. He couldn't get his breath, even though he was heaving deeply, and he immediately unbuckled his seat harness, opened the turret, and climbed out of the ship.

Frank grabbed his arm and helped him down. "Are you okay, Max? What happened in there?"

"I'm okay, Frank. I don't know what happened. All of a sudden I couldn't breathe. I felt like I was tied up and couldn't get out, move, or get my breath. I've never felt like that before. I guess I must be claustrophobic."

"I saw that happen to my wife during an MRI once. She nearly punched a nurse who tried to keep her in the machine. She would have punched the nurse too, except they had her restrained on that little cot they used to push her into the machine. She was like a different person."

"I guess you'll have to fly the thing, Frank. Do you know how to fly a helicopter?"

"Well, sort of . . . I guess I can learn."

"This should be really something. Well, let's see how it goes, Frank. Just put it on auto. The toggle switch is on the left."

As Frank climbed in to the ship, Genie inquired of Max, "Are you all right?"

"Sure, Genie. I guess I'm a little claustrophobic, that's all. Feeling such panic sure surprised me though." Max was a little shaky as he walked to the refrigerator and got a small bottle of orange juice and sat down to watch the show.

Genie quietly said, "I'll take Frank for a test drive. You can take it easy and just watch." Genie took Frank all over the assembly hangar and then opened the door and even took him outside. Up, down, forward, reverse, left and right: Frank was like a kid with a new toy. Everything worked perfectly. They now had themselves a thirty five-ton flying tank, impervious to everything and everyone. The new craft was the master of the sky.

Max let Frank play for about thirty minutes and then, without further explanation, Max guided the ship into the hangar and put it back on its pylons. "Frank, we need to give her a name. What do you think?"

"Well, I'm just a ride-along pilot. You're the boss. Naming her should be your prerogative."

"Let's call her "*Sky Goddess*."

"Yeah. That has a nice ring to it, Max."

Genie quietly agreed. "I think Nute will be pleased too. That's one of his names, you know."

That night, Max called Susan via communicator as usual. She was in Australia winding up her collection efforts in the South Pacific. Max told her of their success with the Goddess and wanted to know how much longer she'd be.

Susan replied, "I don't know. I don't think I'll ever be done completely. There are literally millions of species. I just want to get down to representative family or genus level for some of them. For example, there are thousands of species of bacteria that I will never be able to collect. I'm just going to have to be satisfied with what I have. Time is running out. When are you going to New York to meet with the United Nations?"

"Next month. I think I'll call the Secretary General before then to give the Security Council a heads-up on what I have for them. He may want to beef up security when I come there in person. Do you think you can be back by then? I really want you to go to New York with me."

"Yes, of course. You know I wouldn't miss it. Besides, I could visit Rachael while I am there. Maybe you and I could take in a show or something. You know, like a real date. I miss our quiet time together, we haven't had much lately."

Max replied with exasperation in his tone, "I know. Once we get this weapons stuff over with, maybe we can relax a little before Nute gets back. He is due on December 10. Things should really start popping after that."

The real phone rang, which caused Max to jump a little. Max answered, "Hello? Oh hi, Steve. Yeah, we had our maiden flight this afternoon. How did you know? . . . What! How did that asshole find out about the flight? . . . Why? What does he want with both of us? Do we have to go? . . . Military police, huh? This really stinks, Steve. I thought we were rid of him, . . . I know that's what you said. When do we have to go? . . . In the morning! Now that really sucks! . . . Okay, okay. I'll be ready. See ya in the morning."

Returning to the communicator, Max asked, "Did you get that, Susan? I guess we are not done with General Potter after all. I'll call you when I know something. I think you should just pack up and come home — things are going to heat up fast. All right, I'll talk to you tomorrow."

The next morning, Max and Steve Clark were on their way to the Pentagon to see General Potter. This time, they had two security guards each with them. The General's security detail met them at the airport, and a helicopter took them to the Pentagon. At the entrance to the Joint Chiefs' section, they were stopped at a Marine checkpoint and the body guards had to surrender their weapons. At Clark's insistence, however, their security guards accompanied them to the General's office. Potter was finishing up some paperwork that a very attractive female Marine officer was collecting from him.

As they came into the room, Potter said, "Sit down."

Max immediately replied, "No thanks. We will stand."

The General signed the last papers, and the Marine captain left the room.

"I want to know just who the hell you think you are to have technology in your possession that could mean battlefield superiority and not turn it over to your country."

Max started to reply, but General Potter cut him off. "Shut up, you little shit! All you civilians think you know more than the military. Let me tell you: you don't know jack-shit. You are a disgrace to your brother's memory and your father's career. You make me sick."

Max was devastated by the remark about his brother. It actually made him feel ill, and he looked pale standing next to Clark. Of all things he could have said to Max, this hurt the worst, and the General obviously knew it. He was all but gloating over a direct hit to Max's psyche.

Potter continued his tirade. "I want the plans and specifications to that aircraft right now or you'll be arrested for treason. We'll slam your ass in Leavenworth and throw away the key. You won't see the light of day for at least forty years. I'm going to laugh my ass off while you rot in jail."

Max recovering his emotional footing from the comment about his brother, said with defiance, "General, you *can kiss my* ass! I am not giving you anything. Furthermore, if you try to arrest me, I'll turn my aircraft loose on you personally and destroy everything you own. I will fry your fat ass along with it, if I feel like it. I suggest you learn to live with the fact the aircraft is not in your possession and you will never lay your slimy hands on it."

Max turned to the rest of his entourage and said, "We are done here."

They left the room. At the checkpoint, his bodyguards retrieved their weapons and proceeded toward the exit with a new sense of danger. They were all on full alert now.

When they reached the chopper and got in, Max suddenly realized the General didn't ask for the aircraft. "*Oh shit, he already has it!*"

Max phoned Frank at the lab. No answer. He then called Genie at the cabin. She reported she had detected that someone was trying to fly the Goddess and she had shut it down. Since Frank was the only one there, it was clear that Frank had betrayed him and sold out to the General.

He told Genie "That's why Potter thought he had the aircraft. Unfortunately for the General, you were on duty and stopped the theft."

When Max and Steve got into the plane to return home, Steve said, "I can't believe you had the balls to tell the General to kiss your ass. He really is going to be pissed now."

"I don't care. What he doesn't know is that my brother . . . " Max's voice cracked and he got teary eyed as he spoke. "God rest his soul, he'd be proud of what I am doing. I know my father is. It is the General who should be afraid. The memory of my brother is something he can never use against me, no matter what he says. He should be afraid of what I might do to him right now. How do you think he found out about all this?"

Steve replied, "Max, I think the General knew from the start. I should've realized when the bankers gave us all the money we wanted with no questions asked that Potter was behind all of this. He's been paying off the bankers and probably Frank and Raytheon all along."

As soon as Max and Steve had left his office, the General picked up the phone and said, "Get me the President."

The President was informed of the weapon's existence, and he signed a National Security Finding that Max was an official threat to the peace and security of the United States and presented a clear and present danger to the Union. General Potter and other military personnel were authorized to use whatever means necessary to counter this perceived threat. The Finding was placed in the Top Secret memorandum file. After his conversation with the President, Potter called the Chief of Special Operations, Colonel Taylor, and laid out the problem.

"Colonel Taylor, this is Barney Potter over at the Joint Chiefs. We have a situation. There is a brilliant renegade scientist who has developed a device that can neutralize gravity. . . . Yeah, I know. What is worse, he's built an aircraft that weighs over thirty tons and flies around without a sound. He's also developed some kind of microwave weapon that melts everything it is aimed at.

"He's kept this weapon and the craft to carry it under wraps at a company called Astrolabe Systems and now we think he is going to give it to the United Nations or some such bullshit. We are trying to get the plans and specs now, but we don't have them yet. The inventor's assistant says he can fly the damn thing and is on my payroll. The President and the Joint Chiefs are worried that the device, or plans for it, might fall into the wrong hands. The President has authorized a maximum sanction if we can't get control of the situation.

"You're authorized to make contingency plans to target the inventor, Dr. Max Gibson. He already has good security by the company guys, most of 'em ex-Secret Service. So put your team together and start your research. I'll keep you informed. I'll have our people send over his file."

CHAPTER 19

When Max arrived at the lab, Frank was frantically trying to fly the Goddess by overriding the software. Needless to say, Frank vs. Genie was no contest. When Max entered the room, Frank quickly stood up with an embarrassed look on his face.

Max began in a low tone of voice as if he had caught a child in the cookie jar. "Frank, how could you do this after all the work we have done together?"

Without looking up, Frank quietly responded, "It was just the money, Max — a lot of money. They offered me a million dollars a month. Greed got the best of me, I guess. Besides, I didn't see the harm in it. It's our own government that wants this thing, for God's sake."

"Harm? Don't you understand those guys are vultures and don't have anyone's interest in mind except their own? Oh, well, never mind. You're fired, Frank. Get out of my sight. Take your money and get the hell out of here. Go. Just go. And don't come back, you greedy shit."

Max was hurt by this betrayal, of course, and he felt a little sick at his stomach as he watched his former best friend gather up his personal stuff and leave the lab. Fortunately, more important matters needed his attention now, and he didn't have time to grieve or be angry over Frank's departure. He phoned Susan and brought her up to date on the day's events.

"Hi Susan. I just found out Frank has sold us out and took a bribe to tell the military everything he knew. Fortunately, he didn't know too much, but now General Potter is determined to take the ship. This makes me realize that my dad was right, and I'm more convinced than ever to give the Goddess to the United Nations."

"You're right, Max. It is a good thing I wasn't there or I would have kicked his ass myself," Susan said. "I can't believe he is such an ingrate. I guess money changes a lot of people. I'll be home in two days and we'll take those bastards on together. I'll see you soon, sweetie."

Max couldn't wait for her to return. After betrayal by a friend, he could use a friendly face and the moral support.

Max then phoned Roger and asked him to come over to the lab. He assured his security agents that he needed Roger's help to clean up. Roger was obviously awestruck when he saw the Sky Goddess. Max lined out his needs, and while they were cleaning up the lab and after the body guards were out of hearing, Roger quietly asked, "Doc, what is that big shiny thing?"

Max replied like a father explaining something beyond the comprehension of a child. "A special kind of airplane, one that's very quiet and can go in all directions."

He looked in the direction of the security team to make sure they were indeed out of hearing range. Then Max got very close to Roger and in a whisper said, "Keep everything you see here and what I am about to tell you to yourself. You know how we've been sending those boxes to you and you have been hiding them at Wollum Ford?"

"Yeah, there must be two-hundred-fifty or more of them boxes down there. I had to dig a new hole last month."

"Good. In about a week, we may be going on a trip and taking all those boxes with us."

"Do you want me to help ya load 'em, boss?"

"No, that won't be necessary, but I may need your help with something else."

"Whatever ya need, Doc. You just say the word."

Max was startled when he saw the intensity in Roger's face. His eyes narrowing into a singleness of purpose that revealed a loyalty and unspoken commitment that Max was not accustomed to, especially after his recent experience with Frank. He realized that Roger wasn't fooling around and would take someone out if he said so. Unlike Frank, Roger had a purity, an unquestioned devotion and trust that had been forged between them over the years. He was uneducated, but he was a storm-trooper who displayed the kind of unflinching allegiance that was a little scary to see up close.

"I may need you to meet Susan and me and float us down the river to Wollum at night. Can you do that? We'd need a rubber raft or something quiet. An aluminum canoe would make too much noise."

"Naw, Doc. You don't want no rubber raft. Them damn things are like a flat bottom steamboat, and unless you got a lot of fast movin' water, you'll never get down the river, 'specially at night.

What you need is one of them there PVC canoes. My cousin Jimmy over at Jasper makes them in his backyard. They've got two layers of plastic sandwiched over a layer of foam. They're just slicker than snot and slide over rocks real quiet."

"As always, Roger, you have an answer for me. If I do need you for this task, I'll call your girlfriend Edna's house because the Feds will be watching you and your family, I am sure. All I'll say to her is 'Plan B.' If you get that message, here's what I want you to do: Get the canoe and some food, water, flashlights, and warm winter gear and meet us at Mt. Hershey access off 65 Highway. In case it is really cold, you'd better bring my little mountain backpack tent and down sleeping bags for Dr. McKinney and me.

"Take all this stuff to the river and hide it at Mt. Hershey access. We'll come in from the northeast, on the back roads from Maumee. From Mt. Hershey down to Wollum is only about six miles by river. I don't want to go there directly and tip the Feds as to our location. We're meetin' some people there, and I think we can arrive undetected if we come by river. Understand?"

"Right, boss. How are them other people goin' to get there?"

"They're going to be flying in, probably up Richland Creek valley, which joins the Buffalo there at Wollum. Are we all clear on the plan?"

"You bet, Doc. I don't think we will have any trouble with them fellers. If I get caught, I'll just play dumb. That's easy for me, you know."

"Roger, you are anything but dumb. You've been my best and most trusted friend since I came to Arkansas. It's been a privilege for me to know you and be your friend. I'll never forget you. I appreciate you more than you'll ever know."

Roger got a queer look on his face at the suggestion that Max was going away, but he was also obviously proud for having helped the man he called Doc in whatever his big plans were.

"I've got to get going now. I am meeting Susan at the airport in about two and a half hours. I probably won't see you again until we get back from New York."

Max shook hands with Roger and gave him a hug for good measure. He gave a high sign to his bodyguards, and they headed to the car — Max had to ride in a bulletproof Mercedes diplomatic sedan now — for the trip to Little Rock. Roger continued to sweep up and look busy until they were out of sight.

When Susan saw Max waiting for her at the airport, she broke into a run, plunged into his arms, and planted one of her famous kisses on him. She finally exclaimed after she satisfied her need for that kiss, "God, it's good to see you. I've been so worried ever since you met with that ass Potter. Have you heard anything else?"

"No, not really, not since I found out about Frank. I did talk to Roger about our getaway plan, and he'll have everything ready if we need to leave town in a hurry."

The two of them walked arm in arm slowly through the airport toward the parking lot. It was obvious to everyone they passed that they were hopelessly in love and didn't care who knew it. They didn't see anyone else in the terminal, only each other. When they got into the car, Max and Susan continued their conversation in private, via communicators. Max reviewed their plan to go to the United Nations to make a gift of the Goddess, his world police force that could enforce the laws of the United Nations without question or argument from anyone, and explain the conditions of the gift.

They'd call the United Nations tomorrow and set up their trip. They planned to first speak to the Security Council and later to the General Assembly. Then the entire world would know about the Goddess and its capabilities and they would know if they had a chance to pull it off before Nute arrived on the tenth. They dropped Susan off at her apartment and continued on to the Max's cabin.

The next morning, Max called Susan at her apartment. "I thought you might want to listen in on my call to the United Nations. I'm going to make the call from Clark's office. He said he wanted to go to New York with us, and so I wanted him to know what we planned to do. I thought it would be better to keep you out of this part of the deal until we get things settled in New York."

"Okay, Max. I'll be standing by via communicator. I think you're probably right about keeping my role in this quiet for now. No one knows I'm in on this, do they?

"No, and I think you will be safer that way, don't you?"

"Yes, but you know I don't like being away from you during all this."

"Yes, I know."

Max and his security detail arrived at Clark's office at about nine-thirty. Max gave Clark the rundown on his plan and asked if he still wanted to go to New York with him.

Steve replied, "Are you kidding? After seeing you tell General Potter to kiss your ass, I wouldn't miss this for the world. I spoke to Astrolabe's board of directors by conference call last night, and they're with you 100 percent. They were also impressed by your remark to the General.

"They'll be providing some additional security in New York, they authorized fifteen agents in six vehicles to be waiting at the airport for us. We'll split up our people into various class eight armored cars and sport utility vehicles at the last second. We'll do this so no one who might be watching will know where any of us are located. Then, we'll motorcade to the Waldorf-Astoria on 50th and Park Ave.

We'll settle in there for the night and speak to the General Assembly on Wednesday morning. I'll have to admit, the directors are really excited about what you've done here, Max, and everyone is looking forward to applying your technology to all kinds of equipment and devices; the applications are endless. Max, you and Astrolabe will be famous."

"Okay, let's make the call Steve."

Steve buzzed Glenda. "Could you get the Secretary General on the phone, we're ready? All right, Max, go ahead, I'll put him on speaker. I called earlier, and Secretary Duvalle should have the entire Security Council with him."

Max had done his homework and addressed each member of the Security Council in his own language, even down to the regional accent.

In perfect French for the Secretary General, he said, "Good morning, Mr. Secretary. My name is Dr. Max Gibson and I work for the Astrolabe Systems Corporation ."

"Yes, Dr. Gibson. Thank you for calling. I have the entire Security Council here with me. I understand you have a proposal. So go right ahead."

"Thank you, Secretary Duvalle. I have what I think is good news for the United Nations. I have developed an airborne device that will be able to enforce the resolutions and sanctions of the United Nations all over the world without regard to any nation's armies or weaponry. Even nuclear weapons will not be able to stop my aircraft. I believe, in a short time, the world will become a safer place to live, work, and prosper without the worry of stronger nations taking forcible advantage of the weak. This will allow complete disarmament of all nations, which in turn will free billions of dollars in defense expenditures to be directed toward peaceful endeavors like eradicating hunger and poverty and providing education for everyone. In short, Mr. Secretary, I have the ultimate policeman for the world. I would like to come to New York and address the General Assembly and to present the device to you."

"My God, sir. You can't be serious. How can such a device exist?"

"Not only does it exist, Mr. Secretary, but I would be happy to demonstrate it for you later this week if you desire."

The Russian delegate interrupted in English, "Please, Dr. Gibson."

Max said, "You may speak in Russian. I understand perfectly, Mr. Cameroff."

Speaking in his native Russian with a Ukraine accent, the delegate continued. "Thank you, Dr. Gibson. How do we know this new weapon is what you say it is? Perhaps your government is baiting us to disarm and actually has many of these weapons hidden to take over the world at some later time. Excuse me, but I think you may be a little naïve to think the world will disarm just because you have a new weapon."

Max responded in Russian, and in the same accent as the Russian delegate, "I don't believe you understand, Mr. Cameroff. This aircraft weighs thirty-five tons and flies at supersonic speeds without noise, radar signature, or fuel consumption. It can be flown manned or unmanned and is totally impervious to any weapon system on the face of the Earth. It can destroy any weapon or any structure with impunity. It can absorb any bullet, missile, or explosive device used against it. There is only one ship in existence, invented by me, and me alone, and owned by Astrolabe. There are no other such ships in existence let alone ships like it owned by the United States government."

"Dr. Gibson, this is Harold Adams of the British foreign office. Do you wish us to believe that the U.S. Government doesn't know about this weapon or have access to it?"

"That is correct, Ambassador. The U.S. Government knows of its existence, but definitely has not had access to it."

"Excuse me for saying so, Doctor, but in some quarters this might be considered treason against the U.S. Government. Certainly the weapon would be considered a state secret in most countries. Aren't you afraid they might take it from you and use it for their own agenda?"

"Not as long as I have the ship, sir. It would be impossible to overcome the ship."

"Dr. Gibson, this is Wo Dung Zu, People's Republic of China. I think we all would like to see this ship in action."

Max spoke to him in perfect Cantonese. "Ambassador Zu, are you familiar with Sun Tzu and his advice to the emperor on matters of war?"

"Yes, of course. He is one of China's greatest military philosophers. Why do you ask?"

"Master Sun's contribution to our discussion would be as follows: 'you only have to use the big weapon once to show what destructive power you possess; fear of reprisal then controls your enemy.'

"This is the principle of deterrence, Ambassador. Eventually, when everyone is convinced of the power of my ship, they will comply with the resolutions and sanctions of the United Nations. Most countries ignore United Nations resolutions now because there is no consequence of their rejection of said resolutions and sanctions.

"If you could send the ship to enforce compliance, the results of UN resolutions would be vastly different. You would just have to destroy the leaders of the opposing nation, who could not hide from you and the ship. You could punish them with impunity until you gained compliance. The ship would be relentless and pursue noncompliant nations twenty-four hours a day, seven days a week until they were either destroyed or agreed to comply."

"Yes, I see what you mean, Dr. Gibson."

"Gentlemen, with your permission, I look forward to addressing the General Assembly on Wednesday. I will be able to answer all of your questions at that time. I just wanted the council to know what I had in store before I came to New York. Thank you for your consideration of this proposal. Good bye." Max then hung up the phone and let out a long sigh of relief.

Max went home to pack and as soon as he was in the cabin, he phoned Susan via communicator and asked her what she thought about what had happened at Clark's office.

Susan replied, "It scares me even more than I am already when I hear you and Steve talk about the weapon. It sounds like it is you and the Sky Goddess against the world."

"Yes, I know. I guess all this does sound pretty dramatic, naïve and foolish, but what else is there? How do we convince the governments of the world this could work?"

Max was clearly worried now, and he suggested he and Susan travel separately. He told Susan to take Genie with her, just in case there was a kidnapping or assassination attempt made on him. She agreed and said she would go to her sister's place, which was only about twenty blocks from his hotel and thirty blocks from the United Nations headquarters building. She didn't want Max to be without Genie, but he insisted, pointing out that, if he were detained or intercepted, it would be a little hard to explain Genie. He also said that Genie might be able to help them more easily if Susan had her. Susan reluctantly agreed and booked an earlier flight to New York.

Max's entourage then went over last minute details of the security arrangements. The briefing was conducted by Gerold Pendergrass, the agent in charge. They would travel in several cars from the airport and not decide which one to put Clark and Max in until the last minute. They would exit LaGuardia airport at about 1455 hours for the thirteen-mile trip to the Waldorf. From the airport, they would take Grand Central Parkway West, over the Triboro Bridge onto FDR Drive South, and then make a right on 49th Street. Then they'd turn right on Park Avenue to the Waldorf.

The advance team would clear the hotel of any threats before they arrived. Once in the hotel, they'd occupy rooms in one entire section of the hotel, twenty rooms on the eighth floor.

Wednesday morning, they'd reverse the process and motorcade to the United Nations headquarters, about ten blocks away. Pendergrass, a former Secret service Agent, obviously knew his stuff and Max was impressed if no less worried.

Pendergrass reminded the security team that Max and Clark would be most vulnerable when they were in the open and by themselves. He told Max and Clark to be especially vigilant when they got out of the plane and the ground vehicles. These would be the most logical times for a hit.

At Fort Bragg, North Carolina, Colonel Taylor was also holding the briefing for his special covert operations team. "Okay, men, here's the latest intel. The target will arrive at the Waldorf-Astoria at 1530 hours tomorrow. I've reviewed the itinerary and feel this is our best spot to take him out. We'll need three teams for a standard urban triangle setup.

Riggs, you and Powell will take the taxi setup and park it on the east side of Park Avenue. Try to take a trunk-shot at street level. They'll be traveling with twelve to fifteen in the entourage, and your shot will have to be quick. Take the H&K and forty rounds of Federal .308 168 grain premium.

Kester, you and Billings take the uptown roof shot from the west side of Park Avenue, from the roof of the Palmolive building over Schwab's E*trade. Take the hide and set it up. I think you can use the phony electrical transformer up there."

As he spoke, he pointed out the various hide locations on the three dimensional virtual reality screen on the wall. Each location was shown from all angles as the point of view rotated.

"You'll have to set up tonight while it is still dark. The lower level rooftop is six stories up, so do your math on the trajectory. Palmer, you and Clifton will have to take a window shot from the office building on the downtown side toward the end of the block near 49th Street. We have secured an empty office on the thirty-fourth floor of the building that has a good view of the drive up to the Waldorf. You high-angle shooters will need the M-24 300 Winchester mags for the long shots — too much wind for anything else. Take ten rounds each of the 200-grain match ammo. Use your range finders and do the math when you get in the hide.

"Remember, you'll only have three to five seconds to acquire and get off a shot. So make it count. The taxi shot will need a suppressor as well as the lower power, wide angle scope. At that range, you should take as many torso shots as you need to take out the target and security. Riggs, afterwards, just drive away slowly and make a right on 50th at the corner, a one-way headed east, and meet me at the checkpoint.

"You guys with the high shots, make your first shot a head and, if you get a follow, take a torso. Palmer and Clifton, break your rifles down and put them in the toolboxes you'll have and walk out of the building. Remember you were just there to work on the air conditioning and don't know anything. This logo will match your coveralls and the toolbox. We will pick you up at the checkpoint at 1600 hours.

"Kester, you and Billings you'll need to stay in the hide until after dark. It is too risky for you to leave in broad daylight. I'm sure they will have police up there right after. So, just stay put. They won't even know you are there. It will be completely dark at 1800 hours this time of year, so I'll pick you up at that time in the alley behind the building. Use the same routine as the others for your rifles. We'll be on tactical channel D. Even though it is scrambled, let's keep radio silence unless we have a real emergency.

"All right, men. Listen up. Here are your rules of engagement. This is a photo of the primary target, Dr. Max Gibson. He is six feet two inches tall and weighs one hundred eighty-five pounds. He has dark hair and a full beard."

Pointing to the photo, Taylor said, "This man, Steven Clark, will probably accompany Gibson. He's five feet nine inches, 165 pounds, and has red hair. He's also a target. The rest of the entourage are all professionals, consider them combatants and fair game. If they get in the way, take them out.

"Okay, are there any questions? . . . Yes, Riggs."

"This Gibson looks like a regular guy. What did he do?"

"I don't know and don't care, and neither do you, soldier! Any more questions?" They all answered in unison, "NO SIR!"

"Your flight will be leaving from Pope Air Base at 1900 hours, so get a move on. I'll meet you at hanger 48 at 1845 hours.

"One more thing: standard covert rules apply, so leave all I.D.s and dog tags here. I want nothing in your pockets — no pictures, no nothing. Got it?"

CHAPTER 20

Rachael picked Susan up at LaGuardia at 10:50 Tuesday morning, and they went back to her apartment on 54th Street. When they got inside and closed the door, Rachael inquired nervously, "Susan, what's going on? I've never seen you like this."

With a deep sigh, Susan responded, "It is a long story, but the bottom line is that Max has invented something that is very valuable to the government and the military. Dad built most of it in Canton. Max is going to give it to the United Nations. He'll address the General Assembly tomorrow morning."

"Wow! The General Assembly. Man, only presidents and prime ministers address the General Assembly. This must really be big. Do you think there's any danger for Max?"

"Yes, I do, and so does he. He pissed off some big-shot General, and Max thinks the General is out to get him. Max is supposed to get in later, around 3:30, with some other people from Astrolabe. They're staying at the Waldorf."

Rachael, being her mother's daughter, asked, "You want some lunch?"

"Yes, I'm starved. I've been so worried about Max that I haven't been eating much lately."

"I thought you looked like you'd lost a little weight."

"I don't know. I haven't even weighed in a month or more. All I've done for the past few months is travel, and I'm about worn out."

After finishing off sandwiches and milk, the sisters plopped down in the living room. Susan told Rachael all about her long-

223

distance romance with Max, and Rachael filled her in on what she and Tom had been doing. They had been visiting for about two and a half hours when Susan looked at her watch and asked, "What time do you have?"

"About 3:25. Let's see if there is anything on the news."

Rachael turned on CNN. The news anchor was reporting the latest story: "A little known defense contractor known as Astro-labe Systems has come up with a super weapon, and the inventor is arriving today to speak to the United Nations General Assembly tomorrow at 10 a.m. We have word that he is about to arrive at the Waldorf-Astoria. Let's go live to Shirley Plimpton at the Waldorf."

A woman with a microphone appeared on the screen. "Thanks, George. We have seen a lot of activity here in the last few minutes. Security people are clearing a path and checking the identification of all the bystanders. They have blocked off all entrances and the sidewalk . . . Just a moment . . . I see a motorcade arriving from the south on Park Avenue and pulling up in front of the Waldorf. There are several cars and vans in the motorcade.

"The NYPD has blocked traffic to allow the motorcade to unload passengers in front of the hotel. The first two vehicles appear to be carrying security people and the next one as well. The next two, however, appear to be holding the VIPs. The occupants of the two Cadillac Escalades in the middle of the motorcade are getting out and walking up the covered entryway."

Then, the newscast recorded sounds that did not belong in this crowded street scene: Thump! Thump, thump, thump . . . thump . . . thump . . . boom . . . boom . . . thump, thump. The woman with the microphone lost her composure. "Oh! Oh! What was that?"

The sound was the suppressed muzzle blast of a high-powered rifle at close range and the boom of a 300 Winchester magnum as it echoed between the tall buildings. People were falling like bowling pins. Max was down. Steve and three more of the security men were down. The crowd scene became utter chaos as people screamed and ran about, unsure where the weapons fire came from. The reporter was on the deck with blood splattered all over her face and clothes. The camera was lying on its side but still rolling.

Max was face down and motionless on the sidewalk, bleeding from his wounds. Reverting to years of training, a security guard immediately leaped out of the Escalade and took a position over Max with his 9mm Beretta drawn. Then the final boom! The guard protecting Max was killed instantly with a head shot. The impact caused him to fall directly over Max. The scene was like a suicide bombing in Baghdad, bodies strewn everywhere. People were screaming and crying as fear gripped the survivors who were cowering behind any slight bit of cover. The two planters that held small evergreen trees were the only cover in front of the hotel. The TV crew and other bystanders tried to melt into the wall behind even this small bit of protection.

Pendergrass, who had been riding in the last vehicle, ran up to the scene in time to see the taxi slowly drive away. He quickly recognized the classic triangle ambush and reacted immediately. Pumping two fourteen round clips from his Beretta into the trunk and back window of the taxi as it drove off, he killed Powell in the trunk and caught Riggs in the back of the head with the last two shots. The taxi slowly went out of control and plunged into the concrete median in the middle of the street, where it came to rest.

Pendergrass then radioed for ambulances and more backup from the NYPD and began a triage of the casualties. His cool headed actions under fire began to provide some order to the chaos.

In all, four security men were hit: two dead and two wounded. Max was covered by one of the dead agents so his wounds could not be evaluated just yet. As Pendergrass looked on, the other agents began pulling the bodies into the hotel lobby, blood streaming onto the highly polished black and white marble floor.

Finally, Max and Steve were moved and assessed. Steve was dead, the back third of his skull missing. Max had sustained a neck wound about half way between the clavicle and the base of his skull and was bleeding profusely. Two agents were attending to Max as he lay motionless just inside the doors to the hotel lobby.

Six minutes after the gunfire started, the first ambulance arrived from Bellevue Hospital only a few blocks away. The attendants in the emergency department had been watching the motorcade arrive on TV and saw the massacre unfold. Paramedics quickly took charge of the living and tried to stabilize the three survivors. Max had lost a hunk of tissue from his trapezius muscle but was lucky the bullet had missed the carotid artery, only two inches to the left of his wound.

"He'll probably survive," declared one paramedic to another.

Eight minutes after the ambush started, the TV news camera was still rolling. Although the female reporter had lost her composure momentarily, she realized that hiding behind the planter near the entrance would not be defensible later; besides, the importance of the event in front of her simply demanded that it should be documented. With a trembling voice, she told her cameraman, "Get off your ass and get this!" She boldly walked into the entryway to do her job.

Her clothes splattered with blood and her makeup and hair a mess, she was nevertheless determined to get back on the air. Her voice trembling, she began:

"Ladies and gentlemen, this is Shirley Plimpton in front of the Waldorf-Astoria Hotel in midtown, where we have been witness to an assassination attempt on Dr. Max Gibson and Steven Clark of the Astrolabe Systems Corporation.

"We have no information on the dead and wounded as of yet, but we are sure some of the entourage were killed. The ambush appears to have been well-organized and several people were firing from different directions. One of the security agents returned fire immediately after the first barrage. We'll see if he can speak with us. He seems to be in charge.

"Could you tell us your name and what happened here?"

"Okay, but it will have to be quick. I'm pretty busy here. My name is Gerold Pendergrass, and I'm in charge of the Astrolabe security detail. Some of our executives were attacked here today by unknown assailants. I returned fire at a taxi cab thought to be the getaway car of some of the shooters."

"How many shooters do you think there were?"

"I don't know, but weapons fire came from at least three directions. Look, that's really all the time I have right now." He moved away to resume helping the injured.

The newswoman seemed to be more in control of herself now, and her voice barely quavered as she said, "The wounded and dead are being taken to Bellevue and New York Hospital just blocks away. We don't have any further information at this time, so I'll return you to the studio. George . . ."

CHAPTER 21

S usan was in shock at the horror she saw on the television, crying hysterically as she sat right in front of the television trying to be closer to Max. She kept screaming, "No! No! No! This can't be happening. Rachael, we have to get down there. How far is it?"

"It's about twenty blocks from here. It will be faster to take a taxi. Let's go!"

Rachael and Susan gathered up their coats, and at the last moment, Susan thought to retrieve Genie and slip her into a carry-on luggage bag. The "Taxi Gods" were with them as there was a taxi letting someone out in front of their building.

As Susan got into the taxi, she barked, "Bellevue Hospital and step on it." When the driver saw her face in his rearview, he knew she wasn't kidding and complied and punched it out into traffic.

Rachael exclaimed, "How do you know he's at Bellevue?"

"I saw them load him into a Bellevue ambulance. They took the security guys to New York Hospital." The driver took the shortest route to Bellevue and was there by some miracle in twelve minutes. As if by providence — *or perhaps it was Genie*, Susan thought — every light was green.

Susan stuffed three twenties in the driver's hand and said before sprinting to the entrance, "Thanks for the ride, buddy. You did good!"

Susan and Rachael rushed into the emergency department to find out about Max. After Susan showed her Astrolabe ID badge, the attendants were much more accommodating. The nurse explained that Max had been taken to surgery and would be there for a while. Then the emergency room doctor gave Susan the rundown on Max's condition when he learned she was an "Astrolabe" physician. Dr. Hudson extended her normal professional courtesy and took her to the doctor's lounge and explained Max's wound.

"He was hit in the superior aspect of the trapezius muscle, about two and a half centimeters above the clavicle. He lost a lot of blood, about half his blood volume. He had regained consciousness by the time he got here, however. The paramedic had started him on IV saline en route, so his plasma volume had recovered somewhat. He was taken to surgery suite three for repair and possible closure of the wound. We gave him four units of packed red cells and got his hemoglobin up to twelve before he left for surgery. He should be okay in a few weeks. He was really lucky. A couple of centimeters to the left, and the bullet would have blown out the carotid. You can probably see him in recovery in about an hour, unless you want to go into the OR."

Susan was happy just to get the details and thought she would probably pass out if she saw Max under the knife in surgery. Dr. Hudson sensed Susan's anxiety and said, "You guys close?"

Susan quietly said, "Yes, very," and started to cry.

Dr. Hudson put his arm around her shoulder and said, "Hey, take it easy. He's going to be all right."

"Thanks for taking care of Max, Dr. Hudson. It was nice of you to take time to go over all this with me."

Susan returned to the emergency waiting room, located Rachael, and gave her sister the good news. They went to the surgery waiting room for suite three and took a chair. Susan called Max's parents, who had been watching the news and called to see what she knew before the cab arrived at the hospital. She gave them an update on Max's condition and the news that he would recover. After an hour and fifteen minutes, someone in scrubs came out and said, "Anyone here for Dr. Gibson?"

Susan jumped up and said, "Yes, we are!"

"Hi, I'm Dr. Jamison, a surgery resident. I took care of Max. Are you the doctor from the company?"

"Yes, I'm Dr. Susan McKinney. This is my sister Rachael. How is our boy doing?"

"Really well. We were able to close the wound with a small Z-plasty over the shoulder. I think we got a good closure that doesn't have too much tension on it. Once we got the arterial flow stopped, the rest went quite well. We'll see how he responds in the next few days. We'll have to watch the tension on the sutures closely.

You should be able to see him when he gets out of the recovery room in a couple of hours. There was one curious thing though. We found a small piece of what we thought was bullet fragment at first. Then we took it out and found it is some kind of a crystal. Do you know anything about this?"

He handed Max's communicator to her.

"Yes, I know what it is. But it's classified."

"Well, whatever it is, you can have it back. It didn't have any-thing to do with the wound. I'll check back with Max later this evening. It was nice meeting you, Doctor."

Susan learned from the nurse that Max would be taken to room 814, so she and Rachael went there to wait. When they got into the room and Susan was sure they were alone, she said, "Rachael, I need you to do some things.

"I am afraid the people who did this will make another attempt on Max's life, and so we need to get him out of here and back to

Arkansas as soon as possible. The FBI and Army intelligence will get around to you and Tom within a few hours. Max and I need to be out of here before that — for your safety and ours.

"He'll also need some clothes to wear out of here. He's a 40 regular, 32" waist with a 32" inseam, size 11 shoe."

"Are you sure about this? That sounds really dramatic, like cloak and dagger stuff to me. What was that thing the doctor gave you anyway?"

"Rachael, listen to me! Don't you get it? These people who are trying to kill Max will not stop until they succeed! The only safe thing for you to do is to play dumb and not be associated with us at all. Now get some clothes for Max then go home and find out if Tom has any friends who could help us work up a disguise to get out of town. I will call you from a pay phone when Max is well enough to travel. Hopefully, he'll recover sufficiently to leave this evening. We'll have to meet you someplace besides your apartment to do the disguise. Understand?"

"Yeah, I got it. I need to get home soon to take care of the kids and get them to a sitter. Do you want me to bring the clothes back here first?"

"That's a good idea. There should be some shops in this area where you can pick up something. Then, you can get home and take care of your kids. Now get goin', Sis,' and don't tell *anyone* you are my sister."

During the next hour, Susan tried to figure out how to get them out of the city safely. She asked Genie what she thought.

Genie replied, "Susan, you know that the Goddess has already been programmed to act automatically against any perceived enemy. So you don't have to worry about the ship. As I see it, your biggest problem is getting back to Arkansas to be protected by the

Goddess and to meet Nute in three days. You'll need money and an inconspicuous way to get out of the city and to travel back to Arkansas. Commercial flights or trains are out of the question. Don't you agree?"

"Yes, of course. Can we get Max's communicator back in so that it will work?"

"I think so. It seems to be working fine. We'll just have to insert it back under the skin."

"Will that hurt him?"

"No. The procedure is not painful and should be easy to accomplish."

Susan and Genie's patience was soon rewarded by Max's arrival. The orderlies transferred Max to his bed and made him comfortable, checked his vital signs one more time, and finally left.

Susan could not contain herself. As she held his uninjured left hand, she said, "I love you. I was really scared, Max. I'm so happy you were not hurt more seriously." She began to sob quietly as she sat holding Max's hand. "Genie says to tell you she's glad you are going to recover completely too."

Max looked around as if to see if they were alone, and then he struggled to speak. His voice was hoarse because of intubation during surgery. In a whisper, he said, "Susan, where is my communicator? Did they take it during surgery?"

"Yes, Max. I have it right here. Genie says I can put it back and it won't hurt."

"Go ahead. I need to talk to Genie."

Max rolled over with some difficulty and Susan palpated the area where she thought the communicator was supposed to go. She located the indentation and said, "Genie, what do I do now?"

Genie replied, "Is there an incision over the indentation?"

"Yes. It has three small 4-0 gut sutures closing it."

"Okay, just pucker the skin and force the communicator into the wound. If you tear the sutures, it's okay. We'll seal it in a moment."

As Genie had promised, Max didn't feel a thing, and the communicator began working immediately.

Max began speaking via the communicator to bypass his weak voice.

"Okay, Susan. What is our situation? The last thing I remember is getting out of the Escalade at the Waldorf."

"Okay, here it is straight up. You and five other people were shot in an ambush. General Potter is the top suspect. I am sorry, Max, but Steven Clark was killed instantly."

There was a sigh as if the air had been sucked out of Max, and tears began to roll down his cheeks. Finally, he said, "Go on."

"One of your bodyguards, one who had been riding in the Escalade with you, was over you trying to protect you when he was killed. He fell on top of you and saved your life. If he had not fallen on you, you would have taken the next shot. He really did exchange his life for yours."

Max, with despair in his voice, said, " His name is Jeremy Wilson from Clear Lake, Iowa. He told me on the ride to the Waldorf. He has a wife and two kids. He was twenty-eight-years old and worked out of Springfield. What a waste."

The tears continued to stream down Max's face as Susan continued. "Pendergrass returned fire and two of the shooters were killed. One other agent was killed and two are at New York Hospital wounded."

"Have you heard how the wounded are doing?"

"No."

"Susan and Genie, can I be alone for a few minutes?"

"Of course, Max. I need to call Rachael anyway."

"Thanks."

When they left the room, Max brought his left hand up to his face and wept profusely for his friends and colleagues. He should have insisted on better security and, especially, greater secrecy. Steve Clark's death was really hard to take because he really didn't have to be with Max today. He just wanted to support Max in this effort, and now he was dead. Max knew now that the project was a failure and Plan B would not be that easy to implement.

They were twelve hundred miles from home with the Federal government looking for them, and the Army in the person of one General Potter was out for blood. Max was sure that government and military representatives would make up some cover story to demonize him and justify any action they felt was necessary. He and Susan had to get out the city, and fast. After that, Max felt, a little payback justice was in order.

After a few minutes, Susan returned with Pendergrass.

"Hi, boss. How're you doing? I'm sorry we got creamed today. It was my fault. We should have come in the motor entrance on 50th Street and not given those assholes a shot at us."

"There is plenty of blame to go around. I am so sorry about Jeremy. I guess he saved my life."

"Well, Doc, the way I see it, like any other soldier, this is what we get paid for. Jeremy was just doing his job, and this time, he gave his life for that job. I know it's hard for outsiders to understand, but it happens every day. Soldiers are killed in action for their country while just doing their job. There is no difference between us and policemen or firemen. Sometimes you have to lay your life on the line, and everyone who works in this kind of job knows it — they just don't expect it.

Anyway, we are not going to let anything happen to you from here on out. Okay, boss. I'll talk to you later?"

They had placed twenty heavily armed agents in the hospital to thwart any additional attempt to hurt Max, and the NYPD assigned additional police outside the building to complete a security lock-down. The city had taken the ambush as a personal affront, and everyone was looking for the assailants. The NYPD was treating it like a terrorist attack, and all resources were being pressed into service. Reminded of the 9/11 attack on the World Trade Center, everybody wanted a piece of anyone who could shoot civilians in broad daylight in their city.

The news outlets were releasing more details as the story unfolded. The two dead snipers were traced to the midtown hotel the teams had used for a base. They were long gone, of course, but investigators now had descriptions of the shooters and their han-dler, Colonel Taylor, from the hotel staff.

At the hospital, Susan and Max were ready to make a plan.

"Max, I have some clothes that Rachael got for you."

"I'll try them on in a minute, Susan. Right now I need Genie to help me."

"Yes, Max?" Genie piped in. "How can I be of help?"

"Can you help heal this wound?"

"I thought you would never ask. Susan, hold me up and point the globe at Max's shoulder. Hold me about two to three inches from the wound and move the globe back and forth."

Susan complied, and Max started feeling better immediately. After Genie's treatment, he got dressed and was ready for action.

"We need to get out of here and get to the Sky Goddess."

"Are you sure you are up to this, Max? You still look a little pale."

"I'll be fine. We need a plan to get out of town."

Susan replied, "Well, I've been thinking about how to do that. Travel by any means other than personal vehicle is out of the question. So I think we should get a motorcycle, disguise ourselves as bikers, and head out of town. Nobody would expect that."

"You are right about that. It could work"

"Rachael is going to get a makeup artist to help us. In fact, I have the name of one of Tom's friends from the theater and his address. What do you think?

"Let's go for it. I am ready. First, let's page Pendergrass and create a diversion to get the hell out of here."

In minutes, Gerold was at their door. "Man, what a recovery. I've never seen even seasoned operatives take a bullet and get up this fast. Are you sure you're all right?"

"Sure. It was just a scratch. I was wondering if you could help us get out of this place. I think I'll be safer incognito. If I stay here, they'll find me and take another shot. How about if we fake a bomb scare or a fire?"

"A bomb scare is perfect and something they would expect for a high profile guy like you. I'll have one of my guys call it in, and when they evacuate the building, we can put you in a car and be out of here without notice."

"Sounds good."

"I'll have my guy say the bomb is in the bathroom on the 8th floor, and they'll evacuate the entire floor until the bomb squad gets here. That will give us time to hustle you out the back door. Give us ten minutes to set it up."

"As long as you're sure you can get by without the kind of medical attention available in a hospital, we should get you out of here. I was at a loss for how to do that with you bedridden, so I'm glad to see you up and around.

It's always dangerous for the opposition to know where you are, and with unlimited resources, they would get to you if you stayed put for very long." He winked at Max with a wry smile like they were old drinking buddies talking about a beautiful woman who had just walked by. "We'll have you out of here in a jiffy, boss."

In a few minutes, there was a lot of movement in the hallway. Pendergrass came in and said to Max with another wink, "We're being evacuated. Come with me."

In all of the confusion, mostly created by Pendergrass' men, no one noticed them get into the service elevator at the end of the hall and go to the basement of the hospital. The basement opened out on to First Avenue where a taxi was waiting. NYPD security was intent on keeping people out and did not pay much attention to them as they left just as the bomb squad arrived. Max, wearing a hooded sweatshirt, was accompanied by Susan and Genie to the taxi. Susan handed the driver fifty dollars and said, "We want to go to the nearest ATM and then to a Harley-Davidson dealer, got it?"

"Yes, ma'am."

After the driver had taken them about a half block, they passed a second bomb squad truck on its way to the hospital. He commented, "There must be something big going on back at the hospital." His passengers just smiled.

In a few more blocks they spotted a Bank of America branch that had an ATM in front. Susan stood in front of the machine with Genie in her coat pocket. Susan asked Genie, "Can you hack this machine and get some money?"

"Of course. How much do you want?"

"How much does this machine have in it?"

"This machine has seventy-six thousand dollars in currency and some change."

"Okay, let's withdraw it all."

"Whose account shall I take it from?"

"General Potter's, of course," Susan said with a sly giggle.

"The General has money stashed all over the place. Want to see?" Genie projected his accounts on the wall above the ATM. There were accounts in the Cayman Islands, Switzerland, New York, and Falls Church, Virginia. In all, there were six accounts in four different banks. The balances totaled 13.6 million dollars.

"Let's withdraw all this machine has and then clean out the one at the drive-up around the corner too."

The drive-up ATM had more money in it, $150,250 to be exact, plus change. The total take was over $230,000. It took about ten minutes to vend the currency out of each machine. Then, with their newfound wealth—compliments of General Potter—they headed for the Harley dealership. Genie checked her database and found a dealer on Sixth and Lexington twenty blocks from the bank.

Susan told the driver to go to 689 Lexington and to step on it. They arrived in about fifteen minutes. The dealership was well-lit and open for business. Within minutes, Max and Susan were riding out in Harley style, wearing down-insulated leathers and full-face helmets to match their new Harley Road King with all the bells and whistles. They dropped thirty thousand dollars of the General's money on the bike with an extra two thousand for clothes and three thousand for the dealer to fix the title and license. They then headed for Rachael and Tom's friend's apartment with Genie in the saddlebags.

Genie gave directions to reach Bruce's place in Midtown on 56th and Madison Avenue, an older apartment building but well maintained. When they got to the door, Bruce used the peep hole and verified who they were and then let them in. Rachael and

Tom were there and ready to help. Bruce was a makeup artist with the theater where Tom worked a lot, and so they had some history. Bruce was what they called a "Flamer" in Arkansas, an overt homosexual, which gave him the style and sensitivity to be a great makeup artist. Susan thought it a bit of a cliché, but she hoped he was indeed all he was advertised to be in the makeup department. They needed a masterpiece-quality effort from Bruce.

Bruce hustled them into the kitchen where there was better light to start his make-over. "First, Susan, let's do something with this five-foot, ten-inch body-to-die-for and that long blond hair. Let's get that hair off and make it coal black with a spike cut. Rachael, you get started on that. Now, Max, you come with me. Love the leather wardrobe by the way. It looks good on you. Let's get rid of some of the facial hair and make the beard a goatee. Then we can cut your hair very short in almost a butch and make your hair and goatee blond. Now let's find some fake tattoos for the both of you."

When Bruce got done with them, they looked like different people entirely. He had made a new nose for Max out of a very durable latex and silicone that would last for days. Susan looked the part of a biker moll for sure, right down to the leather boots and silver buckles. A tattoo on her neck said "Bite Here" and the one on her arm said "Love at your own risk." Max had an assortment of tattoos and a skull bandana under his helmet. The ultimate part of Susan's disguise for Max was the "insert tongue here" line on the tattoo in Susan's breast cleavage. All together, they presented themselves as a real "class" couple.

They loaded up the Harley with food, water, and an extra set of insulated gloves and an extra wool scarf for each of them. Rachael pampered them like a couple of ghetto-dressed and tattooed school children, bundling them up to go off into winter's harsh weather. With the down-insulated leather they bought at the Harley dealer, they were ready for just about any weather except rain. Fortunately, the night was clear and 38 degrees when they were ready to head for the Midwest. Rachael, Tom, and Bruce gave them a hug before they mounted the Road King. In Rachael's case, a few tears came as they got ready to leave. Susan had insisted she drive and put Max on the back. They made quite a sight as Susan cranked the gas on the powerful bike and they quickly blended into traffic. Genie gave detailed directions to get out of town quickly, taking care of the traffic lights as they zoomed past all the intersections. In thirty minutes, they were well out of New York City and headed west on I-80.

CHAPTER 22

As Max and Susan cruised along, they spoke via communicator. They were becoming one person as Max had a hold on Susan like a clinging vine, nearly wrapping himself all the way around her, and their thoughts were shared almost as a single person. They pitched and weaved in and out of the interstate traffic like they were part of the bike. The engine of the powerful touring bike purred as they kept a steady pace of 80 mph into the night. After about an hour on the road, they crossed the Delaware River into Pennsylvania. They both felt a wave of relief wash over them as if they had put all the terrible things that had happened in New York behind them.

As they got further into Pennsylvania, Max mentioned that he was getting tired. It was 1:30 in the morning, and given the fact that only hours ago he was in surgery to have a bullet wound repaired, it had been a long day for him.

They spotted a no-name motel in the small town of Wingate and decided to stop so Max could rest for a few hours. They rented what used to be called a tourist cabin in the heyday of travel in that part of the state. The small cabins, separated by about twenty feet, were arranged in neat rows like a small town. The painted sign on the road was lit only by a small light bulb, and it simply said "MOTEL". The cabin afforded them maximum privacy as they could hide the bike from the road and rest at their leisure. Genie said there was no radio traffic and she believed the authorities thought they were still in Bellevue Hospital. The second they got inside, Max collapsed on the bed with his clothes still on and went to sleep immediately.

For Susan, the rest was not quite as necessary, so she decided to keep watch and see what was going on at Astrolabe. Genie and Susan went into the small kitchenette, and Susan made the call to Astrolabe, then turned the reconnaissance over to Genie.

Genie began her report: "There are twenty-nine federal agents on Astrolabe property at the moment: twenty-two FBI agents, five CIA, and two Army Intelligence officers. They are trying very hard to get the Goddess to work and to access the computer files. There is actually a CIA agent in the Goddess now trying to turn on the controls.

"There is a group of six agents at Max's house trying to figure out some of the stuff in the storage building. You may remember, the loading robots are in there along with an extra power pack. They probably think the robots are some kind of electronic beach ball or something. There are also thirty-one Arkansas State Police in the area and one Jasper, Arkansas, city policeman on duty."

"Okay, Genie. Let's do a rundown on the shooters," Susan said. "I'm going to assume they're connected to General Potter. See what you can learn."

"I am able to access all of the government computers, which should tell us what we need to know. Since 2008, everything has been kept on computer for security reasons. Unfortunately for the government of the United States, it is not a problem for me to access the files.

"Ah, yes. Here it is, a file marked: Special Operations, Top Secret. The order for the hit was given by General Bernard Potter and signed off on by the Joint Chiefs and President Jackson.

"Lt. Colonel George Taylor commanded the operation, and the shooters were as follows: Sergeant Clifford Powell, KIA; Master

Sergeant James Riggs, KIA; Sergeant Rex Palmer; Staff Sergeant Howard Clifton; Master Chief Petty Officer Phillip Kester; and Sergeant Joseph Billings. The Special Operations headquarters is at Fort Bragg, North Carolina.

"The computer records show Riggs and Powell were killed by Pendergrass at the hotel. The remainder of the kill-team is restricted to quarters pending debriefing at Fort Bragg at 0600 hours today. General Potter is at home in Falls Church, Virginia."

Genie and Susan continued to find out more about the government involvement in the assassination attempt and learned that agents were hot on the trail of the source of the disrupter at Raytheon. Susan let Max sleep until about 5:45, and then she woke him. He needed to know what Genie had revealed to her. Max was like a new man after his brief sleep. Susan laid out a plan to get some justice for what had taken place the day before. She also told him about a discovery Genie made while researching the files about General Potter. She let Genie tell Max.

"Max, I found some disturbing information about General Potter. It seems he was involved in a top-secret scandal with a defense contractor that was providing a weapons system for the fighter that your brother was testing.

"There was a failure of an explosive charge while in flight, which caused the crash that killed your brother. At the hearing, competitors testified that the system wasn't ready and that Potter got paid off to accept it for the test phase when he knew it was defective. Apparently, Potter had a lot of influence with the Board of Inquiry and the whole thing got swept under the rug. Potter later claimed it was pilot error and blamed your brother."

When Max heard this, he was seething and hated Potter even more. There was nothing that could have been revealed about

Potter that could have made Max more certain that he should be dealt with severely. Max gathered his thoughts and formulated his plan for justice.

They would start with Potter and work their way up and down the chain of responsibility. When their plan was finalized, they set the plan in motion from their operations headquarters, an obscure motel bungalow in Wingate, Pennsylvania.

First, Genie called the Goddess to begin the sterilization of Astrolabe. She addressed the agent trying to figure out the craft's controls.

"Agent Turkle, this is the Sky Goddess speaking." The CIA agent nearly jumped out of his skin.

"You have ten seconds to vacate the ship and get out of the building, 10 . . . 9 . . . 8 . . ." Genie made sure Agent Turkle got the message by instructing the Goddess to give him an electrical jolt in the seat of the pants. He scurried out the hatch in the turret, and just as he cleared the hatch, it closed with a distinctive clank and whoosh as the air-tight container sealed.

The Goddess then shut off all radio communication to and from the complex and began to destroy anything and everything having to do with the project: computer files, buildings, equipment — everything. The files at Raytheon were also destroyed, deleted from all computers at their facility. The Goddess then quietly emerged from the burning building, traveled to Max's house and destroyed the storage building. At the Goddess's direction, the robots quickly made their way back to the Kansas bunker, whizzing along at treetop level at four-hundred miles an hour. The Goddess now traveled east to Falls Church, Virginia, for the first installment of real justice.

It was 0645 hours, and General Potter, wearing a bathrobe, was shaving in front of his bathroom mirror. It was still dark and he was thinking to himself that he had "saved" the Goddess from everybody and would be in a position to rule the roost. He was humming to himself as if he were king of his domain. Then, out of the corner of his eye, he noticed the glint of a shiny object outside his window. Half shaven, he pulled the curtain aside and said, "OH, SHIT!"

The Sky Goddess, in all its power and might, floated motionless and silent about six feet from the second story bathroom window of his suburban estate in Virginia. The Goddess then announced her presence. "Good morning, General. We are here to deliver a message from Steven Clark, Agent Jeremy Wilson, Agent Larry Stone, and lastly, Dr. Max Gibson. Here is your message:"

General Potter said, "What the hell," and just as "hell" passed from his lips, a bright flash of light penetrated the window and the General's eyes, leaving him dumb as a fence post. He had a grin on his portly face only seen in mental hospitals and homebound dementia patients. He would never bully anyone again. At headquarters at Wingate, Genie had confiscated his entire nest egg of over thirteen million dollars, which he'd coerced from defense contractors over the years. These funds would mysteriously appear in cash, delivered by messenger, to the killed agents' families. The only message accompanying the funds would be: "This is not sufficient to cover the loss of your loved ones, but perhaps it will help you get on with your lives when you are done grieving. Do not report this gift on your taxes or deposit it in any bank."

The Goddess then made a U-turn and headed for the White House. President Jackson was at breakfast when Genie gave him the same message delivered to General Potter — instant Alzheimer's. This time several Secret Service agents were present to witness the delivery. It was a shorter trip to dumb-land than for General Potter as the President was substantially closer to being a near idiot in the first place. He had been ushered into office by his family connections and good looks, not his brains. As such, he was putty in the hands of people like Potter, and now he was *merely* putty, unblinking and drooling before his security staff.

By this time, alarms had gone off and a serious effort to stop the Goddess was underway. Small arms fire and some anti-aircraft missiles had been leveled at her, but as advertised, the Goddess plowed through it all unscathed as she headed toward the Pentagon. The Goddess traveled just about treetop level at 150 miles an hour, quickly reaching the Pentagon and locating the Joint Chiefs' morning briefing. To add to the dramatic effect and to emphasize the impotence of the military, the Goddess ripped out the side of the building as the defensive fire continued. The "flash" was delivered individually to each of the chiefs as they hid behind furniture or ran down the hallway.

The next item on the agenda for the Goddess was Fort Bragg, the location for the kill-team debriefing. The Goddess arrived at the Special Forces compound near the northeast corner of the sprawling Fort Bragg post perimeter at 0730 hours. Colonel Taylor was explaining to his commanding officer and a panel of other officers why they had failed to kill Max and caused so much collateral damage to his security personnel. He was coming to the reason they had lost two of their own snipers in the aftermath of the ambush when the Goddess plowed through the wall of the building. Each sniper was blasted with a microwave disrupter beam blast to the brachial plexus of his shooting arm for 0.2 seconds, effectively paralyzing his shooting arm and hand. All of the snipers lay on the floor writhing in pain as the Goddess spoke. "Your careers as takers of life are over. Snuffing out those lives yesterday served no purpose, and it is disgraceful that you would mindlessly follow orders to kill your fellow human beings without a good reason. Your punishment is to live the rest of your lives disabled, which I hope reminds you of the children you made orphans yesterday by your actions."

Max and Susan had a ringside seat via the Goddess's battlefield real-time video link, and they were satisfied with their measured response to what had been done to them and the others at the Waldorf. There was no way they could make up for the loss of innocent lives, but at least the perpetrators had been forced to take responsibility for their actions. At least on this day, justice was done to politicians and military brass who rarely even see the consequences of their decisions, let alone pay for them. And it had been done in a civilized way to those who actually deserved a much more severe punishment.

Back at the Topek Ship still orbiting Jupiter, the Council and crew were ecstatic at the way Max, Susan, and Genie were conducting the retaliation. There were even a few cheers from the normally stoic Council members.

CHAPTER 23

t was daylight in Wingate, and Max and Susan needed to hit the road. Nute would be coming for them in just two days on the tenth. They took off for Arkansas on the Harley, Susan reluctantly letting Max drive after he promised to let her know if he got tired. They traveled without incident all day and made it back to Canton. Susan called her parents when they reached the outskirts of town. Her father sounded vague as he said, "We'll see you on the Fourth of July, as always," which she took to mean that either the phone was tapped or the Feds were there now. Susan really wanted to see her parents, but after what the Goddess did to the President, she and Max were being held personally responsible. They were real fugitives now and had to be careful. Rachael had already told their parents all about the situation and they didn't want Susan to risk coming to see them. Her dad just said, "Be careful, honey. See you this summer."

As a precaution, Genie had routed her call all over the telephone grid so it was untraceable. As much as they wanted to stay, they continued to ride, looking for a place to hole-up in Kentucky. Since it was obvious everyone knew they were on the road now, they worried the authorities would be watching the Mississippi River and would probably put up checkpoints at places where they would logically head into Arkansas. When they reached Paducah, they were tired and looked for an inconspicuous place to stay. They pulled into a small motel on Highway 60. Susan got off the bike first and asked Max if she should register for them in case he might be recognized. He agreed, and she went into the office. A few minutes later, she emerged with a *USA Today* newspaper and the key to a room on the first floor of the two-story motel. After they unloaded their meager luggage, they went inside.

"Max, look at this!" Susan laid the paper out on the bed. It had a four-page spread of the Goddess attacking the White House and the Pentagon. Rockets were exploding on the side of the Sky Goddess, smoke and flames everywhere except on the Goddess. Susan read the story via communicator as Max got undressed and ready to rest.

"Pentagon sources tell *USA Today* the attack was apparently connected to the ambush in New York yesterday and was carried out by some unknown terrorist organization. However, United Nations sources have been quoted as saying that the aircraft in the attacks had been offered to them on Monday by Dr. Max Gibson, the target of the ambush at the Waldorf on Tuesday afternoon.

"United Nations spokespersons also indicate that Gibson, who offered to give the aircraft to the UN for use in peacekeeping, was to address the General Assembly Wednesday. The craft is reported to be impervious to attack, which was certainly verified by the pounding it took Wednesday with no damage whatsoever to the aircraft.

"A news photographer at the White House confirmed the craft spoke to President Jackson just moments before he was incapacitated with a blinding flash of light. The loud speaker on board the aircraft said this was for the people killed in New York, and then listed the names of the victims. A flash from the craft then blinded the President. A White House spokesman denied rumors the President is affected mentally by the flash and stated he will resume his duties soon. Vice President Clayton has taken over the day-to-day operation of the government until President Jackson has recovered fully, the spokesman said.

"A similar attack was reported at the home of General Bernard Potter in Falls Church, Virginia. However, efforts to talk to General Potter were hampered by local police, who had arrested the General for running around his burning house in just his tee shirt exposing his buttocks and genitals to onlookers. The General's neighbors speculated he was either drunk or had lost his mind because they had never seen him act like that before."

As Susan continued to read the paper, Max went into the bathroom to take a shower and get some heat on his sore shoulder. She continued to give details as Max stood under the shower and let the water run on his wound. After a few minutes, he emerged in a fresh pair of boxers and sat down on the bed.

"Susan, let's see what is up on CNN." When the television came on, the story was the same: pictures of the Goddess crashing into the White House and the Pentagon and interviews with United Nations officials. Max watched the TV intently as Susan made her way to the shower. Max had to turn away when the footage of the ambush in New York came on the screen because it made his stomach threaten to heave what little it contained. He turned the TV off.

Max was sitting on the edge of the bed thinking about the loss of his friends when Susan came out of the shower wrapped in a towel that barely covered her down to her mid-thigh. In a playful voice, she said, "See anything you like, sailor?"

Max was betrayed by the communicator when he thought to himself, "*My God, you are gorgeous!*"

Susan then dropped the towel. "How about now?"

Max could not take his eyes off of her nude form in front of an open shower door in a second rate motel, her stunning five-foot, ten-inch physique pulsing. Max turned on the bed to face her and said out loud, "You are the most beautiful thing I have ever seen."

Susan walked slowly to him, pushed him back on the bed, and lay down beside him. She snuggled up to him and whispered, "Do you know how much I love you? I thought I would nearly die when I saw you hurt in New York."

Her breathing became more rapid as she began to kiss him gently on the neck. She pulled off his boxers, creating full-body contact.

Max responded, "I don't know what I'd do without you now. When I am with you, everything else seems to stop and it's just you and me."

The couple lay uncovered facing each other, their passion growing. Max pulled Susan closer to him, and she responded by kissing him with her moist lips.

As they came face to face, she said, "I'm in love, Max. What can I say? I missed you so much while we were apart — it was awful. It's been a long time since Kathy's bedroom. I thought about loving you every night we were apart. I think I've loved you since the first meal you cooked for me at the cabin, I just didn't know it at first"

Max, clearly moved by what she'd said, quietly whispered, "Susan, I had a dream about you when I was in the hospital. I dreamed you were in a long white flowing dress and you were running away from me toward the horizon. I thought I was losing you. You turned and looked at me a couple of times, but then you resumed running. When I woke up and you were there, I was so relieved."

"Don't worry. I will never leave you now."

Max gently began to kiss her as she spoke, and they fell into a sexual embrace that lasted for the next two hours. As their physical and emotional passion grew, each gained new respect for, and more pleasure from, the other. They continued to explore the feelings that had grown and matured over the past year, and they began to realize they really did have something special and Nute was exactly right to pair them. They actually felt like their relationship was bigger and more powerful than either of them.

CHAPTER 24

Susan was asleep in a fetal position, in the same spot where she had drifted off from sheer exhaustion last night. Lying beside her, Max thought how beautiful she was and how much she meant to him, especially after his brush with death on Tuesday. He pulled her closer, and when she felt him snuggle up to her backside, she woke up. She gently pulled his right hand around her waist and quietly said, "Hi, sailor. Want to get married?"

When she arched her back and pressed against him, he could tell she was ready for a return engagement of last night's physical festivities. He chuckled. "Let's not start something I can't finish. After our marathon, I am sexually, well exhausted, shall we say."

He got out of bed. Susan lay there in the bed with a disappointed look on her face and said, "Come on, honey. Let's do one more."

Max said in a playful but defiant voice, "No! We need to get on the road. Nute will be here in less than twenty-four hours."

He smacked her on the butt. "Get up! I'm going for a run to blow some of the cobwebs out of my brain. I'll be back in about twenty minutes. Why don't you get some breakfast at the pancake house down the street and bring it back to the room. Okay?"

"All right, but you better be recovered by tonight, buster."

After Max's run, they breakfasted in their room on ham, eggs, hash browns, juice, and coffee. Afterwards, they showered, then got on the Harley and headed for the river at Cairo, Illinois. As they approached the river at Wickliffe, they noticed the traffic was

257

slowing and the Mississippi was not even in sight yet. When the bridge came into view, they saw the reason for the delay — a road block. As they cautiously approached, they could see U.S. Army vehicles and Missouri State Troopers checking each car as they came to the checkpoint.

They rolled up behind a biker riding a custom chopper and pulled alongside. Max struck up a conversation. "What's going on up there?"

"I dunno. I heard this mornin' they were looking for some guy who attacked the White House. He did a damn good job, if you ask me. He zapped that ignoramus Jackson, which is the best thing to happen to this country since seven-dollar gas."

Max thought to himself, and to Susan via the communicator, "Look at the size of that guy. He must be three-hundred pounds if an ounce. The Santa Claus beard and the pillbox helmet are perfect. There's no way they'll suspect you if you're riding with him."

"What! You don't mean you want me to ride with that slob on his chopper, do you? It has no suspension and no power."

"Sure, just 'till we get to Charleston on the other side of the river. You know I can bluff my way through if I am by myself. Remember, they are looking for a couple. Besides, my fake nose still looks pretty good and so I doubt that they'll recognize me. Bruce said I could put this eyebrow piercing set in and look like a real freak. What do you say?"

Well, okay, but just 'till we get to Charleston. I'll take Genie with me in case fatso gets out of line."

Max called to the biker, "Say, man. My girl really digs your bike. How 'bout taking her for a ride over to Charleston?"

The biker took one look at her and said, "Sure, baby. Climb on, I'll give you a real ride."

Susan rolled her eyes at Max as she threw her leg over the backseat of the chopper and clamped her arms around the three-hundred-pound hunk of a man. The biker and Susan then rode off, weaving in and out of the stalled traffic until they were in sight of the checkpoint. As they came upon the bridge, they slowed down and got in line with all the other cars and trucks. When it came their turn, the sergeant at the checkpoint took one look at the couple and waved them on.

He turned to the other MP and said, "How in the hell did that slob get that babe on the back of his chopper?"

"He must have something, Sarge. He's probably hung like a show pony. She has those long warm legs wrapped around his fat ass for some reason besides looks, that's for sure."

When Max saw them clear the checkpoint, he maneuvered his Harley closer. When his turn came, he rolled up, and in a perfect Australian accent said, "What's the trouble, mate?"

The MP replied, "We're looking for some terrorists. Where're you headed, sir?"

"Las Vegas. You aren't looking for that bloke Gibson are you, the one that has been all over the telly lately?"

"Yeah, that's the one."

"Well, if you ask me, he didn't do anything wrong."

"No one's asking you, buddy. Move it! You are holding up traffic."

"Whatever you say, Sergeant."

Max powered off on the Road King, quickly reached his cruising speed, and purred along to Charleston, Missouri about twenty-five miles away. As he entered town, he saw Susan and the biker on the side of the road in front of a McDonald's. When Max was alongside, Susan said, "Thanks for the ride, big boy. We'll see ya around."

The biker had a disappointed look on his face as Susan climbed on behind Max and they rode off with that thrilling Harley power. Susan told Max via communicator the biker was having romantic aspirations when Genie zapped his bike with an EMP to kill the electrical system. They both had a chuckle, and Susan snuggled around Max and said aloud, "I like this bike and you a lot better."

The roadblock had been sobering. It was obvious now the authorities were looking hard for them and they had to be careful. They took Highway 60 through Dexter and turned off on 160 at Poplar Bluff. Then they took a series of small lightly traveled back roads through the mountains.

They decided to stop for lunch at Salem, Arkansas, just east of Mountain Home on State Highway 9. They pulled into the only place in town to eat, a bar at the edge of town. The parking lot was full of pickup trucks covered with mud, some with hunting dogs in the back. "Our kind of place," Max said as they dismounted.

They came into a dimly-lit, smoke-filled room with a pool table in the middle and a juke box playing a Waylon Jennings song in the back. The sides were flanked by a dozen booths covered with red vinyl, a green Formica table between the seats. They took seats facing each other, and Susan put Genie in her cloth bag next to her. Needless to say, their leather biker outfits didn't exactly match the décor of the establishment, which was early "redneck" and reeked of stale cigarette smoke and beer.

Soon a waiter came over and asked, "You are not from around here are you?" in a tone indicating disbelief that they were even in the place. "You two want something?"

Max replied, "Yes we'd like some lunch. A couple of burgers with everything, fries and two draft beers — whatever you have on tap."

The waiter then asked in a rather belligerent tone, "You got the money for this?" indicating he had been stiffed before by bikers.

Max smiled and pulled a wad of hundred dollar bills out of his leather pants. "You want it in advance?"

The waiter was taken aback by the display of such wealth in the Ozarks and sheepishly replied, "No sir. Your order will be right up."

After Susan had gone to the restroom, Max took his turn to relieve himself and wash his hands. The hot water didn't work, of course, and the towels were gone. It seemed the most important thing in the room was the array of condom dispensers, eight of them in a room only four by six feet. When Max emerged with his wet hands, he found two large Ozark-types talking to Susan.

"Hi, boys," Max acknowledged as he sat down and wiped his hands on the table cloth that partially covered the lime green table-top.

Susan said, "These gentlemen were just inquiring about my tattoo and wanted to know if it was for sale. The one that says, 'insert tongue here.' I was politely telling them to 'fuck off' when you got here"

"It's a good idea to follow the lady's advice, boys. Have a nice day." It was clear the two were not pleased with the brush off as they slowly walked to a booth across the room and consulted with three of the other great minds in residence.

Max and Susan were just finishing their lunch when four of the rednecks aggressively came across the room toward them, obviously to lay claim to Susan and teach Max a lesson in the process. What they didn't know was that Susan had slipped Genie to Max under the table. The largest and most lustful of the locals stepped between Max and Susan and said, "Get out of the way, pee wee."

Just as the "wee" came out of his mouth, Max quickly got up and, holding Genie like a baseball bat, hit the 240-pound redneck with a home-run swing. Genie's globe caught the man squarely in the genitals and dispatched him to the floor in agony. The second blow hit the number two man in the knees and dropped him like a sack of potatoes. As the third genius approached, Max blasted him with an uppercut to the mid-line of the mandible, breaking his jaw and putting him on the floor as well.

The last of the local gentlemen begged off and said, "It was their idea, and I'm sorry if I bothered you in any way, sir. Excuse me. I'll be leaving now."

The last of the four stooges left by the back door, presumably headed for home, looking back to make sure that Max wasn't behind him. Genie disabled all the vehicles in the parking lot and disrupted the phones and the CB radio the bartender had behind the counter with a guided electromagnetic pulse. Max quietly stepped up to the waiter and said, "Now, how much was that tab?"

The waiter nervously said, "$17.60."

Max was in a generous mood so he gave the waiter a hundred and said, "You might want to get some ice for Casanova's testicles, and I believe the fat boy has a broken jaw. Ice will help them both until they can see a doctor."

Susan, after examining him, sang out, "Number three has a nasty contusion on his knee caps, but they're not broken. Mr. 'hot nuts' with the broken jaw also has some teeth missing, so you might need to find an oral surgeon for him."

Max and Susan then confidently strolled out of the establishment, got on the Harley, and took off for Mt. Hershey to meet Roger. Max phoned Edna, Roger's girlfriend, and simply said, "Plan B." As instructed, she didn't say a word in response, but she called

Roger and told him Plan B was on. Roger immediately gathered up the gear Max wanted and headed for Mt. Hershey.

Max and Susan traveled southwest from Salem, through Mountain Home and Yellville, cruising along on 235 headed for Highway 65 just south of Harrison near Pindall. There was almost no traffic on this mid-week winter day. As they rounded a curve, a roadblock came into view just east of 65. The patrol car was across the road and the check point was manned by two Searcy County Deputies.

Max didn't want to attract any more attention, so he decided to try to bluff their way through the roadblock. He told Genie to disable their radio as he slowed to a stop in front of the deputies' car, which was positioned across both lanes. He took off his helmet confidently said in his newly acquired Ozark accent, "What's up, fellers?"

"Roscoe, I believe we got ourselves a couple of real desperadoes here. They fit the description of them two that beat up them fellers in Salem about noon today. You better call it in and see what they want us to do with 'em."

"Jed, this here radio ain't workin' a tall!" Nothin' coming in or goin' out neither."

"Well that figgers. They said they messed up the radio and telephone over in Salem too."

Suddenly the situation grew ominous for Max and Susan as Jed pulled his service weapon and drew down on them. Max and Susan instinctively raised their hands and gave each other a panicked look. The deputy then demanded that they climb off the bike, and they complied as well as they could with their hands above their heads.

Jed then commanded, "Stand still! Roscoe, cuff him." Roscoe roughly shoved Max face down on the hood of the patrol car, put him in handcuffs, and patted him down for weapons.

All right, little missy. Take that there helmet off, and you just put your hands on top the car and spread them long legs. I'll need to check you for weapons"

Roscoe opened the back door to the car and shoved Max in head first. He then closed the door and turned to watch Jed check Susan "for weapons." He gave out a perverse giggle and said, "Go ahead, Jed, check her good. You never know what you might find in them leather pants."

"Shut up, Roscoe!"

Jed holstered his pistol and said, "Now honey, let's see what you got underneath them leathers."

He pushed her legs even farther apart and leaned on her from behind to keep her off balance. He reached around her and unzipped her coat and gave a rough squeeze to both of her breasts. He then moved even closer to her from behind and gave her a firm and sustained pelvic thrust, moving up and down on her buttocks while holding her against the car.

Max let loose an angry outburst by his communicator, "Genie, we need some help here!"

At the same time, Max struggled with the handcuffs and was just able to get his torso out of the back door window. He screamed, "Take your hands off her, asshole!" That immediately prompted Roscoe to smack him on the bridge of the nose with his pistol, causing Max excruciating pain as well as a bloody nose.

Genie replied, "Just maneuver him over here and I'll zap him with a Potter treatment."

Susan was disgusted by the oaf manhandling her and more concerned about Max, but she was able to say with amazing conviction, "I have a blanket in the bike's saddlebags that we could take over to the woods if you want to really see what I have up close."

As if he had just uncovered a treasure, Jed said with a self-congratulatory tone, "I could tell that you was a fiery bitch right off when I saw you ride up. I thought you might like a tussle with a real man for a change. Let's see what you got in them saddlebags.

Cover her Roscoe while I check out the bike. I may have to question her some before we take 'em back to the jail. She's got a nice set of tits and a firm ass. I'll let you question her too, if you act right, Roscoe."

Roscoe pointed his service revolver directly at Susan and held the collar of her coat to keep the forward pressure on her, pushing her against the car. Jed slowly walked to the bike and looked in the saddlebag. When he uncovered Genie, he got the surprise of his life. Expecting to find a "love blanket," he got a laser pulse that rendered him unconscious. Roscoe quickly came to his aid and got the same treatment. They both lay in a heap on the pavement.

As Susan stepped over Jed, she said, "Nice tits, huh?"

She kicked him in the groin with her heavy motorcycle boots and then rolled him over and located his handcuff key on his service belt. After she released Max, she tended to his nose.

"Oh honey, I'm sorry, but he really whacked you. I think the rubber enhancement Bruce put on your nose may have kept it from being broken though."

Max replied, "This really hurts. Genie can you give us a hand here?"

"Of course, Max. Susan, bring me to Max and I'll stop the bleeding and the pain."

After Genie treated Max's nose, they were able to relax a bit and Susan said, "I have the perfect lesson for these two hillbilly jerk offs"

Max and Susan stripped the deputies completely nude and handcuffed them together in the backseat of the car. When they had finished their dirty trick by posing them, Jed on top of Roscoe, Susan said, "Let those two clowns try to explain this to their buddies."

Roscoe was face down on the seat, his arms behind him, and Jed was on top. Susan stepped back to admire the overall effect and commented, "They sure make a pretty couple. They'll have a real surprise coming when they wake up, since Genie said they won't remember how any of this happened."

Susan drove the patrol car to a nearby side road and parked it. Susan then called the sheriff's office via Genie and a cell tower and reported that she had seen two deputies doing lewd, obscene, and licentious stuff in the back of a patrol car. She gave them the location of the patrol car and quickly hung up. Then she and Max folded the deputies' clothes neatly and put them in the front seat as if they got undressed deliberately before their play time.

Before Susan got out of the car she leaned over and gave Jed an indignant slap. "That was for feeling me up, you creep!"

As they drove off, Max commented to Susan, "Bruce's disguise is almost too convincing. It makes you attract a lot of attention from these macho Ozark types. I sure hope I never make you mad, Susan. You've got a mean streak."

"They just got what they deserved, that's all, Max."

They continued on the Harley to well-traveled State Highway 65 and made a right. It was only a few miles from there to County Road 21, which led down to the Mt. Hershey access on the Buffalo River. Max and Susan arrived at 4:15, just as the sun was setting over Bolin Mountain to the southwest. The weather had turned colder, and the temperature in the Buffalo River Valley was below freezing by the time they spotted Roger in his old, full-sized pickup. He had a broad grin for them when he realized who they were. He certainly didn't expect them to arrive on a Harley.

"Boy, you had me fooled for a minute, boss. I thought you was some kind of biker looking for trouble."

Max took off his helmet and the rest of his damaged fake nose and gave Roger a big hug. "Man, is it good to see you, Roger!"

"Did you have any trouble, boss? Everbody's lookin' fer ya."

"No, but we did have a run-in with a couple of Searcy County deputies over on 235."

"Boss, you got to watch out for them fellers over there in Searcy County. They like to beat up on their prisoners and such. They killed a guy in the jail last year with nightsticks, ya know."

"Well, I don't think those two will be bothering anyone for a while — they may be in jail themselves tonight."

Roger turned his attention to Susan. "You sure look different, Miss Susan. I don't think I would've knowed ya on the street."

"My God, it's good to see you, Roger!" Susan gave him a hug. Roger was embarrassed momentarily but enjoyed being greeted as if this were a family reunion.

"Well, do you have all the stuff, Roger?"

"You bet, boss. I got it all, right down to the last rivet. The canoe is over here in the brush, and the other gear is underneath the canoe. I got some hot coffee here in the truck if you want some. Miss Susan's cat, Cosmo, is in the truck too."

"Roger, you're a wonder. How do you always know what we need." Susan ran over to the truck and squealed with excitement to see her pet. Cosmo even showed a little reserved affection toward her, which was unusual for the customarily aloof cat.

Roger was proud of the job he had done for Max. In fact, Max was about the most important thing in Roger's life. The quiet pride he had for his relationship with Max can only be understood by two close friends. This has sometimes jokingly been called male bonding.

But this kind of pure trust and friendship can only be known when it develops from hardship and adversity. Shakespeare's band of brothers is the archetypical example of the way Max and Roger felt about each other. Roger would protect Max to the death, especially now that he knew he was in real danger. He welcomed the chance to work for Max and provide for his safety.

They got into Roger's truck and enjoyed a cup of strong Colombian coffee that Max always drank. It began to snow as they sat there in quiet contemplation of the upcoming trip down the river. Roger told them that federal agents and the State Police were all over the Astrolabe complex and Max's house. They were all trying to find something that could lead them to where Max might be hiding. He said that everywhere between Astrolabe and Harrison was crawling with police of one variety or another.

The Feds continued to make Max out as a terrorist in the news, and the various agencies were all operating under "shoot on sight" rules of engagement. The United Nations and the media, except for the right-wing, talk-show guys, were on Max's side. The reporters continued to press the government to learn who had ambushed Max in New York and why rumors continued to circulate that the shooters were American soldiers. The Pentagon denied this, of course, saying the attack was part of a conspiracy to destabilize the United States government. Army spokesmen labeled the snipers as "foreign mercenaries."

After they finished two cups of coffee each, they loaded the canoe and shoved off down the river. Due to recent rain, the river was up slightly from the level of previous weeks and so the going was easier than expected. Max was in front with Genie, and Susan was in the middle taking care of the gear. Roger was in the back steering and keeping the canoe moving when it did drag occasionally. Max shined a spotlight ahead so Roger could see the water. Roger had a head lamp to aid their navigation too, but he didn't need much guidance. He knew this part of the river well enough to navigate it in near total darkness and handled the canoe with ease through the riffles and eddies.

In just short of two hours, they arrived at a landmark known as the Narrows, a rock formation only a few yards wide and 150 feet tall that had been carved out of the limestone by two ancient rivers flowing together eons ago. Now, the Buffalo was clearly the larger river and the other river to the south was merely a wet weather tributary known locally as Richland Creek. This was the rendezvous point for their meeting with Nute. Near the end of the rock formation was Wollum Ford, where a small dirt road crossed the Buffalo River. At this spot, the two river valleys came together in a Y-shape to form the larger Buffalo River Valley.

Max and Roger unloaded the gear and pitched the tent. The snow was coming down with intensity now, making the work more difficult. With this weather, they didn't expect anyone to come down the river and so they camped right out on the gravel bar next to the water. It was clean of vegetation there and easy to make a camp. After they got the camping gear situated, they were able to drag up enough driftwood to make a fire so they might be a little more comfortable in the cold. Genie told Max the valley temperature was 14 degrees Fahrenheit. Everyone sat down by the fire to get warm, and then Max began a serious talk with Roger.

"Roger, you cannot stay here. If we get caught, you'll be in great danger. I want you to have the Harley we left at Mt. Hershey. The papers were faked, so you'll need to get a new title and license, but you told me once that your cousin Raymond knows how to do that.

Roger tried to interrupt, but Max cut him off and said, "Don't even say you don't want the bike because I know you do.

"Next, in the cabinet at my house on top of the roll-top desk, is a signed deed to my house transferring it to you. Mr. Donavan, a lawyer in Harrison, knows all about it. He will help you with the paperwork. Finally, I want you to take this money we have, two hundred thousand more or less. Don't ever tell anyone where you got it and never put it in a bank. Hide it at the house or someplace safe and use it for you and Edna. Consider it a wedding gift from Susan and me."

Roger was quiet for a minute, as if considering his newfound wealth. Then he asked, "What's gonna happen to you, boss? How are you gonna to load all that stuff?"

"Don't worry. There'll be people to do that when they get to our location. They'll be here at 3:30 to pick us up. All we have to do is sit tight 'til then. How are you getting back to Harrison?"

"I got my cousin's truck over there. I hope the thing will start in this cold weather. Maybe we'd better check it out, boss."

Max and Roger took a flashlight and Genie to the truck, which was parked in the brush next to the stash of genetic materials. Roger got in and tried to start the old Ford truck. Nothing! Max raised the hood and held Genie a little closer. He said, "Try it again," and the truck started immediately.

Max said to Genie telepathically, "Thanks."

She said, "You are very welcome, Max. It's nice to be of service."

Roger and Max loaded the canoe into the pickup bed, and Roger reluctantly prepared to leave.

"There is one other thing, Roger," Max said. "Susan and I believe there will be a nuclear war soon and there may be radiation fallout that could kill anyone caught in the open. Remember the hidden vault that you and I built in the basement of the cabin. The combination for the lock is in the top drawer of the roll-top desk. Open it after all this blows over and you'll find everything you need to survive a nuclear war for at least a year: food, water, weapons, survival books, radiation measuring equipment, and so on. There are enough supplies for eight to ten people.

"Decide ahead of time who you want to be in there with you and stick to your guns. Don't even tell anyone else about the shelter, or they'll take it away from you by force in an emergency. If you think war is coming and you have some time, lay in more supplies and encourage your extended family to build and stock their own shelters.

"There's a metal footlocker near the back of the vault that's full of radio gear and instructions for using it. The antenna is hidden in the tree in the front yard and the leads are underground. Hook the radio up if there is any trouble, but don't hook up the antenna until you actually need it because it'll pick up any stray electromagnetic pulses and bring them into the radio and fry it. So, if there is danger of an attack don't hook up the antenna and leave the radio equipment in the metal footlocker to shield it from any EMP. Don't run the generator unless you have to. There's about fifteen hundred gallons of fuel to run it, which should last a long time if you only use it when necessary.

"My dad will have a similar shelter built out west by now, and you can reach him by radio on the frequencies I've listed. Just turn to those and transmit at the times I've marked. He'll answer if he survives the attack.

"Do you understand? If you don't want to use the shelter, that's okay, but I want you and Edna to have the option. It's your house now, so you do what you want with it.

"There's also a package in the vault for Susan's family. When things settle down, I want you to ship it to them. The address is already on the crate. It has some important information and gear in it that they will need. They'll have a radio similar to yours so you can get in touch with them at the times and frequencies listed on the radio sheet I left for you.

"Roger don't worry about remembering all of this. When you get into the vault, all of these instructions will be in the note book that says Roger Hatfield on it."

Roger had tears in his eyes, and Max knew that he had nearly overwhelmed his friend with all this bleak information.

Susan joined them and gave Roger a big hug. "It's been a pleasure to know you," she said, then gave him a big wet kiss, her specialty.

Max gave him a hug and a pat on the back and said, "I hope you enjoy the house and the bike. You've earned it. I don't know of anyone who'd take better care of my house than you."

Roger had tears streaming down his face now as Max spoke. For once, Roger was speechless. All he could muster was, "Thanks, boss. I'll never forget you." Then, choking back his emotions, Roger got into the old Ford and took off up the hill back to State Highway 74 toward Harrison.

The snow was coming down with intensity now, and the ground was covered with two to three inches. Susan had loaded the tent with all their gear while Max was helping Roger with the truck, including sleeping bags, blankets, and Cosmo. Susan informed Max that Roger had even put some candy bars in the food kit, and so they crawled into the tent, got their leather clothes off, and slid into the sleeping bags that they had opened, using one for a mattress and the other for a blanket and ate a candy bar apiece. The two love birds were just as consumed with each other as they were the night before. And when the candy was consumed, they fell into an embrace as soon as they touched each other under the sleeping bag cover. Susan was not disappointed as Max was indeed recovered. He performed like the marathon runner he was.

When they had both reached a point of sexual exhaustion, Max lay quietly with his arm around Susan. They opened the tent flap and gazed out at the campfire for a few minutes, and then he said, "You know, we should probably say goodbye to our families before we leave."

"You're right, Max. They are probably worried sick about us."

"Genie, are you there?"

"Of course, Max. I am always here. How can I help you?"

"We need to speak to our families without the call being traced or putting them in danger. What do you think?"

"Actually, it is about time for a communications blackout anyway due to the arrival of the mother ship. It is so large that it can be seen with the naked eye, and if this information were to be reported, we might have casualties. I'm not worried about the ship, of course, because it will automatically protect itself. It would be better if we kept news of the arrival confined to people who accidentally see the ship. It will not be detectable otherwise since it is invisible to radar and all military sensors.

"After the blackout, I can then bounce your conversations off the satellite to your respective homes. Would you want me to do that now?"

"That would be great. Let's call Susan's folks in Ohio first."

"Very well."

Genie then performed some of her technical magic and shut down all the phones, radios, and televisions in North America. No one could send or receive. She then called Susan's parents and said, "Talk as long as you like. It is perfectly safe now."

"Hi, Mom. We are great. We are safe, and no one can bother us now."

Susan continued telling them all about their ordeal and how they made their escape with Bruce and Rachael's help and so on. She left no detail untold. She did omit the episode of the deputies and their bad behavior and subsequent punishment.

She talked for about forty-five minutes and ended with, "Mom and Dad, I love Max, and we are going to be married someday soon. We are leaving on a long trip and we may not be back. I hope you understand this, but it is the only way we can survive. This brings me to a very important topic. Max will be sending you a package in a couple of weeks after things settle down. It will have a plan for survival if there is a nuclear holocaust of some kind. Pay attention to this, Max knows what he's talking about. Dad, I think you'll understand the stuff that'll be in the package.

"I love you both and want you to know how much I appreciated the home you gave me and the love you taught me to have for others."

After a long pause, and with tears flowing, she finally said, "Goodbye, I love you!"

Max then spoke to all his family members, each in turn. When he spoke to his dad, he thanked him profusely for his help with General Potter and the entire military issue. His dad had been exactly correct in his assessment. He also told him about the information that Genie uncovered about Potter, and his dad was not surprised. He was glad to hear his long-lost son who had been blamed for the crash of the test flight was vindicated by the truth. They also discussed the probability of a nuclear holocaust and the need for him to be ready to protect the family. Max suggested they get away from Colorado Springs because NORAD headquarters would certainly be targeted. His dad said that he had already located a place in a secure location near Whitefish, Montana, and it would be ready soon.

The details of the New York ambush convinced his father they wouldn't rest until they got their pound of flesh from Max for embarrassing them in their own front yard, so to speak. Without pressing Max for details on where they were going, he told him he was glad they would be safe, together, and happy. After an hour, with lots of tears and explanations, they said goodbye.

Max went outside to put some more wood on the fire. The snow had let up and it was clearing from the northwest. Now they waited.

CHAPTER 25

Precisely at 3:30 a.m., a slight breeze began to blow up from the Richland Creek valley. Max and Susan stood up and looked southwest. They saw the ship soundlessly coming up the valley until it hovered directly over them. A blinding light lit the area underneath the ship, which was about ten feet off the ground. The light promptly melted the snow under the ship, which had the general shape of the Sky Goddess but was much larger in the center section. It was about a hundred yards in diameter and about sixty-five feet from top to bottom.

A ramp lowered silently to the ground, and Nute, in his male body, made his way down it to where Max and Susan were standing. He greeted them both warmly with a big hug. "Congratulations! I'm so proud of you. You've exceeded all our expectations. It's wonderful to see you here alive and well. Genie tells me you had a close call in New York but were obviously able to escape."

"What happens now? asked Max. "I feel like we failed."

"Nonsense. That isn't true, Max. The plan didn't have much chance of success, but I must say you gave it all you had — a magnificent try. You succeeded beyond what the Council ever thought you would. In fact, we didn't think you'd even get the ship built. However, the government reacted exactly as we thought it would, if indeed you did manage to build the craft.

"Then, you surprised us with your response to the military and the treatment of President Jackson. That was brilliant! We would never have thought of that. The Council wants to meet you. They're all inside. Genie has been giving them regular updates. Genie likes you both very much also, by the way."

"You mean Genie is a person like you?"

"Yes, I am afraid so. You see, you have been on a trial run, so to speak. For the past year, Genie was not only your helper and confidante but also she became your friend, and now she holds you both in the highest esteem. She'll be speaking on your behalf in front of the Council, and I'm proud to say, I will be too."

"What'll happen to the Goddess?"

"She's already back in the storage bunker in Kansas. She will remain there until you, or someone else returns and needs her for something."

As they spoke, the familiar ball-shaped robots loaded the 290 boxes of genetic materials Roger had stored for them. They had the entire batch loaded in a matter of minutes. Max and Susan were bundled in their coats as they carried on their casual conversation with Nute, who was dressed in nothing but a shirt and pants.

When the last box was loaded, Nute turned to them and said, "Are you ready to go?"

They looked at each other and, Max, holding Susan's hand with increasing determination, said, "Yes, we are. There's nothing but fear and a lifetime of hiding for us here."

"Okay, let's go."

Nute led the way up the ramp. Max followed him, and Susan was behind Max holding Cosmo. As they started up the ramp, a sense of panic suddenly gripped Max. His claustrophobia kicked in and he froze. He started to gasp for his breath and was paralyzed! Susan, who remembered his episode with the Goddess, immediately made the diagnosis and provided the treatment.

Susan handed Cosmo to Nute, took hold of Genie, and punched Max in the solar plexus with the globe. She then put him over her shoulder in a fireman's carry and brought him on board. The ramp closed behind them and they gently gained altitude until they were out of Earth's atmosphere and headed for Nute's home.

Roger was waiting on the hillside overlooking the Buffalo River valley and saw the whole thing. He had remained to make sure no one bothered Max and Susan and he wasn't going to miss seeing the ship come down and get them. Roger was awestruck.

After the ship was gone, he collected all their gear and took it to his house. He stashed the cash Max had given him in a cardboard box under his bed. Edna went with him to retrieve the bike at Mt. Hershey, and then she took the pickup back to Roger's house. Roger cruised by Max's cabin on the Harley to make sure the Feds didn't damage anything, and as he expected might happen eventually, when he stepped off the Harley, he was arrested and taken to the police station in Harrison. After about twenty minutes, an FBI agent came in to interview him.

"Hi, I am special agent Tom Lattimer. Could you give me your name please?"

"Yeah."

"Well, what's your name?"

"Oh, you mean you want to know now. Well, my name is Roger."

"Roger what?"

"My name is Roger Duane Hatfield, and yes sir, before you ask, I am from a long line of the famous Hatfields. I have eight brothers and two sisters. They're Hatfields too. Do you want to see a picture?"

After a two-hour interview, Agent Lattimer had the entire history of Roger's family, the tale of the building of Max's cabin, how the grounds were laid out and cared for, the mysteries of drying herbs, and so forth — ad infinitum. However, the agent was totally mystified by Roger's lack of understanding of his questions. Lattimer knew everything except what he wanted to know: What happened to Max and the Goddess?

Susan had placed Max in sickbay, where he was still trying to get his breath after twenty minutes. Susan comforted him. "It'll be all right, honey. Just take some slow deep breaths."

After about thirty minutes, Nute guided them to their quarters and advised them to get some rest. "I know you've been busy the last few days, so rest for a while. We'll talk to the Council tomorrow."

Susan helped Max get undressed and they slept like babies in the luxurious quarters prepared for them. Silk sheets and goosedown pillows added a flavor of home to the intergalactic ship.

Max got up first, as usual, and took a shower. The spacious rooms dispelled any lingering claustrophobia for Max, and he felt right at home. Susan got up shortly after Max and came into the shower with him. Without saying a word, she took some soap out of the dish and washed Max, and then he washed her. By the time they had finished, they were locked in a sexual embrace and proved you could make love standing up in a shower traveling at 98 percent of the speed of light.

When they emerged from their extended shower, they dried off and got dressed ready to explore their new surroundings. When they walked out into the corridor, they discovered all of the crew seemed to know them, each calling them by name. The crew also seemed to be impressed that Max and Susan were on board and treated them like celebrities. Just outside their room was a directory that said the mess hall was to the left. They proceeded down the hall and found a cook at a short order counter just inside the mess hall. As they approached, the cook said with a bright cheerful smile, "What'll ya have?"

Max inquired, "What do you have?"

"Anything you want, sir. Just say the word."

"Really? Okay then, I'll have two eggs over easy with sausage and toast and a little blackberry jam on the side. Also, you better get me a cup of Colombian-grown Arabica coffee."

"And for the lady?"

"I will have two Belgian waffles with whipped cream and maple syrup. Also, I'll have an order of bacon and some of that Colombian coffee."

"Excellent choices. Your orders will be right up." He wasn't kidding. About thirty seconds later, the waitress brought out the breakfast. She quietly said, "You don't know what an honor it is for me to serve you. I hope your food is to your satisfaction."

As Max and Susan were eating their breakfast, Nute joined them in the dining room with a somber look on his face. He inquired, "How are you feeling, Max? Susan gave you quite a punch there on the ramp last night."

"I'm okay. I don't know how I got to be so afraid of enclosed spaces. I didn't even know it bothered me until I climbed inside the Goddess last Fall."

"How's the food?"

"Wonderful!" Susan exclaimed.

Max added, "It's really great, first class."

Nute, having dispensed with the small talk, became very serious and spoke quietly to Max and Susan. "We received a message from our observation post on Earth this morning by special sub-space communication while you were asleep. I am very sorry."

Nute handed a copy of the message to them and slowly walked away.

Susan took the paper and read via the communicator to Max. "March 10, 2024, at 0130 hours local time, a nuclear bomb exploded over Tel Aviv wiping out the city. Within minutes, the Israeli Air Force attacked Baghdad, Tehran, Riyadh, Damascus, Karachi, and Cairo. Initially, the United States, Britain, and France urged restraint. Then, at 1100 hours, local time, London and Paris were attacked simultaneously. Two hours later, Washington was destroyed by a nuclear device that had been pre-positioned perhaps years before. Los Angeles and San Francisco were also extensively damaged by two more devices probably on board ships in the harbors. At this time, approximately two-hundred megatons of nuclear detonations have taken place. Smaller tactical nuclear weapons have been dropped on North Korea, Libya, and Pakistan by the United States in a preemptive strike. Radiation has reached lethal levels in most of Europe and the Middle East, and radiation in the rest of the world, carried by the prevailing winds, will certainly reach toxic levels within days.

"Max, I don't understand. We just left but it's already March. How can this be?"

"It is our speed, Susan. Because we are going so fast, time is moving at least fifty times slower for us. Two days here is like a hundred on Earth.

"I guess it had to happen. The Muslims and Jews had to start it, both wanting to be martyrs. Well, I guess they have their way now. This makes me sick. I always thought that someone would come along and put a stop to all of this nonsense of religious warfare. I sure hope Roger and our families keep their heads down and survive this."

Nute returned to their quarters about an hour later and asked if he could be of any help. Max said, "No. But it was nice for you to offer." Susan just nodded in agreement.

Nute had them sit down as he had more news he wanted to give to them personally. "According to our observation team, the detonations in America were restricted to the east and west coasts. South America and Australia were untouched by any blast effects. Europe, the Middle East and Asia were all damaged heavily and the radiation reached deadly levels within hours. The main worries for the survivors would be fallout and starvation.

"There was also a biologic attack designed for the United States that has had serious consequences. As it turned out, in the third world and in the southern hemisphere the pandemic was cata-strophic. It was apparently designed to wipe out the people without damaging the infrastructure. It seems to have worked well on that front but killed nearly everyone in developing countries and in the southern hemisphere as an unintended side effect.

The fallout caused a nuclear winter in the northern hemisphere due to the massive dust cloud drawn up by the blasts. Weather patterns would tend to circulate the cloud mostly in the northern hemisphere for several months until gradually the radiation would spread worldwide and then dissipate. Unless someone was capable of staying underground for at least six months and had sufficient food and water, the radiation would be fatal for them. The biologic pandemic probably will outlast most of the population that survives the nuclear blast and fallout. I realize this probably means the end of your families and everyone that you knew on Earth. For that, I am deeply sorry."

He offered to put off their meeting with the Council until the next day, and they both agreed they would probably be in a better frame of mind. They agreed to meet the Council the next morning at nine o'clock shipboard time.

Until then, Nute offered them the run of the ship and told them to feel free to ask any questions they wanted. He said, "I will meet you in your quarters at 8:55 a.m. Okay?"

"That will be fine,"

Max and Susan strolled around the ship and even looked outside, trying to forget about the holocaust on Earth. Susan finally broke down and sobbed quietly as Max held his arm around her and they gazed out a portal of the ship. Max's comforting reassurance was unspoken, but the deep commitment they now had for each other seemed to be even more poignant. There was a good possibility they would be the only surviving members of the human race. Max realized he didn't recognize any of the constellations and so they must be deep in space now, far from Earth. He told Susan as much, and they felt so totally alone now, except for each other.

They completed the tour of the ship and returned to their quarters to rest up for their meeting the next day. Before going to bed, Max got the latest news report from the communications center and brought it back to the room. He summarized the details for Susan: "Radiation fallout has indeed killed most of the surface life forms on Earth, but some radio transmissions have been monitored by the observers — probably ham radio. It's now about four months after the war, so there is a slight chance there may be survivors when all is said and done and the radiation dissipates."

"Not very good news, but not all bad either," Max commented as he got into bed. Neither Max nor Susan slept very well that night.

The next morning, Nute arrived exactly on time, as usual, and escorted them to the Council chambers. The Council consisted of five members, two men and three women, all dressed in golden robes. They were seated in a semicircle and all their attention was directed to the two chairs they had placed in the center for Susan and Max. Nute escorted them in and introduced them to the Council. Chief Councillor Clacton was a middle-aged woman who spoke with a sweet drawl found only in southern Georgia. She began an explanation of what was to become the shock of their lives, and considering what they had been through, it took a lot to shock them.

"I cannot tell you how much it means to have you honor us with your presence here. We are especially thankful because we know you are distressed by the news from Earth. If you feel up to it, we would like to explain our civilization to you and why we have taken such an interest in your species.

"We have borrowed some of Nute's costumes to make you feel more at home. I must say, I can see why he enjoys dressing up like this so much. The sensation of having a body is wonderful, especially the food."

Max and Susan both nodded their approval for her to continue.

"You represent a species that has fascinated us for many thousands of years. Nute has kept us informed as to your progress, and he believes you are ready for the most important event to affect our species in over three million of your years.

"Let me explain. Our species evolved and developed over many thousands of generations. We evolved far beyond where your species had reached before you left, before the nuclear holocaust.

"We were able to reduce our work by producing machines and computers and, eventually, we became less dependent on our own bodies to think and move about. Approximately three million of your Earth years ago, some of us decided to convert to pure energy and leave our bodies behind for good. We left them behind to die.

"This was not an easy decision for our society, and many of our friends and relatives opted not to make the conversion. We watched with sadness as they grew older and died, until only those of us who had left behind our corporeality remained. I myself watched my parents and all of my siblings age and die while I went on unaffected. Those of us who converted were able to conquer a relatively short lifespan and live virtually indefinitely in this state. We were able to stop the aging process in ourselves and our environment.

"Unfortunately, over time, we began to question the wisdom of our decision for living as pure energy. This way of living gradually caused a type of reverse evolution. That is, we are regressing as a species and our culture had stagnated. We found no challenge in life and began to wither due to sheer boredom. We have lost not just the emotional stress of losing loved ones to death but also the thrill of having and raising children. We are alive but not really living. There is no adversity and therefore no challenge in our existence. There is just us.

"We know your culture is self-destructive, but it is also vibrant, creative, and passionate. The arts, beautiful buildings, and the love of your families and children all have great appeal to us.

"The exploits you have endured on our behalf have thrilled us beyond any measure. Over the last year, we followed your adversity and triumphs with keen interest. The genetic material you collected will aid us, and you, to form a new society made of a new species, to inaugurate a new life for all of us. In effect, you will be the Adam and Eve of a new civilization. If you agree, you will be the prototype for regenerating both our species in a new world."

When Clacton said that, Max gently took Susan's hand and gave her a look of pride and excitement.

"We can give you the long view of history and vast technology, and you can give us back the dynamic resourcefulness, passion, and creative genius of your species.

"We knew the chance for the long-term success of your species was small, under the present circumstances. The species simply could not endure because of the number of established institutions like the military and governments run by the wrong people, selfish and stupid people. You have proved the wisdom of Nute's choice. When given the chance, you chose reasonable punishment rather than total annihilation, as many of your fellow humans would have done. For this, you have earned our total respect and admiration.

"We would be honored if you would teach us to be more human, to help us awaken within ourselves our long forgotten past. We want you to help us to be more like you. Not only have you passed the test, you have astounded us with your integrity, your sense of justice, and your love for each other. The members of the Topek civilization salute you and honor you. Be apprised that there is no other entity we admire more.

"If you agree to help us, from this day forward, you will be known as the father and mother of our combined civilization. We will await your decision."

The entire ship's complement cheered as Nute led Max and Susan out of the Council chambers and back to their quarters. Each crew member bowed when they passed by.

When they reached their quarters, Nute said, "Please take your time to decide if you want to do this for us. I know it is a lot to contemplate. Call me when you're ready."

Max and Susan were overwhelmed and sat in silence. After a few minutes, Susan said, "I don't think anyone has ever honored me in this way before. Just think, we were unwittingly being tested to become the parents of a new civilization. Some job interview!"

"I know what you mean, and remember, we can't go back home to Earth right now. Besides, there may not *even be* an Earth anymore. I say we go for it. We'll have the chance to bring Nute's species to life the right way and do things as they should be done. What an opportunity. Let's sleep on it and let them know tomorrow."

The next morning, Max and Susan, having discussed various scenarios during their pillow talk the night before, informed Nute they wanted to go ahead with the plan. They only had one request, a short ceremony they wanted Nute to perform. He said he would be honored.

After breakfast, Susan and Max, in formal attire, made their way to the main assembly area. The entire ship's complement was in attendance to witness the ceremony.

Nute stood before them with obvious pride, even a little choked up with emotion in his human body as he began, "Dearly beloved, we are gathered here in the presence of these assembled to join in matrimony these two humans: Dr. Maximilian James Gibson and Dr. Susan Judith McKinney." As the ceremony proceeded, the crew was fascinated by the radiant happiness etched upon the faces of Max and Susan. The cook stood with pride as the best man and the waitress stood with Susan as her maid of honor. At the end of the ceremony, when Nute said, "You may kiss the bride," the crew gasped as Susan planted her famous open-mouthed kiss on Max. They all cheered the couple as Nute turned the beautiful couple around like a proud father to introduce them.

Nute announced with great fanfare, "May I present, Doctors Max and Susan Gibson."

The Council and crew eagerly greeted them in a hastily formed receiving line. They were greeted not only as husband and wife but also as their new stepparents. First in line was a tall beautiful woman with dark flowing hair and pale blue eyes that sparkled when she talked. She approached Susan and said in her rich west Texas accent, "Congratulations, Susan"

When she heard the voice, Susan squealed with delight and immediately grabbed the woman and gave her a hug. "It's you! It's you! Look, Max, it's Genie!"

Max came forward and gave Genie a hug as well and kissed her on both cheeks. "I'm so glad to finally get to see you. You are so beautiful! Just as I imagined you!"

Next in line was a stocky balding man of about forty. When Max turned to greet him, he was shocked and exclaimed, "Pete Bradley! How did you get here?"

"I flew, of course." Suddenly, Max realized his friend Pete from the lens grinding lab at Astrolabe was a Topek. He turned to Susan, who was still giggling with Genie, and said to her, "Would you look at this. It's Bradley from work."

Susan, equally shocked replied, "You're not one of these guys are you?" Pete smiled and said, "Yes, I'm afraid so. Welcome aboard."

Susan gave him a hug. "I always knew there was something about you that was different. No wonder our date didn't go so well, Pete. Genie, you devil, Did you know about Pete?"

"Of course, Susan. I don't want to hurt your ego, but Pete's interest in you was purely scientific." The four of them put their arms around each other and laughed. The rest of the crew marveled at the four friends as they seemed so excited to all be together again.

Nute, acting as the gracious host, was busy making sure everyone had a glass of Champagne. When everyone had a full glass, Max asked for their attention, then proceeded to propose a toast: "We are so pleased, and relieved, that we are with friends again to start this new adventure."

Then, raising his glass, he said in a loud and confident voice, "Here's to our new civilization." The entire ship's compliment cheered.

End of Part 1

Wayne Goodin had a private practice as a general dentist for forty years in Springfield Missouri. During his professional career, he did a lot of technical writing for his practice and for training purposes at the hospital where he worked taking care of the oral problems of patients being treated for cancer. During this time, he worked on his novel and when he retired, he finally had enough time to finish it and write more fiction including a second novel and several short stories.

For information about other works by Wayne Goodin:

Wire Road Press
PO Box 663
Republic, MO 65738-0663